A nother horrific wail filled the sky. Closer this time. Kara didn't move.

"Do as you will," Mary Kettle said, eyeing the nearby ridge. "But I won't waste my life waiting for your decision."

"We're not afraid," Kara said. She wanted the words to sound brave and defiant, but she could hear the quiver in her voice.

"Not afraid of what?" Mary asked. "Death? Is *that* what you think will happen?" Her gray eyes grew wide. "You're even more foolish than I thought."

With that the woman threw her tinkling sack over one shoulder and started along the path, never once turning her head to check that the children were following her. *What choice do we have?* Kara thought. Seeing the same question in Taff's eyes, she lifted him onto Shadowdancer's back, and they quickly followed the old witch deeper into the Thickety.

ALSO BY J. A. WHITE

The Thickety: A Path Begins

THE
THICKETY
The Whispering Trees

J. A. WHITE

Illustrations by
ANDREA OFFERMANN

KATHERINE TEGEN BOOKS
An Imprint of HarperCollins Publishers

Katherine Tegen Books
is an imprint of HarperCollins Publishers.

The Thickety: The Whispering Trees
Text copyright © 2015 by J. A. White
Illustrations copyright © 2015 by Andrea Offermann

Library of Congress Cataloging-in-Publication Data

White, J. A.

The whispering trees / J.A. White ; illustrations by Andrea Offermann. — First edition.

pages cm. — (The thickety)

Summary: "Deep within the dangerous Thickety, Kara and her brother, Taff, must figure out
who and what to trust in order to escape and stop the evil Sordyr"— Provided by publisher.

ISBN 978-0-06-225728-4

[1. Magic—Fiction. 2. Brothers and sisters—Fiction. 3. Human-animal communication—
Fiction. 4. Fantasy.] I. Offermann, Andrea, illustrator. II. Title.

PZ7.W58327Whi 2015   2014022226

[Fic]—dc23   CIP

                                                                                              AC

Typography by Amy Ryan
16 17 18 19 20 CG/RRDH 10 9 8 7 6 5 4 3 2 1

First paperback edition, 2016

For Jack, Logan, and Colin—
a book of monsters!

PROLOGUE

Safi shifted beneath her blankets, waiting, as she did each night, for her father to return home. If only she could fall asleep, there would be none of this anxious tossing and turning, no imagining the thousand injuries that might have befallen him during the Binding. Safi would simply close her eyes, and when she opened them again Papa would be sitting by her side.

Like magic.

Tonight he was even later than usual, however, and Safi was scared. Of course, Safi was scared of lots of things: thunder, fire, those insects with too many legs that waited until she fell asleep before crawling across her bedroom floor. But the thing that scared her most was losing Papa, so despite her fear of the dark Safi decided to walk to their neighbor's hut to see if their son, another Binder, had come home yet.

Besides, she thought, *I need to tell Papa what I've seen.*

She was just sliding out of bed when she heard her father's telltale footsteps, heavy and slow. With a gasp of surprise, Safi leaped back beneath the blankets and smoothed them. Papa entered the room and she opened her eyes groggily, as though he had just awoken her.

"Papa?" Safi asked.

Her father's long white beard was matted with sweat and dirt. A vicious, crescent-shaped burn swelled across the dark skin of his chin.

"You're hurt," Safi said, sitting up to touch his cheek.

"It's nothing," said Papa.

Safi supposed that was true. Papa's entire body, especially his hands and arms, had already been marred by similar injuries. This latest burn was hardly the worst of them.

"You need to go to sleep," he said. "It's late."

"I've been asleep."

Papa raised his eyebrows.

"Well," said Safi, "I *have* been in bed."

"Sleep, darling one. Sleep."

"Could I have a story first?"

"I'm well past tired," Papa said, but already he had pulled a stool to Safi's bedside and taken a seat. "And I haven't eaten yet."

Safi smiled. Truth be told, now that her father had returned she felt sleep tugging at her like a fishing line. But she sensed Papa's need to tell her a story, how sharing this time with his only child might heal wounds beyond the reach of any poultice.

Safi said, "Tell me how he came to be."

"Again? This is a dark tale, love."

"It's a good story."

"It's not a——"

"I'm not scared."

And despite the many fears that dominated Safi's life, it was true. In a story, the Forest Demon was just words, shackled to the tale as securely as any other character. In a story, he couldn't hurt them.

"Tell me," Safi said.

Papa stretched his arms into the air, the stool creaking beneath his weight, and began. The tiny room was enveloped in his sonorous voice.

"In a castle on the edge of a cliff lived a princess who did not find joy the same ways as other children. She had no desire to play with the fine toys that surrounded her; only breaking them brought her the slightest satisfaction. The princess could not bear the laughter of her playmates; only their tears could make her smile. Nothing, it seemed, could fill the emptiness in her heart, and so her father, a good man but blind to his daughter's true nature, held a competition: half his kingdom's treasure for something that would bring the princess joy."

"You forgot about Rygoth," said Safi. "She could control animals and was the only one who warned—"

"It's late," Papa said, "and you know all about Rygoth. Besides, she comes back at the end."

"But it's better when you tell it right."

Papa made a motion to stand. "It's better when I tell it at all, no?"

Safi nodded eagerly.

"Now where was I?" Papa asked, easing back into his seat. "Ah—the competition. Word of it went out to every corner of the World, and from distant shores came inventors and toymakers, talespinners and gamesmiths, poets and architects, all eager to win the king's prize. Each morning the princess sat in her throne and was presented with a dazzling array of treasures. There was a metallic child who could play every game ever invented but always let the princess win; a dollhouse with large windows through which the princess could watch the inhabitants talk and play, argue and grow old; and a loom that could weave the princess's dreams into beautiful tapestries.

"At each of these remarkable gifts the princess simply turned away, offering not a word. Forty days passed in such a manner. And then, on the forty-first day, a man came bearing a book wrapped in black leaves."

"Sordyr," Safi whispered, and though she had promised not to be afraid, her voice trembled just a bit.

"He promised the princess that this book could give her the power to do anything she wanted. The king's adviser, a powerful *wexari* named Rygoth . . ."

"Finally," said Safi.

". . . pleaded with him not to let the princess keep the book. But the king, at last seeing true happiness in his daughter's eyes, refused to listen." Papa sighed. "Sordyr had not lied—the grimoire gave the princess the power to make all her dark wishes come to life. In a few short days the kingdom was nothing but ruins, and the princess was no more."

"Only Rygoth survived," Safi said.

"And tracked Sordyr to the island he had made his home, intent on stopping him from hurting anyone else."

"She should have killed—"

"No," said Papa. "Rygoth believed in the sanctity of all life, and no one should ever be faulted for that. Besides, it was Sordyr's *power* that was the true danger, and so Rygoth created a beast called Niersook. Just a single bite from its fangs and Sordyr would be no different from any other man."

Safi closed her eyes. No one knew exactly what Niersook looked like, so every time Papa told this story she envisioned something different. Tonight Niersook was a giant centipede with horns on its feet.

Her father continued. "Sordyr was more powerful than Rygoth had imagined, however. He held dominion over the plants and trees, and slayed Niersook with a hail of black thorns before it could get near him. A great battle commenced. Sordyr attacked Rygoth with strangling vines and monsters made of roots and branches, and Rygoth fought back with birds and beasts and the insects beneath the earth. The island shook. In the end, however, Rygoth was no match for Sordyr's viciousness, and knowing that her life was coming to a close, she used all her magic on one final spell, imprisoning Sordyr on the island where he could hurt no one."

"Except us," Safi said.

Papa nodded. "Except us."

He placed a kiss on Safi's cheek, and she giggled at the touch of his scratchy beard.

"Now go to bed," he said, placing the stool in the corner of the room. "One of us needs to make breakfast tomorrow."

"I had a vision."

Papa froze. "What did you see?" he asked.

"A girl journeying through the Thickety," Safi said. "Tall with black hair. There's a boy with her. They don't know it yet, but they're coming here."

Papa's mouth twisted into a nervous grimace. He peeked out the window, checking for movement.

"Did you tell anyone about this?" he whispered.

"No! Of course not!"

"These dreams—we can't let him find out—"

"I didn't tell *anyone*. I promise."

Papa stroked his beard and considered her words. "Do you know who she is?" he asked.

"I know some things," Safi said. "She comes from a distant village just outside the Thickety. And she has great magic, yet carries no grimoire."

"Interesting," said Papa. Tucking the covers beneath Safi's body, he leaned forward and spoke softly into her ear. "Perhaps she is *wexari*. Perhaps she is coming to save us from him at long last."

Safi shook her head. "It's not like that. I saw what happens after the girl gets here," she said. "Destruction. Fire. Death. Not just here, but in the World itself." Safi clasped her father's hands. "This girl is not coming here to save us. She's the one who's going to destroy us all."

BOOK ONE
WEXARI

"Witches spread evil
by instructing children
in the ways of darkness."
—The Path
Leaf 12, Vein 49

ONE

Though she was only twelve years old, Kara Westfall had known many kinds of darkness. The smothering darkness of a potato sack as it knotted tightly over her head. Watery darkness so absolute she could lose herself in it. The darkness of temptation, blotting her mind with promises of power and revenge. All these darknesses, in their own specific ways, had left their imprint on her soul. They were all different. They were all the same.

She had never known darkness like this before.

After the branches closed behind them, Kara and Taff

were set adrift on an ocean of starless night. All was silent save the muted sound of horse's hooves against the soft surface of the Thickety.

Kara clung tightly to Shadowdancer's mane and closed her eyes, trusting the mare to guide them. She could do little else.

"They tried to kill us," Taff whispered in her ear. His breath was warm and came in quick, needy gasps; the air here was thin and strange. "Why didn't Father stop them?"

"That *thing* is not our father."

Kara felt his body tremble against her back.

"Our father is gone," she continued. "Grace used her Last Spell to change him. He is Timoth Clen now."

"*The* Timoth Clen? From the stories?"

Growing up they had been taught the legends. The Mighty Clen. Vanquisher of witches. Creator of the One True Path.

"Yes," Kara said.

"But that doesn't make any sense."

"*Magic* doesn't make any sense."

"Not that part. The part about Timoth Clen. Even if he was Father—even if he was *anyone*—he would never hurt us. He's *good*!"

"Maybe to some," she acknowledged. "Not to witches."

Kara thought she heard a sound in the darkness but it was only Taff shifting into a better position on Shadowdancer's back.

"Is Father dead? Dead forever? Or just gone?"

"I don't know."

"You'll bring him back."

"Taff."

"I've seen what you can do. You're a witch. A *good* witch. You'll cast a spell and fix this."

The hope in his voice was a dagger driven deep in her heart.

"My spellbook is gone," Kara said. "And even if I had it, I couldn't use it. It's not safe. You saw what happened to Grace."

"You're different."

"Not different enough."

"But there has to be something we can—"

"I'm not a witch anymore."

"But—"

"Shh," Kara said. "Let's just ride for a while."

Taff linked his hands around her waist and rested his head between her shoulder blades. "I hate magic," he murmured.

They journeyed deeper into the darkness of the Thickety. Kara wondered if they would ever see the light of day again.

When Taff began to snore, Kara smiled at her brother's ability to fall asleep and stroked the back of his hand, the skin as soft as chicken feathers. Although she would wish the boy to safety if she could, Kara was grateful for his presence.

The Thickety was no place to be alone.

Looking to either side she tried to distinguish any kind

of outline against the utter blackness. Some landmark, some hint of shape or form. Some . . . *something*. But in every direction stretched nothing but absolute darkness.

If this were the other part of the Thickety, she thought, remembering her first visit, *the webspinners might light a path to guide us. I could call them here, if I could still use magic.* But she couldn't, not anymore, and she felt its absence as keenly as a lost friend.

A light mist began to fall, tingling her cheeks. At least she wasn't cold. Though it was nearly winter in De'Noran, the temperature here was more like the sticky warmth of summer just after a thunderstorm. Sweat rolled down Kara's forehead and matted her clothes to her back.

The warmth, and Shadowdancer's steady cadence, allowed her mind to drift to the events preceding their flight to the Thickety. *Grace, dragged down into the impossible abyss of the grimoire. Lucas's face growing smaller as his ship disappeared into the distance. Rocks and pebbles buzzing past her head, the savage hatred of the villagers she had saved.*

And over it all, words spoken in her mind with the timbre of rustling leaves: *Your power cannot be bound in a book. You are not like the others, Kara Westfall.*

She awoke.

For a single, terrifying moment she was certain that Taff had fallen from the horse. Then the fog of sleep dissipated and Kara felt his comforting weight against her back.

This relief was short-lived, however, once she realized how difficult it was to breathe.

Kara's chest burned as she tried to suck stubborn air into her lungs, but she was limited to short, meager breaths, as though she were pulling air not from the outside world but the tiny opening of a reed whistle. Taff, who had been the picture of health since the Jabenhook rescued him from the brink of death, sounded even worse.

"Taff," Kara whispered, and even this tiny exhalation of air was difficult for her oxygen-deprived body. "Taff," she repeated. "You need . . . Wake up."

"I'm hungry," her brother muttered, still drowsy. But then he jolted upright in panic. "Can't . . . breathe."

"Shh," Kara said. "Shh. Don't talk. Save."

Although she couldn't see Taff nod in the darkness, Kara knew he understood. His heart, which had been pounding like a drum, settled into a less frantic rhythm.

"Air," Kara said. "Wrong."

On Kara's first journey into the Thickety, the air had been fine—better than De'Noran, actually. *But that was two hours south of here. Maybe the air is different in this part of the Thickety. Maybe it's not meant for people.* If that were the case, what should they do? She had no idea how many hours they had traveled. At the rate they were losing oxygen, turning back might be futile. Besides, even if she *wanted* to go back, she didn't know which way to turn. The darkness devoured all sense of direction.

She heard a sickly rumble and realized it was Shadowdancer's heaving chest, desperate for air. *How far has she carried us like this?* Kara thought, patting the mare's flank, longing to speak reassuring words but unwilling to spare the oxygen. Instead she slid off Shadowdancer's back to lighten her load.

The moment Kara's feet touched the surface, she knew that this section of the Thickety was even stranger than she thought.

The ground was moving.

This slow, steady motion had been easily masked when they were riding Shadowdancer, but there was no doubt about it now. Kara felt the ground and found that it was not dirt at all but something ridged and slippery and as smooth as skin. It tickled her fingertips as it passed, like a lily pad floating along a rolling stream.

Impenetrable darkness. Moving ground. Mist.

Kara remembered what Mother had taught her about certain Fringe weeds, and in her mind an impossible thought began to form—though surely she would have to reconsider the meaning of the word "impossible" in a forest capable of blotting out the sun.

If we're even in the forest at all.

She pulled Taff off the horse, her chest aching with the effort.

"Come," she said. "Hold hands. Don't . . . let go." She guided him through the darkness, Shadowdancer close behind.

"The ground," Taff said. "Do you feel—"

"Yes."

"What is this place?"

Kara longed to explain, but there wasn't enough time.

"Trap," she said.

The ground pulled them in a certain direction—she couldn't have even guessed which one—but Kara led Taff perpendicular to the moving surface. Each step was exhausting, like walking through water. No matter how deeply she inhaled, only a trickle of air wisped through her lips.

But when their progress was impeded by a wall-like structure, Kara's spirits lifted. *I was right!* she thought, and then chided herself for such overconfidence. They weren't out of this yet.

She put her ear to the wall's slippery surface and heard the muffled patter of raindrops outside.

"Help," Kara told Taff. She took him by the hands and guided them over the fleshy wall. "Feel . . . gap. Dig . . . fingers into it."

Taff squeezed his sister's hand to acknowledge that he understood.

They traced the wall with their fingertips, inspecting the slightly moist surface for openings. The search would have been more efficient if they parted ways, but Kara wouldn't risk sending Taff off on his own. Besides, she wasn't even sure this was going to work. *Just because I saw Mother do it in the Fringe doesn't mean anything here.* Kara ran her fingers across a particularly smooth patch and found her hand continuing to travel downward. It took a few moments for her to realize that she had fallen to the ground. She lay there, her breathing raspy and quiet, wondering why she wasn't getting to her feet. All she could do was listen to Taff's footsteps vanish into the darkness.

He thinks I'm still beside him, but he's all alone.

The world spun.

Taff screamed something in the distance, but though she heard the words Kara could not make out their meaning. She tried to take a breath so she could call out his name, but her lungs had finally closed up completely and the first wave of true panic hit her.

And then the ground dropped and Kara was sliding backward down a sudden slope. Cold rain pounded her face, and air, sweet air, filled her lungs. She heard Taff scream with exuberance. Turning her head she watched him tumble down what appeared to be a shiny green mountain, his hands held aloft as though this were some sort of festival ride.

A few moments later Kara was rolling across the soft soil of the Thickety. It was black and granular and nothing like the fertile soil of De'Noran, but it was still dirt and she had never been happier to feel it. Her breathing came free and easy.

High above, black treetops coiled together and swallowed the vast majority of late-afternoon sunlight, but errant beams speared the forest floor, providing Kara with just enough light to observe her surroundings.

Their former prison hung overhead, suspended by ocher vines. It resembled the type of Fringe weed Mother called a *tulinet*, except you could hold those in your hand and this was large enough to hold hundreds of people, its massive weight distributed among a perfect circle of trees. Black petals fitted together at its center, giving it a dome-like appearance similar to the frame-skirts some girls favored during Shadow Festival. The petal that had provided their escape route retracted into place like a giant tongue.

"What is it?" Taff asked. He stroked Shadowdancer, who looked quite put off by her sudden tumble but was otherwise uninjured.

"A gritchenlock, of course," said a female voice behind them.

Kara and Taff turned to face her.

The woman was as tall as Kara, which was very tall indeed, and wore a tattered cloak that had been patched together from different sources. Her hair was cut as short as a man's and stuck out in jagged clumps. Based on her dry, wrinkled skin and slightly stooped back, Kara put her at just north of seventy, but there was an ageless quality to her flinty eyes that spoke of lost kingdoms and forgotten lands.

Over her left shoulder drooped a simple rawhide sack. Whenever the woman moved, it rattled mysteriously, as though filled with marbles or shards of broken glass.

"Drink," the woman said, nodding to a nearby creek.

"Is it safe?" Kara asked.

The woman's eyes narrowed with amusement.

"As safe as it gets here," she said.

Before Kara could stop him, Taff was ankle-deep in the stream. He plunged his face beneath the water.

"It's delicious!" he shouted, coming up for air. He bent down to drink more, but Kara held him back.

"The water's *fine*, Kara," he insisted.

"You don't know that."

Cupping her hands, Kara took a hesitant sip, then a longer one. The water, cold and refreshing, soothed her parched throat. Though her body yearned for more, Kara stopped herself; she would give it time to settle first and see how her stomach reacted.

"How long have you been watching us?" Kara asked warily, leading Shadowdancer to the stream.

"Since the gritchenlock first snatched you up. I was waiting to see if you would live or die." She shrugged. "It passed the time."

"You could have helped us!" Taff exclaimed.

The woman shook her head. "Today is not a day for tree-climbing, I'm afraid. If you had caught me yesterday— well, that would have been a different story."

Taff put his hands on his hips. "That doesn't make any sense."

"And yet it's true," replied the woman. "Rather like a gritchenlock."

"That's nothing like a gritchenlock."

"Also true. How did you know you were inside one? Most just walk around in circles, all oblivious-like, until their air runs out and the digestive process begins. The spinning, you see. Makes the prey think it's still moving, when really it has not moved at all." The woman clucked with appreciation. "Rather clever."

"It's terrible," said Kara.

"No," said the woman. "Not terrible at all. Most of the gritchenlock's victims die in their sleep. In the Thickety, that passes for kindness."

The rain, until then a soft drumbeat against the leaves above, began to fall harder. Taff glared at his sister stubbornly while catching a few drops on the tip of his tongue, as if daring her to forbid him a drink from this water as well.

"Look," the woman said.

Vines creaked and stretched as the gritchenlock

descended from the treetops. Upon striking the surface its massive petals slowly unfurled across the ground, their interior darkening from green to the precise shade of the soil: a perfectly camouflaged trap.

"Works better at night," said the old woman, "but you aren't the first to be caught during the day. Don't blame yourself. Things are disorienting here, especially for new-comers."

"Who are you?" Kara asked.

The woman scratched the side of her head, pinching something between her fingers and flicking it away. "You still haven't answered my question. How did you know how to escape?"

"My mother and I used to pick weeds in the Fringe," Kara said. "She was a healer, and there were many plants there that could be turned into medicine. But she also taught me what to *avoid*. Tulinets and dirt maidens, meat-eaters like that. One night—we had been picking cabbage all day; I remember because my hands were stained green and I kept wiping them against my frock—she took me deep into the Fringe and we knelt next to what I thought were just some petals that had fallen to the ground. My mother dimmed the lantern and we ate sunflower seeds in the dark." Kara's voice cracked, and she took a moment to collect herself. It was, as always, the small, specific memories of Mother that pierced her heart with loss. "Finally a mouse scuttled across the leaves and the trap sprung, lightning fast. The petals came together, just off the ground, and began to spin around a short stalk. My mother brought me close so I could hear the mouse moving inside. 'Poor thing thinks it's still running free through the night,' she told me. 'Doesn't realize its air is running out as we speak. Soon it'll be gone.' I begged her to save it, and though it wasn't my mother's practice to interfere with the workings of the Fringe, that night she listened. 'The strongest man in De'Noran couldn't pry these leaves apart,' she said, 'but watch this.' She ran a single fingernail between the petals and they stiffened before unfolding, giving the mouse a nice little hill to tumble down."

"Is that what you just did in the gritchenlock?" the old woman asked. "Parted the petals? That old trick—nothing more?"

"Actually, it was my brother."

Taff, still trying to catch raindrops with his tongue, smiled brightly and waved.

The old woman sighed. "The Fringe is an unusually dangerous place for children."

"We've had unusual childhoods."

"What is your name?"

"Kara Westfall. This is my brother, Taff."

The old woman gave a slight nod, as though Kara had simply confirmed something she already knew.

"Who are you?" asked Kara.

"My birth name, if you're interested in those sorts of things, is Margaret Allweather. But you might know me by another moniker, given to me much later. Mary Kettle?"

A soft gasp escaped Taff's lips. He moved to Kara's side.

"Ahh," said Mary. "I see you've heard of me."

Cold rain streamed down Kara's back. Wind whistled through the trees like a keening sigh, as though on the verge of saying something but unable to form the necessary words.

"You're dead," Kara said. She stepped protectively in front of Taff and withdrew her penknife. "You died centuries ago."

"I *vanished* centuries ago. Substantial difference."

"You can't still be alive."

"And yet I am. Wonderful thing, magic."

"I won't let you hurt him."

Mary Kettle regarded Kara with undisguised amusement. "And why would I want to do that?"

"I've heard the stories. I know what you do to children."

"You know what I *did*. But you need my help. You're all

alone in this place, and you are already in danger. There are creatures here that can smell magic, that live for the taste of it—"

"I have no magic."

Mary Kettle smiled, her teeth yellow with age but still sharp enough to bite.

"I doubt that very much, Kara, daughter of Helena."

A gust of wind swept through the treetops. Instead of rustling, the leaves *whispered*, a rushing stream of almost-words that fell just short of intelligibility. The whispers were the opposite of bells, songs, the coos of newborn babes. They were the absence of hope itself.

"What is that?" Kara asked, surprised to find her eyes brimming with tears.

"The Thickety is different than other forests," Mary said. "It is not rich soil and the rays of the sun that make these trees flourish, but pain and suffering, heartache and despair. Their leaves will never turn golden or red, nor will they crackle on a cool autumn evening.

But sometimes, if the wind hits them just right, they whisper."

The wind stopped, silencing the trees and exposing the sound of snapping branches as something plowed through the forest, heading in their direction. A moaning wail echoed through the trees, followed by a chorus of high-pitched chitters.

"Something's coming," Taff said.

And then the forest exploded with motion as creatures small and large rushed past, a whole world that had remained hidden beneath the underbrush and in the canopy above now fleeing in a crazed exodus. Kara watched in wonder as they passed, far too many to register at once: winged batlike animals with drooping silver faces, two-footed dragons no larger than squirrels, a flat circle of eyes pinwheeling its way along the ground. These were not animals accustomed to traveling together, but they were united in one basic need: to get away as quickly as possible.

"He knows you're here," said Mary Kettle.

Neither of the children bothered to ask who she meant. They knew.

"How did he find me so quickly?" Kara asked.

"This is his Thickety, child. He knows all."

Above them the treetops crept together in huddled masses, darkening the forest to a false dusk.

"Come with me. I know a place he cannot reach you. It's safe there, for you and your brother."

"Why should I trust you?"

Another horrific wail filled the sky. Closer this time.

Kara didn't move.

"Do as you will," Mary Kettle said, eyeing the nearby ridge. "But I won't waste my life waiting for your decision."

"We're not afraid," Kara said. She wanted the words to sound brave and defiant, but she could hear the quiver in her voice.

"Not afraid of what?" Mary asked. "Death? Is *that* what

you think will happen?" Her gray eyes grew wide. "You're even more foolish than I thought."

With that the woman threw her tinkling sack over one shoulder and started along the path, never once turning her head to check that the children were following her. *What choice do we have?* Kara thought. Seeing the same question in Taff's eyes, she lifted him onto Shadowdancer's back, and they quickly followed the old witch deeper into the Thickety.

TWO

They raced through the forest, spurred onward by a crescendo of footsteps and cracking branches. A muffled boom of thunder shook the treetops, and Kara glimpsed a flash of lightning through a gap in the canopy. For a heartbeat the black leaves sizzled green and revealed the Thickety in its entirety: monstrous tree trunks, gnarled roots bulging out of the ground like ancient veins, a pulsating patch of amber moss. Then the sky turned dark and once again their only lights were the green eyes that dotted the false sky, watching them from high above like cursed stars.

Mary Kettle and Taff rode Shadowdancer, while Kara followed them on foot. The darkness and uneven ground hindered the mare's speed, allowing Kara to keep pace. A stitch was beginning to form in her side, however, and her legs shook with exhaustion. She would have to rest soon or collapse.

"We're almost there," said Mary, as though reading Kara's thoughts. Given what she knew about the old witch, Kara supposed this was a possibility.

They descended through a patch of knee-high weeds with blue bulbs that dangled low and whistled tiny puffs of steam as they passed, Kara's feet soggy and cold in her soaked-through boots. *What am I doing?* she thought. *We're following an evil witch who's as likely to steal our souls as save us.* Kara started to lag behind, Shadowdancer now just a vague silhouette between the trees, the stitch in her side growing fearsome teeth. Then Mary leaned over and whispered something in Shadowdancer's ear, and they came to a sudden stop.

"Here," said Mary. She slid from the mount and nearly lost her balance upon hitting the ground. Taff reached over to steady her.

"Thank you, little gentleman," she said.

Before them a stone bridge stretched into the darkness. Kara cautiously peered out over the expanse and saw nothing below, the light through the canopy squeezed to the faintest trickle in this part of the Thickety.

"It'll be dark on the bridge," said Mary, handing Kara Shadowdancer's reins. "You'll have to lead her."

Thunder crashed and the treetops flashed green once more, revealing their pursuers. Their appearance was vaguely wolflike, but with features exhumed from the ground: hollow, branch-boned bodies, ruby-leaved mouths and bright, flowering eyes. At their head was Sordyr, his face concealed beneath the folds of a pumpkin-orange cloak that stretched into the distance as far as the eye could see, flowing through the trees like mist.

Kara stepped backward onto the bridge. The monstrosities edged closer. Though Sordyr's eyes remained hidden Kara could feel them trained on her every move.

Shadowdancer's reins pulled taut in her hands.

"Shadowdancer," Kara whispered to the unmoving horse. She yanked the reins harder. "Shadowdancer, come on."

At first Kara thought that the mare was reluctant to step upon the bridge, this man-made thing that spanned impossible spaces in the air. That wasn't the case, however. Shadowdancer was *trying* to move with all her might, her sinewy muscles straining with effort. Trying, but unable.

Looking down, Kara saw the reason. Four thick roots coiled tightly around Shadowdancer's legs, shackling her to the earth.

"Hold on, girl," Kara said, unclasping her penknife.

Before she could step forward and make the first cut, however, a strong hand grasped her arm. "Don't step off the bridge!" Mary exclaimed. "The Forest Demon must remain rooted to the earth at all times—he cannot cross stone. You are safe here."

"I have to help her!"

"No! If you place a single foot on the earth he will take you as well."

Shadowdancer watched Kara with trusting eyes, waiting for her to do something. To save her.

"She is lost," Mary said. "I'm sorry."

And then Sordyr was before them, no more than an arm's length away. He craned his neck forward so that Kara caught a glimpse of his eyes, moss-green wells that held bottomless depths of pain and cruelty.

Sordyr ran a branch hand over Shadowdancer's flank. His surprisingly nimble fingers were as long as broom bristles and segmented into dozens of barely perceptible joints.

"Kara," he said. "You have returned to me. As I knew you would."

"I had no choice."

"Yes. They would have killed you otherwise, no? The same gutless sheep whose lives you saved."

Kara said nothing.

"Come to me," Sordyr said, inching forward until his cloak danced along the edge of the stone. "Just one step. That's all it takes. Close your eyes if it will make it easier. I have such things to teach you. You think you know magic. You think you've learned the extent of your power. You know nothing."

"Let Shadowdancer go."

Sordyr paused, confused for a moment, before following Kara's eyes to the mare. Something in his throat clicked with amusement.

"You've named the beast that carries you on its back? How very human of you."

"She's my friend."

"I see."

Reaching beneath the folds of his cloak, Sordyr pried apart the bark-like plate of his chest. His hand dug deep, loosening a waterfall of soil and black mud, then deeper still, searching for something.

Finally he produced a single black seed and offered it to Kara.

"You can save her," he said. "Your *friend*. Simply swallow this and I will set her free."

The seed vibrated eagerly between his branched fingertips.

Taff pulled on Kara's hand.

"No," he said. "Don't do it."

"I can't let him hurt Shadowdancer."

"Listen to your brother," added Mary. "I've seen what happens. Swallow that and you'll belong to the Forest Demon forever."

Kara stepped forward to the very edge of the stone bridge. In the soil just beyond her boots, dozens of wormlike roots probed the air, ready to pounce the moment Kara's foot touched earth. Sordyr's cloak snapped at the air and strange odors overwhelmed her: a tree stump swollen with decay, rotten flora scraped from the bottom of a swamp.

"Come to me, *wexari*," said Sordyr. "I will not ask again."

"Please," Kara said. "Don't hurt her."

Sordyr shoved the seed down Shadowdancer's throat. The mare gagged and shuddered but ivy slithered from within the arms of Sordyr's cloak and clamped Shadowdancer's mouth shut. "No!" Kara shouted, trying to rush to Shadowdancer's assistance but unable to escape the grasp of Mary and Taff, who pulled her backward onto the bridge.

The mare became very still. Kara looked into her eyes and saw the life there flicker and extinguish like a candle flame left too close to an open window. In less than a moment Kara's companion was gone forever.

A new life began.

Shadowdancer's beautiful chestnut-brown flank disintegrated, revealing not bones but a skeleton frame composed of twisted branches. Black orchids burst forth from her eyes. The creature that was once Shadowdancer looked up at Kara without any sign of recognition, her flowered gaze now dark and malevolent, and whinnied—soft and choked, as though forced through a mouthful of dirt. The branchwolves responded in kind, not a howl of anger or hunger but something far worse: a cry of immense suffering. Kara covered Taff's ears and he clamped his hands over hers, shaking his head from side to side.

Sordyr waved a hand and all sound stopped.

"You could have saved her," he said, stroking the mane of red ivy still growing into place. "You chose to save yourself instead. Perhaps we are not so different, you and I."

Kara wanted to be angry. She wanted to tell him he was wrong. But words and emotions would be meaningless to the Forest Demon, a dark force as implacable as the sun abandoning the world to night.

He will win eventually. Even if I had my magic there is no way to fight him. All I can do is run.

"Good-bye, Shadowdancer," Kara said, forcing herself to look straight into the horse's orchid eyes.

She took Taff by the hand and began to back away; Mary Kettle had already vanished into the darkness of the bridge. "It's all right," she told Taff. "He can't cross the bridge. We're safe."

But then Sordyr raised a branch hand and pointed in their direction.

"Bring me the girl," he told the branchwolves gathered around him. "As alive as you can. The other two you can do with what you will."

THREE

The five branchwolves that spilled onto the bridge seemed slightly unsure of themselves at first, like children learning how to ice-skate. Kara took this opportunity to open some distance between them. She longed to sprint, but the bridge was narrow and there were no walls to guard against a sudden spiral into the depths. Besides, even though Taff was fast for his age, he still wouldn't be able to keep up with her long strides, and there was no way Kara was going to leave him behind to fend for himself.

Quickly, however, the branchwolves found their footing and began to gain ground. Over the thudding of her beating heart, Kara heard their approaching nails clicking lightly against the stone.

"Run!" Kara exclaimed.

"I am!"

"Run faster!" She pulled Taff's hand as hard as she dared. If he stumbled or fell over, the branchwolves would be upon them. The stone blurred beneath her feet, darkness squeezing against them on all sides.

Suddenly Kara felt a sharp pain. A branchwolf—only a runt, but clearly the fastest of the pack—had jumped up and nipped her forearm, losing its balance in the process. Almost immediately it found purchase on the stones and charged again, leaping gracefully through the air. At the last possible moment Kara kicked it as hard as she could. It was light, like a sack full of leaves, and with a muffled yelp flew backward along the bridge, knocking into a second wolf. The two plummeted over the edge, their choked whines followed, a long time afterward, by a cracking sound no louder than a foot stepping on a branch.

The remaining three wolves withdrew, and the bridge grew silent, even the rain slowing to a drizzle.

"Are you hurt bad?" Taff asked.

Kara shook her head. She could feel a thin trickle of blood running down her arm, but the pain was no worse than a bee sting. It was the least of their worries right now.

They proceeded through the darkness, their pace slower, more deliberate. The bridge, cracked with age and wear, narrowed considerably. Lifetimes ago the stones might have been smooth enough for wagon wheels, but now jagged fissures made even walking difficult.

Taff slipped his hand from Kara's grip and peered over the edge.

"I wonder how far it goes," he said, picking up a stone from the debris that littered the bridge.

"Taff!"

"I just want to see!"

He tossed the stone over the edge, and it seemed to hover in midair for a moment before an undulating shape carried it away. Kara glimpsed what might have been the eye of a great leviathan floating in the darkness, far too large to notice something as insignificant as a stone on its back.

"Let's go," said Kara.

"Yes," said Taff, nodding in agreement. "Let's go."

Sunlight was fading fast. Kara had no idea how long this bridge was, but if they didn't reach the other side by nightfall, the crossing would become far more dangerous.

"What happened to Mary Kettle?" Taff asked.

"She left us," said Kara. "Just like everyone else."

"I don't know about that," said Taff. "She might be waiting for us at the end of the bridge. I think she went ahead to make sure it was safe."

"Taff—you need to understand. No one is going to help us. We have to get through this by ourselves."

"That's not true. There are good people. They'll help us. You'll see."

Kara sighed. *How can he think that after all we've been through? After everyone he's ever known turned against him— even Father.*

"It's probably for the best anyway," Kara said. "You know the stories about Mary Kettle. She's even scarier than Sordyr."

"No," Taff said, and there was a terrible timidity in his voice that Kara had never heard before. "Nothing's scarier than him."

She squeezed his hand, hating the Forest Demon more than ever.

Their jog settled into a slow and steady walk, Kara constantly glancing downward to make sure each step met stone and not empty air. Finally Taff exclaimed, "I can see the other side!"

That was when they came. A dozen branchwolves, maybe more.

They didn't flee. They went back for reinforcements.

"Go!" Kara told her brother. "Don't turn around! Just run!"

Taff sped ahead, vanishing into the dark. Kara hoped he was far away by the time he realized his sister was not by his side.

I need to buy him some time. It's me they want, after all. Besides, I handled two of these wolves pretty easily. Maybe they aren't as scary as they look.

The pack crept toward her, noses low to the ground, like walking skeletons constructed from branches instead of bones. Within the rib cage of each monstrosity beat a clump of black mud.

Were these once real wolves? Did he change them like Shadowdancer?

At that moment one of the wolves leaped over her head and slid along the stone, turning nimbly to block her path. This one was larger than the others, with two broken branches where its ribs should be. Battle scars.

Kara took a step backward and heard dirt-choked growls just behind her. Though she was loath to take her eyes off the pack leader, Kara glanced over her shoulder long enough to see a semicircle of approaching wolves.

She could go neither forward nor backward. To either side of her loomed a long fall into nothingness.

There was no escape.

The pack leader arched his back and watched her expectantly, his eyes wilted roses. Behind the wolf she heard sounds of struggle, the participants obscured by darkness. "Let me go, you old hag!" screamed Taff. "We have to help her!"

"No," replied Mary Kettle, the words meant more for Kara than Taff. "She needs to do this on her own."

After this the old woman was silent, and though Taff had a lot more to say—including several words that would have earned his mouth a good soap-washing back in De'Noran—Kara blocked him out. Her concentration remained on the pack leader. *There's no point trying to go back the way I came*, she thought, *with Sordyr waiting at the other end of the bridge. I have to somehow get past this big one.* Kara feinted to the right and then sprinted forward, thinking she could slip past the pack leader. The wolf remained still. She thought she saw the hint of a smile part the leaf where its mouth should be.

Then the wolf grunted something, lower and more guttural than the previous sounds she had heard. At first Kara thought it was trying to communicate with her, but then she turned and saw a member of the pack behind her step forward, stick paws clicking against the stone. Though not as large as the leader, this branchwolf was still fierce-looking, with a broken twig at the top of its head that extended like a sharpened horn.

They're not going to attack me all at once, Kara thought. *It's too narrow. They don't want to fall.*

But even as Kara thought this, she knew it wasn't true. They weren't worried about their own lives. They were worried about something happening to her, what their master would do if they harmed his prize.

They feared Sordyr more than they feared death.

Kara scanned her surroundings for a weapon and found a loose stone, as large as a brick, jutting from a crack in the bridge.

A hush of anticipation fell over the wolves. Bending its head so low that the pointed branch atop his head scratched the ground, the champion that the pack leader had chosen pounced forward.

For a moment, Kara considered throwing the stone. The branchwolf was hollow and probably weighed less than Taff; one solid hit might shatter him to bits. Before she could decide, however, the champion was already leaping through the air, headed straight toward her. Kara stepped to the side, thinking to dodge its horn, but the branchwolf surprised her by turning its head at the last minute and snapping at her calf instead.

Kara felt the bottom of her dress dampen with blood. She pricked a black thorn from her leg.

The champion gave her no time to rest. This time it slid across the stone bridge, using its momentum to knock Kara off her feet. It stood over her and drooled a handful of black earth onto her face. Without breaking eye contact, Kara grasped for a weapon and felt something solid. A stone. She drove it into the monster's left paw. The branchwolf howled in pain. Broken twigs scattered across the bridge. The champion fell, tried to rise, then fell again. Kara got to her feet and raised the stone high in the air but had no heart to destroy the creature, injured as it was.

A soft jingle filled the air: Mary Kettle's sack, swinging from side to side as she emerged from the darkness. Taff followed close behind, dragging a too-heavy stick along the ground. Instead of attacking them—as Kara was certain it would—the pack leader backed away warily, moving past Kara to rejoin the other wolves.

"Why aren't you using magic to fight them?" Mary asked.

"I'm done with magic."

"Hmm," said Mary. "I wonder, though. Is magic done with you?"

The pack leader growled and two new wolves stepped forward to face Kara, the petals of their eyes opening and closing.

"They're not going to kill you," Mary said. "But they are going to tear the muscles from your legs and drag you back to their master. Unless you start acting like a proper witch and stop them, that is."

Kara thought of the Forest Demon waiting for her at the end of the bridge. He would enfold her in his impossibly long cloak and thrust a seed down her throat, changing her into something else altogether.

The thought of using magic again frightened her. The thought of becoming one of Sordyr's minions frightened her more.

"I don't have a grimoire," Kara said.

"So? You are *wexari*."

"What's a—"

"Lesson later," Mary said. "For now, just cast."

"I—"

"Just. Cast."

Kara closed her eyes.

Focusing on the branchwolf directly in front of her, she thought: *Stop this. Leave us alone.* When she opened her eyes the branchwolf was a few steps closer, having rudely ignored her feeble attempt to enchant it. She tried to remember a spell from the grimoire—any spell—but the words that had once come so easily to her were now nothing more than a jumble. She could recall some individual sounds but the order of them was well beyond her.

The wolf continued to approach.

Kara grunted with frustration. Without the grimoire, casting a spell was impossible, like trying to read without using words.

"I can't," Kara said.

"Not yet," said Mary. "But I felt something. Something

weak and insignificant and pathetic, like a kitten trying to topple a mountain." The old woman sighed and dropped the sack to her feet. "I guess it's up to me this time."

Humming under her breath, Mary pulled the sack open and shifted through its contents, seemingly unperturbed by their current predicament. Kara thought the branch-wolves would use this opportunity to attack, but instead they backed away, eyeing the old woman cautiously.

They're scared, Kara thought. *Of Mary . . . or whatever's in that sack.*

Finally, Mary withdrew a battered glass lantern. It was set into a cracked and faded red and blue wooden base. Mary blew away its shroud of dust and placed the lantern carefully on the ground.

"You're going to fight them with *that*?" Taff asked.

"What did you expect?"

"I don't know. A sword or something."

Mary shooed him away. "Bah. Boys and their swords."

She removed a paper shade from her sack. Several

elaborate shapes had been cut into the material, though Kara could not determine their identity in the dim light.

Lucas told me about these lanterns, she thought. *They spin and project images onto the wall, matching the shapes cut into the shade. A bauble of the World, far too magical for De'Noran.*

Mary placed the shade over the lantern.

"Don't worry," she said, taking a few steps backward. "This will take care of them. Watch."

The branchwolves stopped, waited. Then, their confidence growing, edged closer. The one nearest to Kara bared its teeth, revealing a mouthful of razor-sharp thorns and a tongue speckled with black fungus.

Taff turned to Mary. "You're just crazy, aren't you? You're just a crazy old lady with a sack full of junk." He shook his head in exasperation. "Figures."

Facing the wolves, Taff tried to raise his giant stick into attack position but could barely lift it off the ground. He looked about as threatening as a boy toasting marshmallows.

"Wait!" Mary exclaimed, producing a key from the folds of her cloak. "I always forget this part." With surprising speed, she inserted the key into the base and cranked it three times.

The lantern began to turn.

Kara heard a whooshing sound. Looking up, she watched wisps of early evening sunlight slip between small gaps in the treetops. These threads of light gathered together in swirling whirlpools that rocketed straight through the slight opening at the top of the lantern. The lantern revolved faster, spinning like a top now, sucking more and more light into it.

Behind the lantern's shade a small flame flickered to life, revealing what had been cut into the paper. Kara gasped. The lantern began to spin even faster, just a blur of fiery motion now, and against the sky a dragon of light appeared, a larger version of the shape in the shade. Flickering in and out of existence, it bore down on the branchwolves with a hideous roar. The bridge became a cacophony of piteous whines as the creatures fled, quite a few slipping over the side.

Moments later the dragon dissipated with a puff of white smoke. The lantern shook away any unused sunlight like a dog after a bath and then came to a creaking halt.

"Still want your sword?" Mary asked Taff.

She slid the lantern into her sack and knotted it tight.

FOUR

They followed Mary along a narrow path lined with foul-smelling weeds and irises whose petals looked disturbingly like skin. Kara thought she saw the branches of one tree bend closer to the ground, as though to snatch her away, but it could have been her imagination. It was hard to tell anymore.

"Your lantern," said Kara. "I've never seen such magic."

"You haven't lived long."

"In the stories you use a grimoire."

Mary Kettle winced at the word as though Kara had struck her.

"My spellbook was involved in the lantern's making. But now it's just a tool, like everything else in here." She shook the contents of the sack. "Almost anyone can use them. No magic required."

"What else is in there?" Taff asked.

"Toys."

His expression brightened.

"What kind of toys?"

"Enchanted toys."

"What kind of—"

"Shh," whispered Mary. "In this part of the forest, there's a terrible monster that feeds on little boys who ask annoying questions. We don't want to awaken it."

"I know that's not true," Taff said, but he remained silent until they reached Mary Kettle's encampment, little more than a fire pit and lean-to built from some rotting pieces of ashwood.

"Rest for a bit," she said. "Sordyr will have to travel days before finding a place he can cross. He needs earth, the Forest Demon does, two feet planted in the ground at all times. He cannot cross stone, as you know, nor can he cross water. He cannot ride a horse."

"Why?" Taff asked, but Mary swatted the question away like a troublesome fly.

"The important thing is that Sordyr does not travel quickly—our one and only advantage." She paused, biting her knuckle in consideration. "He'll try to cut us off at Brille, I wager."

"What's Brille?" asked Taff.

"A village."

"There are villages in the Thickety?"

Mary smiled but did not meet his eyes.

"Of sorts," she said.

After checking Taff for wounds, Kara lifted the bottom of her dress to examine the place on her calf where the branchwolf had bitten her. The fabric was matted to her skin with dried blood, but the wound was not deep. It would heal. Her pale-green dress, however, was another story. It had been the finest dress she ever owned, a surprise from her father three days before his coronation as fen'de.

Now it was torn and tattered beyond repair.

Was it really from Father? she wondered. *Or was he already Timoth Clen, even then?*

"It's brighter now than it was during the day," Taff said. Kara looked up at the canopy. Just an hour ago she could have glimpsed a hint of sunlight through the net of branches—not much, but enough to remind her that it was daytime in the world outside. Now only night peeked between the gaps of the canopy, and while this should have plunged the Thickety into an even deeper darkness, their surroundings had actually become *brighter*, courtesy of a new, green-tinged light that hazed around them.

"One of the quirks of the Thickety," said Mary. She hung a small cauldron over the fire pit. "If you look up at the treetops there, you'll see that most of the light comes from the leaves themselves. During the day they suck up the sunlight. At night they set it free."

"Day is night and night is day," Kara said. "Everything's backward here."

Mary said, "That's one way of looking at it."

While Mary reheated some stew left at the bottom of the cauldron, Taff went to gather water from a shallow brook bubbling nearby. Kara warned him to stay within sight, and he mumbled his assent.

Finally she was alone with the witch.

There were so many questions Kara wanted to ask. *Are the stories about you true? Do you know why Sordyr is so intent on capturing me? What do the other things in your sack do?* But feeling a warm weariness settle into her body, Kara decided—for now—to ask the only question that really mattered, the one that couldn't wait: "How do I get my brother out of this place?"

Mary stirred the cauldron, her eyes closed. Kara would have thought her asleep were it not for the steady motion of the wooden ladle.

"You cannot leave the way you came," she finally said. "Sordyr will not allow it."

"There must be other ways."

Mary Kettle's ancient head rose and fell a single time.

"I know of only one path that leads out of the Thickety," she said. "There is even a ship there, I've heard tell. A relic from an ill-fated journey of exploration."

"Is it far?" Kara asked.

The old woman fixed her with a disappointed look.

"If you're going to survive this place, child, you need to ask the right questions."

"The path," Kara said after a moment's thought. "Why does Sordyr allow it to remain open?"

"But it's not open, not truly. Just closed in a different fashion. See, there's a guardian of sorts at the end of the path, and I think it amuses Sordyr to feed her, like a pet. She's called Imogen, or at least she was when she was still human."

"What is she now?" asked Kara.

"A foul and hungry beast who has lost every trace of humanity."

"She eats people?"

"In her way."

Mary stopped stirring and took a sip from the ladle. Her cloak drooped downward and Kara saw the whole of her arm, blue with veins.

"Perhaps we could sneak by her," Kara suggested.

"Impossible," Mary said, sprinkling something into the bubbling stew from a pouch inside her cloak. "But if you take the time to learn magic properly, you might be able to bend her to your will. When all is said and done, Imogen is nothing more than a monster now, and it is my understanding that controlling such creatures is your area of expertise."

"How do you know that?"

The old woman smiled, her eyes glinting with childlike mischief. "I haven't left the Thickety in a long time—a *very* long time indeed—but I have my ways of checking in on the outside world. A nosy old woman needs her entertainment, after all." Her face grew serious again. "But no matter where your talents lie, you must learn to use them properly before facing a creature like Imogen. There will be no grimoire to help you win this battle."

Kara wasn't anxious to use magic again, but if it was the only way to escape this place, she supposed she didn't have a choice.

"Do you think I can really use magic without a spell-book?" she asked.

"Your first lesson's tomorrow. We'll start with something small and go from there. But we must keep moving. Sordyr may have lost a day or two, but he will not rest until he's found you."

"You are putting yourself at great risk on our behalf. Thank you."

Mary did not answer but continued to stir the stew, looking up only when Taff returned, dragging a bucketful of water along the ground.

"You aiming to spill more than we drink?" Mary chided him, taking the bucket from his hands.

She ladled the stew into clay bowls and they ate greedily. It was unlike anything Kara had ever tasted, and as she ate, Mary told her of herbs and vegetables that grew only in the Thickety.

"Plus there's some diced dramal in there," Mary said. "Caught one just yesterday. Most people don't eat them on account of how they smell when you slice them open, but I think those inside parts taste just fine."

"What's a—" Taff started, but Kara shushed him, telling him it might be better if they didn't know.

After dinner, Kara washed the cookware in the brook. By the time she returned, Taff was fast asleep. She pulled a blanket over her brother and kissed his forehead. He looked older somehow, aged by experience and not years.

Mary sat by the fire pit, stoking the flames. Kara yawned into her hand, her eyelids suddenly heavy.

"Tired?" Mary asked.

Kara nodded. "How about you?"

"I'm always tired. I just don't like to sleep. Bad

dreams." She watched the dwindling flames with haunted eyes. "With the things I've done, I suppose that's a small price to pay."

With the things I've done . . .

Kara swallowed hard. Given how much the old woman had helped them, it was easy to forget that she was *Mary Kettle*. Kara had heard all the stories, especially during Shadow Festival. The children of her village had even made up a rhyme: *"Run and hide, run and hide / Mary's coming to take you inside / Her black kettle knows your name / You will never be the same."*

"Stories are just stories," Kara said. "People used to speak ill of me all the time. Doesn't make it true."

"Sometimes lies do grow in the telling," Mary said. Then she leaned forward, her gray eyes flickering in the firelight. "But in my particular case, everything you've heard is true. Every unimaginable horror happened just the way the talespinners say. It's important you know that, Kara Westfall."

Despite the warmth of the fire, Kara's body had

suddenly grown cold. It took her a few moments to gather the courage to speak again.

"But if you're truly as evil as people claim," she said, her voice cracking, "then why are you helping us?"

Mary chewed her lower lip. "Chances at redemption do not come so often in the Thickety. I might not get another. You need me to survive, but I need you as well. I know it's far too late for me to balance the scales completely, but maybe if I can counter all the evil I've done, just a little bit, I can find some sort of . . ." The old woman paused, shaking her head. "What are you, fourteen?"

"Twelve."

"Tall for your age."

"I've been told."

"In any case, far too young to understand all this."

A series of images flashed through Kara's mind. *Simon Loder's face, bloated by stings. Grace's crystal-blue eyes as she falls into the grimoire's abyss.*

"I understand just fine," Kara said.

Mary Kettle opened her mouth as though to disagree, but then met Kara's dark eyes and nodded. Reaching into a side pocket she withdrew a clear vial and poured its contents into the flames, which flashed silver for a moment before bursting into a pure, warming light.

Kara yawned, mesmerized by the flickering flame, a sanctuary in the encroaching darkness.

"It'll burn through the night now," Mary said. "Just so you know, I might not be here come morning. At least, not this me."

Before Kara could ask what she meant, sleep took her.

Kara was not a dreamer by nature, but when she did dream, it was often of her mother. Images, mostly: Mother scrubbing Kara's nails clean after a day gathering herbs in the Fringe; Mother packing a poultice in a calf's wounded nose while whispering a song in the animal's ear. Or just Mother's face, Kara trying to hold the features in her head, fighting against the day when she could no longer remember what Helena Westfall looked like at all.

Tonight, however, Kara did not dream of Mother.

She dreamed of Father.

He was walking through a field she had never seen, the soil already tilled and ready for seeding. His beard was neatly trimmed, and on his head he wore the black hat he used to favor when Mother was alive. By the way he carried himself Kara knew that this was her real father and not Timoth Clen, and she longed to run into his arms and drink in the farmer smells of dirt and coffee.

Father scooped up a handful of earth, then let it run through his fingers, watching it carefully as it fell to the ground. Stroking his beard he pulled a black pouch from his inside pocket and shook it in his hands. It rattled.

The dream ended.

Kara awoke to the sounds of swordplay.

The rain had stopped but little remained of the hazy

green glow; the canopy leaves, having used up their stored light, needed to be replenished by the sun's rays before they could be effective again. In the meantime, Mary had encircled their camp with a dozen blazing torches.

"I got you that time!" Taff shouted. "I'm getting better!"

"Oh yes," said a girl's voice. "I bow before your masterful skill."

It took Kara's eyes a few moments to adjust to the light, but once they did she saw Taff and a girl about eleven years of age. They were fighting with wooden swords, the girl's sharp gray eyes tracking Taff's every move. He swung his sword and she slid out of the way with feline grace.

"Almost hit you!" Taff exclaimed.

The girl turned to Kara. "Note the use of the word 'almost,'" she said. "Important distinction, don't you think?"

There was something familiar about this girl, Kara thought, especially in the eyes, as flat and expressionless as stone. And then she remembered the words spoken to her before she fell asleep: *I might not be here come morning. At least, not this me.*

It couldn't be. . . .

The girl dodged another one of Taff's blows, dancing past him with ease and smacking him on the bottom.

"Hey!" Taff exclaimed, his ears turning red.

"Would you rather I hit your sword arm? Perhaps knock some skill into it?"

Grunting with exertion, Taff turned and swung the wooden sword wildly. He was growing frustrated now, and it was making him careless.

"Keep your feet balanced," the girl said, dodging every blow, "and your arms raised. You look tired."

"I am tired!"

"Fine. Just don't show it. Perception is all."

Taff brought the sword down, and instead of dodging the blow, the girl met it with her own weapon. The clack of wood reverberated throughout the forest. Branches shook as a flock of tri-winged birds spiraled into the sky.

With a shout of pain Taff dropped the sword. He rubbed his left elbow, his arm hanging loosely by his side.

"Is this your pathetic way of yielding?" the girl asked.

"I think that's enough," Kara said. "You're going to get hurt."

Taff rolled his eyes. "We're having fun, Kara."

"Yes," said the girl. "You did well. Considering."

"Considering what?" Taff asked.

"Just considering."

The girl knelt by the bucket and ladled water into a cup. She handed it to Taff.

"Drink. The ringing in your arm will pass." She took a step back, taking stock of him. "You should forget about using a sword. You will never be large enough to wield it."

"I'm not done growing, you know!"

"If you see the stem of a rose, do you suspect it will turn into an oak tree?" She lifted his arm, ran a hand along his back. "The thinness of the wrists, the slope of your shoulders. You're not meant for size." She tilted his chin upward so his eyes met hers. "Besides, you have a gentle heart. Not a good quality if you plan on plunging a blade through a man's chest with any regularity."

Kara stepped into the conversation.

"You can change your age," she said.

The girl nodded and picked up Taff's sword. Withdrawing a penknife she carefully whittled away the splinters.

"It's a good sign that you realized it so quickly," Mary Kettle said. "Such a willingness to embrace the impossible will help you in the days to come. Your brother figured it out right away as well. But saying I can *change* my age is not exactly true. It's nothing I can control. My years are a fickle thing, slipping and sliding as I sleep. Even I don't know how many years younger I'll be when I wake. Or older."

"How is that possible?" Kara asked.

"A long story," she said, "best left for another time. We need to start moving."

She handed the sword to Taff.

"You're fast," she said. "That's good."

Taff beamed. "A swordsman needs to be fast."

"You misunderstand. I meant you could use your speed for running away."

"I don't want to run! I want to fight!"

"No," said Mary. "I think you're too smart for that. I see it in your eyes. A blazing intelligence."

Kara wrapped an arm around Taff's shoulders. "The schoolmistress back in De'Noran said she couldn't teach him fast enough. That he could do with a boatload of books from the World."

Mary regarded Taff carefully. She might have looked like a child, but there was no mistaking the wisdom in those old eyes.

"Perhaps that can be your weapon, then," she said.

Taff did not look convinced. "Being smart?" he asked.

"How can I fight with that?"

"If you have to ask, then I was wrong to think it. Feel free to practice your sword work, futile as it may be. But for now we must break camp."

Taff slid the wooden sword through the belt loop of his mud-stained breeches.

"Where are we going?" he asked.

"I will take you to the path that leads out of the Thickety. It is a long journey, but this is good, in a way. You will need the time to train. Only then will you have a chance against Imogen. But first there is another problem of a more pressing nature."

Mary crouched next to her sack and, after rummaging quickly through its contents, withdrew a simple slingshot. She lowered her voice so that only they could hear.

"We're being watched. Come, children. It's time to go hunting."

FIVE

They edged along a rise overlooking the stone bridge from the previous night and wound north through a tangle of black-leaved trees. A thick carpet of moss gentled their footsteps.

"Is it Sordyr?" Taff asked. "Is he the one watching us?"

"Don't be foolish," Mary said. "It'll be days before he reaches the end of the ravine and is able to cross over. I told you—"

"His feet need to touch the earth at all times," replied Taff. "I remember. But why?"

"Is the why of it so important?" she asked.

"It is to me!" he exclaimed.

"How strange," Mary said. "In the Thickety we are simply happy to survive. But I will answer your question. Beneath his feet lies a network of roots that anchor him to the Thickety. They stretch out of the dirt to allow him enough freedom to move but never part his body entirely, for if they did he would wither and die. He is as much a part of the Thickety as these trees you see before us. And, like them, he is a prisoner here and longs to make his escape. After so many years, it is the only thing that matters to him anymore." She sighed, looking out at the shifting shadows beyond the chasm. "It wasn't always like this, you know. Once the sailors sang songs of this island, its great beauty. But then Sordyr came and the Thickety spread like a sickness from one shore to the other. De'Noran is the only part left untouched."

"Our village has its own brand of sickness," Kara said. "Besides, I think you can find beauty anywhere if you look hard enough. Even here."

"Perhaps," Mary said, "but it's a dark, diseased sort of beauty."

To their left hung a throng of brownish, sagging bracken. *In De'Noran*, Kara thought, *such plants would be a vibrant shade of green.* Here, however, the palette was limited to black and brown and gray and all the hues between. The smells Kara usually associated with the woods of De'Noran—soothing pine, moist earth, the fragrant perfume of blossoming flowers—were nowhere to be found. Instead, decay permeated every breath. The Thickety looked like a forest but lacked its most essential qualities, like a person with a smiling face and all the right words but an empty cavity where the heart should be.

A dark, diseased sort of beauty.

The bracken rustled.

Lightning fast, Mary turned in the direction of the noise and aimed her slingshot. She waited, the empty pocket pulled taut between two fingers.

"You forgot to load it," Taff whispered. "I'll get you a stone."

"I don't need one," Mary replied.

She swiveled in the direction of a nearby tree and released the pocket. There was a soft whizzing sound, and a branch cracked at its center and fell to the ground.

Mary retrained the slingshot on her original target, ignoring Taff's astonished expression.

"It's magic, isn't it?" he asked.

"That's right."

A toothy grin lit Taff's face.

"Can I try?"

"No," Mary said. She turned to Kara and nodded toward the bracken. "Flush it out."

Kara picked up a long branch and nudged the clump of vegetation. Nothing happened. She heard Mary's slingshot stretch even farther.

"Do it again," Mary said.

Kara jumped backward as something with five legs

and black mushrooms sprouting from its body exploded out of the undergrowth, wildly gnashing its teeth. Mary trained her weapon on the creature but paused only a moment before lowering it. The animal zipped off into the forest.

"That's not what was watching us," she whispered. "I was tempted to fire anyway for the sake of tonight's stew, but I'm not sure how you two would feel about stitch-rat. It's more of an acquired taste, and it spoils quickly. Not a good catch for a morning hunt. Besides, it's Blighted. I'm hesitant to eat those." Noting the confused expression on Kara's face, Mary elaborated. "The black mushrooms? Sordyr's evil courses like poison through many of the plants and trees of the Thickety, and it has infected that creature. Could have been something it ate, the scratch of a thorn as it passed. Anything, really."

"Is it going to die?" Kara asked.

"No. Physically, it's probably never been better. But . . . do you believe animals have souls?"

"Of course!"

"Well, not that one. Not anymore."

They continued onward over a knoll overgrown with gummy grass that stuck to Kara's boots and past a boulder dimpled with recesses, as though something had tunneled its way in and out again. As they walked, Kara caught glimpses of animals squeaking through the undergrowth or prancing from branch to branch. Many of them had been scarred by sickly yellow fungus or withered flowers.

I'm not the only one he torments, Kara thought. *Everything he touches is diseased.*

"This path leads up the hill here," Mary said. "At the top—that's where the spy was watching us. I'm hoping we can catch him unawares, but there's a good possibility he's long gone by now. Then again, what we're dealing with might not even be human." She nodded in Kara's direction. "You sense anything?"

"Me?" Kara asked.

"Yes, *wexari*! You!"

"That word again. I don't even know what it means!"

Mary buried her face in her hands. "I'm sorry. I forget how little you know sometimes. A girl with a talent for witchcraft is rare enough, but for every thousand witches there is only one *wexari*. One who does not need a grimoire to cast spells."

"But I *do* need a grimoire! I've never used magic without one."

"Don't be so sure. My guess is that you've been using magic for years without realizing it. See, *wexari* are different from other witches in a number of ways. They aren't beholden to a grimoire—though they can certainly use one—and their magic is more specific. Some *wexari* can control the weather. Others can create illusions. Your talent involves animals—though that may evolve as your powers grow."

Kara thought about this. "I think you're half right," she said. "It's true that every spell I've ever cast involved some sort of creature, and I guess that makes sense. I've always been able to somehow . . . *communicate* with them, ever since I was a little girl. But it's the *grimoire* that made that connection magical! I can't just wave my hand and make animals do my bidding, not by myself."

Mary Kettle gave Kara the same look a schoolmaster might reserve for a particularly slow student.

"Have you ever tried?"

Kara was about to respond when Taff spoke instead. "Remember when poor Shadowdancer came to help us?" he asked. Of course Kara remembered; the villagers, under the spell of Timoth Clen, had been on the verge of overtaking them. She had called the mare in her mind and Shadowdancer had simply appeared. "That was definitely magic, and you didn't have the grimoire then!"

"You can *use* the grimoire, but you don't *need* it," Mary continued. "Not when it comes to animals. That is your special gift. This is *true* magic, not magic stolen from the pages of a spellbook. You will have to learn how to wield it. It will not be easy."

"Anything would be better than using a grimoire," Kara said.

Mary Kettle's old eyes narrowed with pity. "Poor girl," she said. "You really don't know anything at all."

In less than an hour they reached the top of a large hill that gave them an excellent vantage point. It reminded Kara of the place she had often met her friend Lucas for lunch.

By now he should have reached the mainland, she thought. A weak smile touched her lips. *At least one of us is safe.*

Creeping on soft feet, avoiding the snap of branches and crackle of leaves, Mary Kettle leaned over the side of the hill.

"It was watching us from a tree down there," she whispered.

"How do you know?" Taff asked.

"You don't survive in the Thickety for as long as I have without developing a sense for these things. My guess is Sordyr himself sent it to spy on us."

"What is it?" Kara asked.

"I thought you could tell me. Maybe *where* it is, while you're at it."

"But . . . even if I *can* do magic without a grimoire, I don't know *how*!"

"Nor do I, child. Remember, I'm just a common witch . . . albeit a common witch who has traveled the World a bit. I've read a lot of forbidden books, talked to others far older and wiser than myself. Knowledge is power, they say, and truer words have never been spoken." Leaning on one elbow, she turned to face Kara. "A *wexari*'s power is a personal thing, an extension of who she is—or he, for though only women can use grimoires, a *wexari* can be either gender. The manner of casting may change, but the first step is always the same." She pulled on her lower earlobe. "Listening. *What* you're listening for may change from witch to witch, but in your case—"

"Animals," Kara said.

"That's right. Before you can control an animal, you need to recognize its presence. Its *true* presence."

"I'm not sure I understand."

"All I'm asking you to do is listen closely. Just that. Listening for a sound only you can hear: your first lesson."

Dozens of questions swarmed through Kara's mind, but she pushed them away and focused on the midmorning sounds of the Thickety. The creak and sway of branches. The wind whistling through knotted trees. And then smaller sounds. A single droplet of water, falling from the rounded top of a stone to a tiny puddle beneath it. The crinkle of a leaf as a beetle with spindly legs skittered along its veins.

"I don't hear anything," Kara said.

Mary grunted. "How strange. I hear so many things, and I am not even *wexari*."

"I meant nothing out of the——"

Mary held a finger to her lips. "Shhhh," she whispered. "Listen *closely* this time. For the sounds beneath the sounds."

"The sounds beneath the sounds," Kara said, nodding

slowly as though she understood.

Maybe Taff was right, she thought. *Maybe she is just a crazy woman.*

Nonetheless she squeezed her eyes shut and listened closer. For a few minutes there was nothing more. But then Kara *did* hear something different, a faint scratching behind the wall of audible noises. Pressing her fingertips into her temples, Kara muted the everyday noises, scraping them away like skin and bones to reveal the hidden heartbeat of the Thickety.

RUN.

HIDE.

FEED.

SLEEP.

These words, unleashed from a hundred different sources, from insect and bird and unspeakable beast, swirled in her mind, rising in intensity.

"What do you hear?" Mary asked, her voice distant through the other sounds, a footstep in a thunderstorm.

"Thoughts," Kara said, then shook her head. "No. That's not right. More like . . . needs."

Mary nodded. "These are simple creatures. What more did you expect?"

Kara listened closer now. There was something else. An undercurrent of pain. Torment.

"They hurt," she said. "So many of them are sick. Suffering. Like the stitch-rat."

"Focus, Kara. There should be one whose needs are different from the others. Can you find it?"

"I'll try," Kara said.

Locating a unique need proved impossible, however, like trying to find a specific drop of water in the ocean depths. Instead Kara *muffled* groups of similar sounds, never quieting them completely, but sealing them away until they were little more than whispers. Soon only a few scattered thoughts remained, including one that rose above the others with a unique intelligence.

Watch, it thought. *Wait.*

Once Kara had latched on to the animal's mind, trailing it to its location was surprisingly simple.

"Over there," she said, pointing toward a branch concealed by a particularly thick patch of crimson-colored leaves. Far below them she saw their campsite. They had left all their supplies behind so the spy, knowing they had to return, would remain in its position.

Mary got to her knees and raised the slingshot.

"Do you have to?" Kara asked.

"If not, it'll continue to follow us and report our movements to Sordyr. He'll find us that much easier." Mary pulled back the slingshot, grimacing with the effort. "Why couldn't I be twenty-three today? I'm a dead shot when I'm twenty-three."

Kara heard Mary's breathing slow as she lined up her shot. At that exact moment, the wind exhaled and pushed the crimson leaves to one side, revealing folded wings and a midnight-blue patch of down.

Kara recognized the one-eyed bird instantly.

"Wait!" she shouted. She threw herself into Mary Kettle, intending to knock the slingshot from her hands, but it was too late. Mary released the pocket and an invisible stone whizzed through the air.

"No!" Kara screamed.

Wincing, she anticipated the squawk of pain, the rustle of leaves as the one-eyed bird fell lifelessly to the ground below. Instead, a deep gash appeared in the trunk of the tree, just right of the slingshot's intended target.

"You ruined my shot!" Mary exclaimed.

The one-eyed bird stared down at Kara, unperturbed by its brush with death. Its single eye revolved to forest green.

Thank you.

Color was the bird's language, and Kara spoke it fluently.

"This is my friend," she said, lowering Mary's upraised slingshot. Kara's other hand strayed to the shell-embossed locket around her neck. She remembered how the one-eyed bird had taken it from her, leading Kara into the Thickety for the first time.

"Friend?" Mary asked. "That *thing* is a Watcher! They're all over the Thickety—we call them 'the eyes of the Forest Demon.' It's a spy. That's what it does."

"Not this one," Kara said. "It's special."

The one-eyed bird perched on a nearby boulder. The eye in its socket revolved, passing through a number of colors until it was the dark brown of strongly brewed tea.

Friend. Not enemy.

"I know," Kara said. "You don't have to prove anything to me. Is that what you are, though? A Watcher?"

Its eye rotated to orange.

Yes.

"That fits," Kara said, smiling. "I'm going to call you Watcher, if that's okay. I need something to call you, and that's as good a name as any."

"You can talk to this creature?" Mary asked.

"Of course she can!" replied Taff, rolling his eyes. "She's *wixuri*!"

"*Wexari*," corrected Mary.

"That's what I said."

Kara knelt down so her eyes were level with the bird.

"Did Sordyr send you to spy on us?" she asked.

Watcher's eye rotated to orange.

Yes.

"You're supposed to tell him where we are, aren't you? So he can find us."

Yes.

"But you're not going to do that, are you?"

There was a slight hesitation before this next color rotated into place. Kara sensed that Watcher was making a momentous decision. Once made, it would change things forever.

Red.

No.

Kara looked over her shoulder at Mary. "Sordyr thinks Watcher is helping him, but he's not. He's helping us."

"How can you be sure?"

"He's helped me before. I trust him."

Though Mary looked like a child, her sigh was the throaty rattle of an old woman. "Fine," she said, facing the bird. "Where is Sordyr right now, then?"

Watcher's eye rotated again. Eggshell white this time, with a smudge of blue on its right side.

"He's coming from the east," Kara said.

A flash of surprise crossed Mary's face. *She thought Sordyr was somewhere else*, Kara thought. *Perhaps she was inadvertently leading us right to him.*

"You sure you trust this thing?" Mary asked.

"Absolutely," Kara said.

"Then Sordyr has already found a place to cross and is looping back in our direction. He'll be upon us in less than a day. We'll have to cut north—he won't expect that. No one goes that way."

"Why not?" Taff asked.

"You'll see."

Watcher's eye began to spin quickly in its socket, pausing only for a moment on certain colors.

Need. Witch Girl. Help.

"You need me to help you?" Kara asked. She examined him more carefully. "Are you hurt?"

Friends. Forest. Hurt.

"Are you talking about what Sordyr is doing?" Kara asked. "The sickness spreading through the animals?"

Yes.

Kara nodded. Watcher had shown her the truth about her mother, given her hope when she had lost all of it. If there was a way for her to repay the bird, she would.

"What do you want me to do?" Kara asked.

Watcher closed his eye. When he opened it again, it was the mud brown of cemetery dirt after a heavy rainfall.

Kill Sordyr.

"I can't do that," Kara whispered, shaking her head violently.

Only you.

"I'm sorry, I truly am, but I need to get my brother

to safety. There must be someone else—"

Only you.

"He's too strong! He'll kill me! Or change me!"

The eyes rotated again. Faster. Insistent.

Only you. Good witch. End suffering. Save us.

Kill Sordyr.

Kill Sordyr.

SIX

They trudged onward. For the first two days the landscape didn't change, though with every strong breeze the trees whispered so dolefully that Kara had to resist the urge to sit down on the forest floor and give up altogether. On the third day the ground became marshy and unstable, sucking eagerly at their boots. The air hung in dank and noxious plumes. Mary taught them how to grind certain yellow weeds into a paste and smear them along the interior of a handkerchief. This absorbed the foulness of the air, by nightfall turning the paste a tarry black.

They didn't talk much during their journey; making progress through the harsh landscape required all their energy. Mary's unpredictable age posed difficulties as well. After two days as an eleven-year-old she went back to being an old woman, and they were forced to move at a slower pace. The following day, however, she was a vivacious nineteen and had to slow down for *them*.

As Kara walked, she practiced.

Reaching out with her mind, she listened for the hidden sounds of the Thickety that only she could hear. It was difficult at first—since the creatures' needs were often identical, they tended to blend together like voices in a crowd—but gradually Kara trained herself to distinguish one voice from another. The gruff *FEED* of the fat, boar-like creatures that frequently tottered across their path, for example, was quite different from the skittish *FEED* of the winged slugs that slipped away at the slightest noise. Kara grew to recognize the timbre of each voice, and by the end of the third day she could quickly pinpoint an individual creature in the swarm of sounds.

She began to hear other, more complex thoughts as well. A mother *HOPING* her new hatchling would be safe. A lone creature, cocooned in spirals of web, anxious to be *FREE*. A thirsty branch bug *WISHING* for rain.

Unfortunately, even the happiest sounds were tarnished by darkness. The animals lived their life in fear of Sordyr. He had polluted their forest with evil and transformed many of their friends and family into snapping things more plant than animal. Safety was a dream long forgotten.

There's nothing I can do to help them, Kara told herself again and again. *Even if I didn't have to keep Taff safe, I'll never be powerful enough to fight Sordyr.*

She knew she was right, but it did not make her feel any better.

On the fifth day, as they finally left the swamp and entered a new section of the forest, Kara focused her attention on a creature she had never seen before, a spiky ball covered in tongues and eyes that ran onto her out-stretched hand.

"Ew," said Taff.

Kara said, "Don't be cruel. I think she's cute."

"You think all these things are cute."

Kara reached out with her mind, anticipating the usual thoughts: *FEED, SLEEP, NEST* . . .

It wasn't any of those. Kara dropped the creature to the ground.

"What is it?" Taff asked, grabbing his sister's arm.

"It . . . No, I must have just imagined it."

"Imagined what?"

Kara watched the tiny creature slip beneath the under-growth.

"It talked to me," she said.

"What did it say?"

"'Help us.'" She mumbled the words, not wanting them to be true. "It said, 'Help us.'"

That night, Kara awoke to someone pinching her shoulder.

"Wake up, *wexari*," Mary Kettle said. "You've listened enough. It's time to cast a proper spell."

Kara shook Taff awake, then dressed quickly beneath nighttime trees glowing with pinpoints of yellow-red, as though the sun itself had been impaled on the branches above them and bled onto the leaves. They packed their meager belongings, and from her sack Mary retrieved a lopsided ball stitched together with animal skin. She tossed it to Taff. He looked at Kara for guidance, unsure of what to do next.

"Well, it's not going to work if you just stand there," Mary said. "You're a boy. It's a ball. Use that clever mind of yours and figure out what to do."

Taff tossed the ball into the air, and it began to glow faintly. Giggling, he tossed it again and again until it was as bright as a torch.

"Thank you," said Mary, taking the ball from his hands. "Let's go."

Though it flickered erratically and sometimes went out for entire minutes at a time, the glowing ball was a welcome beacon of light as they passed beneath trees bristling with hidden life. Sets of eyes in twos and threes watched them between parted leaves. A snake that was little more than a forked tongue slithered over Kara's boots, while above them a many-clawed creature, thin as a flapjack, stretched tightly across the limbs of several trees.

In time they came to a small clearing.

Knee-high grass just a few shades darker than wheat rustled in the gentle breeze. Past the clearing Kara heard the rushing of a waterfall. She stepped forward, intending to investigate, but Mary gripped her arm.

"Wait," said Mary. She picked a few blades of grass, rolled them into a ball, and sucked it eagerly. "It won't be long now." She found a stump to rest on. Taff plucked a blade of grass and took a hesitant taste before tossing it to the ground. He looked at Mary with newfound admiration, impressed by her ability to ingest disgusting things.

"The thing to remember about magic," Mary said, "is that it's a talent, no different from being a painter, or singer, or teller of tales. They are witches, all, creating something that was not previously in the world."

"There's a big difference between singing a song and casting a spell," Kara said.

"Is there? A talespinner, for a time, will take his audience and transport them to a different place. A good singer as well. And a sculptor uses her craft to reflect reality as she sees it." Mary spat out a huge wad of gunk and replaced it with some fresh grass; her tongue was beginning to turn yellow. "When you use magic, you are simply changing what's real to what you want it to be."

"But that's not possible."

"For most. But have you never looked at something extraordinary—a stained-glass window, a beautiful gown—and wondered, 'How did they *do* that?' Possibility is not universal, Kara. It's a matter of *ability*." Leaning forward, Mary held the glowing ball between them, her features almost pretty in the soft light. "Believe you have the power to change the world, and you will. Forget the Forest Demon. Doubt is your greatest enemy right now."

Something darted through the grass. Taff withdrew his wooden sword.

"Put that thing away, boy. You'll be doing your sister a grave disservice if you scare the grettins away before we even start."

"What's a grettin?" Kara asked.

"Little creatures that come out here every night to eat the grass. They're as harmless as mice. That's not the best part, though. Wait."

They waited. There seemed to be a dozen creatures moving through the grass now—two dozen. And then, muffled by the stalks, came a high-pitched, melodious sound.

"They're singing!" exclaimed Kara.

The chirping rose and fell in perfect time to the wind's rustling, the creaking of the branches, the song's beauty only intensified by its contrast to their grim surroundings.

Kara looked over at Mary. Her eyes were closed, and an expression that was almost peaceful had settled over her features.

"What do they look like?" Taff asked, stretching across the ground on his elbows.

Mary shrugged. "I've never seen one. Grettins have the misfortune of being a tasty treat for predators, so they're understandably skittish. If I were to take a single step toward the grass, they would all run off." She opened her eyes and turned to Kara. "But if you were to use your magic, I think we might get a different result."

"I'm not so sure about that," Kara said, wringing her hands. "Hearing these creatures is one thing. Making them do my bidding . . ."

"You've done it before," said Mary.

"With the grimoire!"

"The spellbook allowed you to cast spells more easily,

I'll grant you that. But nothing has changed. You are *wexari*. A true witch." Mary gestured toward the clearing. "Now go out there and prove it."

Kara took a dazed step forward, the first blades of stiff yellow grass scratching her knee, before a question occurred to her. She looked back over her shoulder, taking a moment to brush long strands of black hair from her eyes.

"You said a witch was like an artist, creating something that wasn't there before. But I just communicate with animals. What am I creating?"

Mary clapped her hands together. "Well done, *wexari*. You're asking the right question. Or close enough, at any rate. A better question would be, 'What do I *need* to create?'"

"That doesn't help."

"Nor should it. Asking the right question isn't enough. You have to ask it at the right time."

"How will I—" Kara started, but Taff cut her off.

"They won't hurt her, will they?" he asked.

"Of course not," Mary said. "Kara, if you truly intend to face Imogen, you need to master your powers, but I would never put you in a situation where you might get hurt—not yet, at least. Then again . . ."

Mary withdrew a curved dagger from a sheath hanging from her side and handed it to Kara.

"Probably best to be cautious. This is the Thickety, after all."

With hesitant footsteps Kara entered the clearing. At first the grass rustled as startled creatures fled her approach, but Kara moved slowly toward the center of the field, humming a song her mother had taught her, and the creatures returned. She sat down and crossed her legs, the blades of grass rising over her head and obscuring everything but the treetops. It was like sinking into a secret world.

You've called animals to you before, she thought. *You can do it again.*

"Come here," Kara whispered. "I won't hurt you."

Her words were anchored by doubt.

What if Mary is wrong? What if I'm not special after all?

"You get one yet?" Taff asked after only a few minutes had passed. Mary shushed him.

In the following hour Kara asked, commanded, cajoled, and begged the creatures to come to her, with no result. Kara could hear the true voices of many grettins, but even these were vague, no more than brief snatches of *SING* and *HIDE* peeking out from beneath the telltale sounds of the night.

She had begun to nod off when the grettins' song rose in intensity. Now, however, it bore a slightly mocking quality, as though it knew what Kara was trying to do and found it amusing. The grettins were playing with her in their fashion, and for a few moments she forgot all about magic in light of this strange and wonderful animal.

You want to come to me, don't you? You're curious . . . but you're afraid it might be a trick. How can I prove that I won't harm you? If you were a person I would just use words, but you're an animal. Human words mean nothing to you. We need a different kind of connection.

(Ask the right question at the right time. . . .)

What connects two things?

"A bridge," Kara said.

She closed her eyes and imagined a simple wooden bridge that began in her mind and stretched out toward the voices of the grettins. *I offer this connection between us,* she thought, hoping that they could understand the words. *You can trust me.* In her mind Kara felt the grettins get closer, like indecisive dogs sniffing a path, and braced herself for whatever might happen next.

They refused to cross.

Something's not right, Kara realized. *I need to make a link between us—I'm sure of it!—but I'm not giving them a good enough reason to trust me. How can I prove I mean them no harm?*

The answer came in a flash of insight, as though the canopy had suddenly peeled open and let in the afternoon sun.

Real bridges are built from wood or stone because that makes them safe—but that's only true in the physical world. A mind-bridge needs to be built from a different sort of material altogether, one that makes these creatures feel safe in their minds, just like wood makes people feel safe in reality.

Kara remembered the times in her life when she had felt the safest. Falling asleep on the porch and waking in Father's strong arms as he carried her to bed. Walking through the aisles of the general store with Mother's hand in hers. Like a mason baking bricks, Kara transformed these memories into building material and then used them to form a mind-bridge constructed from feelings of warmth and safety.

With renewed curiosity, the grettins milled closer.

"Come," Kara whispered. "You are welcome."

She felt a small tug in her head and gasped softly.

Her invitation had been accepted.

The grass parted, and a creature with large amber eyes peered out at her. Its body was long and pliable, like a fer-ret's, with rust-colored fur and a bushy tail.

"There you are," Kara said.

She held her hand low to the ground and waited. After hesitating for a moment, more out of pride than concern for its safety, the grettin sniffed Kara's fingers, then hopped onto her hand. The tiny animal was heavier than it looked, but not so heavy that Kara couldn't lift it with ease until it was level with her eyes.

"Hello, my friend," Kara said.

The grettin chirped.

From all around her now, they came. Kara felt the creatures slip beneath her legs and over her shoulders and up her arms. She laughed as their tiny paws tickled her skin.

"What's going on?" Taff shouted. And then, hurt accusation in his voice: "Are you *having fun without me?*"

The grettins climbed off Kara and began gathering together at her feet, a growing mass of shifting bodies that ballooned to her height before suddenly shrinking and reshaping, the bodies falling into one another, combining, until a creature the size of a pony stood before her, its face withered and wise and old.

"All of you," Kara said. "You're all part of the same creature."

She stroked the grettin's back, marveling at the lumps sliding beneath its skin like a sack of marbles. From the back of its hind leg protruded a bushy tail that had gotten confused during the transformation.

Kara rose to her feet and waved to Mary and her brother, dim shapes in the approaching darkness of morning.

"You have to come and see!" she called. "It's wonderful!"

"Are you sure that's a good idea?" Mary asked, holding Taff back. "I don't want to scare it off."

Kara bent down so she was eye level with the grettin, and scratched behind its ears.

"Is that all right with you?" she asked, and because the creature was on Kara's side of the mind-bridge she knew it understood. "Can my friends come and see how pretty you—"

A low growl rumbled in the base of the creature's

throat. Kara took a step backward, thinking that she had completely misjudged the situation. *This is a trap*, she thought, snatching her hand back while she still had all her fingers. *It's going to attack me!*

But then she found the grettin's gentle eyes and saw that it held no malice in its heart, for her or any other creature. The growling was meant as a warning, and as Kara realized this, the growl changed into something different, something her mind could latch on to and understand.

Sledgeworm come! Teethsome! Rungofast! Now!

But it was too late.

The ground quaked as a monster thudded to the earth. It had no legs, but instead balanced itself on arms corded with thick, reptilian muscle. The skin of its squirming torso was concealed beneath a garden of moss and fungus.

Blighted, Kara thought.

The sledgeworm bent forward, lifting its maggot-like

body into the air to balance its body weight, and Kara found herself staring into vermillion eyes rank with madness.

"Run, Kara! Run!" Taff exclaimed.

The sledgeworm opened its mouth, revealing a gruesome combination of fangs and thorns. A vine shot from the place a tongue should have been and whipped around the grettin, holding the flailing animal in place.

Through the grettin's half-closed eyes Kara saw a look of somber acceptance.

It is time, she heard it say. *Fate for such as I.*

"NO!" Kara shouted.

Even later, Kara would be hard-pressed to explain what had happened. The best way she could put it was that the grettin was on her side of the mind-bridge, and because of that it had to listen to her. Kara didn't give it a choice.

"Escape!" she shouted.

The grettin exploded, no longer one creature but

hundreds, slipping between the sledgeworm's teeth and into the night, the monster snapping at its prey but unable to catch something so small and fleet.

"Yes!" Kara shouted. "Run!"

She thought she might have heard a chorus of chirps in the distance, coalescing into one last message.

Thank you.

Kara's triumph, however, was short-lived.

The sledgeworm turned its full attention to her. It was too stupid to truly comprehend what had just happened, but seemed to be aware, in a very basic way, that this small human had somehow stolen its breakfast. Heart galloping in her chest, Kara backed slowly away. Her instinct was to turn and run as fast as she could, but she fought it, afraid the sudden motion would spur the monster to attack.

Kara felt a hand flat against her upper back.

"Magic, *wexari*," Mary whispered in her ear. "Control it. Make it yours."

The sledgeworm took another giant arm-step forward. Something stringy and uneaten dangled from its lower gums.

Kara reached out with her mind, feeling for the creature, but whereas the grettin was like a fond memory eager to be recalled, the sledgeworm was a moment better left forgotten: the snap of a broken bone, a sleepless night burning with fever, her mother's face looking away in disappointment.

"I can't," Kara said. "I found what the grettin wanted and made a sort of connection with it, but there's nothing I share with this monster."

"You mean nothing you *want* to share."

The sledgeworm went after Mary then, turning its body with surprising speed and knocking her to the ground. Kara ran to help her but the monster blocked her path. It swung an arm and Kara ducked, feeling the hiss of air as its claw passed just over its head.

Suddenly the sledgeworm collapsed.

"I got it!" Taff shouted, wooden sword in hand.

Kara saw what had happened. When the sledgeworm put all its weight on one arm to attack her, Taff struck it with his sword. The blow hadn't been enough to hurt it, but the timing had caused the monster to lose its balance, buying her precious seconds.

Taff had already helped Mary to her feet, the two of them running toward the shelter of the trees now. Kara, thinking the sledgeworm would follow her, ran in the opposite direction.

Except it followed her brother instead, furious at the little human wielding the biting stick.

"Get back here!" Kara screamed. "Leave him alone!"

She picked up a rock and threw it at the sledgeworm, striking its body. The monster, only a few steps away from Taff now, ignored her.

Build a bridge! Now!

Reaching into her mind, she thought about Simon—not the guilt she felt for killing him but the pure joy she had taken in the act, under the spell of the grimoire but ignoring that now, enjoying his screams as her children bit into him, the pleasure of the kill . . .

. . . and transformed that rush of feeling into a mind-bridge that she followed straight to the sledgeworm. Her passage into its mind, however, was blocked by a solid wall of hate. She concentrated harder, pushing the wall, but it was as hard as stone. Unlike the grettin, the sledge-worm did not know the meaning of trust. It would never come to her. If Kara wanted to stop it, she would have to make her own entrance into its mind.

Taff screamed.

Holding her head between her hands, Kara lashed out with her mind and struck the wall as hard as she could.

The sledgeworm wailed in pain and fire blossomed in Kara's head. Her nose *popped*. Something wet and sticky dribbled onto her lips. The creature faced her, uncertain, but then Kara saw its arms tense as it prepared to charge.

She closed her eyes and struck the wall again. It was

easier this this time, though no less painful.

The sledgeworm flew backward as though caught in a sudden gust of wind.

Withdrawing Mary's dagger, Kara approached the monster. It lay coiled on the ground, struggling to regain its balance. Despite everything that had happened, Kara felt pity for the creature. It had only been hungry, nothing more.

She held its gaze, remembering a moment of blinding fear (*Grace has Taff; where has she taken him?*) and used that to find the monster, feeling what it was feeling right now.

I won't hurt you again, Kara told it. *As long as you leave this second.*

With a weak hiss the sledgeworm righted itself and sprang into the treetops.

Taff watched it go, then turned to his sister with something like awe in his eyes.

"What did you do?" he asked.

"Magic," Kara replied, and collapsed.

BOOK TWO

IMOGEN

*"In time, those who use magic
become monsters.
This is the fate no witch can escape."*

—The Path
Leaf 182, Line 45

SEVEN

She slept for two days.

During this time she was visited by another dream of her father. It started like the first one: Father in the field, folding seeds into the soil and standing back to wait as though they might actually sprout there and then.

They did.

Green shoots stretched to the sky, flattening into stalks as husks of corn blossomed before her eyes, the whole process insanely fast but Father tapping his foot impatiently nevertheless. In just a few moments a cornfield surrounded him. Picking a husk from the nearest stalk, Father peeled the corn in that peculiar way he had, from the bottom up, revealing a perfect ear that would have fetched at least a brown at market.

He took a small bite of the corn and chewed it thoughtfully. Behind him, the first stalk began to wither and die.

The thrumbeetle danced over and under Kara's hand, its antennae tickling her fingers.

"I had another dream of Father last night," Kara said.

"Was he in the field again?" Mary asked. She was young today, younger even than Taff, her auburn hair braided into twin pigtails.

"Yes. Except this time the cornstalks around him died. What does that mean?"

"It might not mean anything," said Mary.

Kara, however, had caught the look of trepidation that crossed Mary's face. "But it might," said Kara. "What do you know?"

Mary sighed. "I think it means that your father is still alive. Your real father, that is. What you're seeing is where he's being kept right now while Timoth Clen occupies his body."

"A field?" Kara asked.

"What could be better? To your father, it's just another day of work, over and over again. A brilliant spell, really. Cold, but brilliant. He's in a prison, but thinks he's just living his real life."

Kara brightened. "Then I can bring him back! It's not too late! I'll have to find a way to get him a message and let him know that he needs to escape—"

"No!" Mary exclaimed. "You'll do no such thing."

"But he's trapped!"

"Yes, and for now that's the safest place for him. In time, he'll realize what's going on himself, and it will begin to drive him mad. No need to rush the process. Once you escape the Thickety, you can figure out a way to break the spell. For now, let's focus on your training."

She nodded toward the thrumbeetle. "It's getting easier, isn't it?" she asked.

"A bit," said Kara. Though she was still weak from her encounter with the sledgeworm, building a mind-bridge to the thrumbeetle had posed no challenge; she simply recalled an afternoon spent splashing in calf-deep puddles. All the thrumbeetle wanted to do was play, and once Kara built a bridge from this simple memory, the insect crossed it willingly.

"The bridges I build to communicate with these creatures," Kara said, "are made up of memories. Images. I think that once I build the bridge, I can go back to it. So from now on, when I see a thrumbeetle, any thrumbeetle, I won't need to make a new bridge. It will already be there."

"You're learning fast," said Mary. The compliment was at odds with the somber expression on her face, however, as though Mary knew what was coming next.

"But when I think back," Kara said, "I can't remember

the memories I used to make the bridge in the first place! Even this thrumbeetle. I built the bridge just a few moments ago, but when I try to think about the memory I used . . . nothing."

Mary nodded sadly. "That's because it's gone, Kara. You can't use a brick to build a house and expect to keep the brick. You've used the memory up completely."

"So every time I build a mind-bridge I lose a memory?" Kara asked. She thought about the bridge she had built to the sledgeworm; though she couldn't remember the specific images she had used, she knew they must have been something disturbing. "I suppose that could be good, in a way. There are definitely some memories I'd rather forget."

"No!" Mary exclaimed. "Never think that! Memories— *especially* the bad ones—make us who we are. You must be cautious. Use too much magic and you'll forget all the experiences that made you Kara Westfall."

Kara's hand began to shake, and the thrumbeetle,

which had been curled contently in her palm, found steadier ground on her shoulder.

"Magic always has a price," Mary said, "but you knew that already, better than most." She cleared her throat. "Let's focus on your lesson right now. Something simple today. That insect in your hand—send it to me."

Kara found the place in her mind where the thrumbeetle had come to visit and asked, *Do you mind gracing my friend with your presence?*

The beetle did not move from Kara's shoulder. It was comfortable.

"She doesn't want to leave," Kara said. "And I don't want to force her. I'm afraid I'll hurt her by accident."

"It's just a thrumbeetle."

"It's a life," Kara said.

Still, she didn't see how dancing on Mary's hand would harm the insect, so she reached more aggressively into its mind, feeling perhaps a slight nudge but little other resistance. It trusted her completely.

This two legs is the same as me, Kara thought, sending an image of Mary standing next to Kara along with other images of safety (*twig, mud, leaf*), helping the beetle to make the connection.

Dance on her hand.

The thrumbeetle crawled onto Mary's palm.

"That was . . . unexpectedly easy," Mary said. Kara tried to hide her smile at the little girl's look of disgust. She shook her hand to get the beetle off her, only to have it crawl up her arm. "Kara. Please. If you would?"

Kara severed her connection to the thrumbeetle, knowing the mind-bridge would be there again if she needed it. The insect spread its sapphire wings and glided into the morning air.

"Well done, *wexari*," Mary said. "There is a meaning to that word, you know, in the Lost Tongue. 'Creator.' Other witches need to channel their magic through the grimoire. But you can create magic out of nothing." Mary laughed slightly. "The grimoire needs *you*."

Kara thought about how the spellbook had worked differently for her, the spells appearing in the book only *after* she had cast them, as opposed to the other way around. The way the pages had grown wings and vanished after she had cast the Last Spell.

Oh no, Kara thought.

"I was feeding it magic, wasn't I?" she asked. "I was making it stronger."

Mary Kettle smiled. She was missing an upper tooth and looked fairly adorable.

"There's a mind behind the talent, I see. A powerful combination."

"The grimoire took what I gave it. All those spells. And then when I was done, the grimoire sent them . . ."

"To other grimoires," said Mary, nodding.

Kara's stomach lurched, disturbed by the implications.

"So you're saying that somewhere a girl with the talent might be tempted to use a grimoire—because of a spell that *I created*?" she asked quietly.

"I suppose it's not beyond the realm of possibility, though it would have been more likely centuries ago. Now she'd have to find a grimoire first, a difficult task indeed."

"So, they're rare?" Kara asked. "Even in the World?"

"When magic was at its height they were *rare*. Now I'd say they're closer to extinct. As Timoth Clen waged his war on witches almost all the grimoires were seized by his soldiers and buried deep within the earth, where they couldn't do any harm."

"Some grimoires are good, though," Kara said. "Right?"

Mary shook her head. "They are inherently evil. Every one."

"But my mother's grimoire helped me save Taff. It—"

"—was perhaps *less* evil than most, only because its influence had been held in check by your mother's extraordinary will for so many years. That's all. Darkness and temptation are what bind the pages of any grimoire together. Only a witch with a truly pure heart can resist its call."

"Like my mother," Kara said.

Mary nodded. "But she would be the exception more than the rule."

"So what you're telling me is that grimoires are evil, and since I'm *wexari*, every time I cast a spell I'm *helping* them seduce new users."

"You're not using a grimoire anymore, so it's *helped*, not helping. And only in a very minor way. Like adding a single log to a massive pyre."

"Fires can't burn without logs!"

"And logs are harmless without fire."

Kara pictured a girl her own age in some distant land, innocently opening a book and seeing one of Kara's spells inscribed inside, no doubt something simple to start— *how to conjure a rat*—the strange words forming on the girl's lips without her even knowing. The first step down a dark and wicked path.

"Why didn't the Last Spell kill me, like other witches?" Kara asked.

"Because as *wexari*, you're much too important. It hopes you'll pick up another grimoire, start the process anew, add even more spells to the library. Now if you were just a common *tay'lom* like me, you would have been dragged to Phadeen, the Well of Witches. There you would have suffered for all eternity, your life force supplying the grimoires with the power they need to ensnare new souls." Mary pulled at her pigtails, considering. "It's actually an interesting word, '*tay'lom*,' often mistranslated. Most scholars think it means 'user' or 'tool,' but that's not quite right. Its real meaning is something closer to 'fuel.' It reminds me of the story about the greedy baker's children who ate all the fruit in the forest, only to find out that the forest was actually a Rath'nuw that was trying to fatten them up. That's what the grimoire does to *tay'lom*. Swells them with magic so they will burn longer in the end."

Kara imagined Grace Stone chained in some dark well, screaming in unimaginable pain.

It's not my fault, Kara thought. *She chose her own path.*
Such thoughts were little consolation.

"That blackrobin in the branches," said Mary, pointing to a nearby tree. "See if you can make it fly over here. They are notoriously stubborn creatures, so this will be a good challenge."

Reaching into the mind of the beautiful creature, Kara allowed her guilt to spread outward, trying to build a bridge. But guilt was not an emotion that animals understood, and the bridge collapsed. Instead she reached out with the fear that someday—*wexari* or not—she would find herself in the Well of Witches, where Grace would be waiting. She pictured the white-haired girl, standing above Kara and taking the grimoire in her hands for the first time. . . .

In a few moments the blackrobin landed on Kara's outstretched hand. The mind-bridge she had created between them held strong.

All animals understood fear.

They traveled at night in order to make better use of the phosphorescent leaves that hung from the canopy. Kara learned which plants were safe to eat and which fruits were indeed fruits and not the hiding spot for a laxid, a parasitic worm that waited for its prey to take a bite so it could slide down their throats.

She missed Father, though she did not have any more dreams about him. She missed Lucas and wondered if he missed her too.

She missed her bed. She missed the monotony of life in De'Noran.

For a few days Mary tried to teach Kara how to use her slingshot but gave up quickly, Kara's aim being "impressively irreparable." Taff, however, continued to practice his swordwork when Mary's age allowed him to do so, despite her insistence that he was not destined to wield a blade.

There was no sign of Sordyr, which meant that

Watcher had successfully led the Forest Demon astray. Kara knew the bird was clever, but she worried about her friend nonetheless.

If Sordyr finds out that Watcher is helping us . . .

One morning, just before they broke camp, Kara caught a glimpse of a tan-furred animal lying at the edge of her vision, its chest rising and falling in sleep. Curious what it would be like to build a mind-bridge to a sleeping animal, Kara closed her eyes and listened carefully for its true voice. At first she heard nothing. *Perhaps it's Blighted*, she thought. Creatures that had been infected by Sordyr's plants were difficult for her to make a connection with, sometimes impossible. She listened harder and identified a faint whisper, unlike anything she had ever heard before. . . .

Mary grabbed Kara by the shoulders and shook her.

"What are you doing?" she asked, her voice frantic.

"Practicing!"

Without releasing her hold on Kara's arm, Mary

dragged her over to the creature. The smell hit Kara first. And then, looking down, she saw that while the stomach of the creature was indeed moving, it wasn't from the steady breathing of sleep. Beneath its flesh swelled a pond of feasting maggots.

"You must *never* use your powers on the dead," Mary said. "You understand me? There are *rules*."

"Why?" asked Kara. "Will it hurt me?"

"No. But the others will." Mary released her arm and said no more.

At last the forest opened up and a sea of boulders spread out across the horizon. Without a canopy of trees to block their view, Kara saw sky for the first time in weeks, a single white cloud drifting across a glorious expanse of blue. *Was it always this beautiful?* she wondered. The sun caressed her back and face. Though she longed to stare into its welcoming yellow light, Kara was forced to shield her eyes, which had long since acclimated to darkness.

"Come on!" Taff exclaimed, jumping on the first

boulder, but Mary—graced with the speed of a woman in her midtwenties today—quickly grabbed his arm and pulled him back.

"Wait," she said. "We have to prepare first. The journey across the Draye'varg presents particular dangers."

"What's out there?" Kara asked. "Another monster?"

"Nothing so simple, unfortunately. Perhaps it will be easier if I show you."

She bent down and picked up a twig, then cracked it in two, tossing away one piece and keeping the second, which was about the size of a pinkie.

"Watch," she said.

Mary leaned over and placed the twig on the nearest boulder, then gave it a gentle push so it fell through the crevice between the rocks.

"There are many stories about the history of the Draye'varg," Mary said. "Many attempts to explain its origin. Some people believe that these boulders around you are the pieces of a stone god who fell from the sky.

Others say that this was a playground constructed by a court wizard for a particularly demanding prince. And of course others claim that this is Sordyr's work."

Beneath the boulder, Kara heard something begin to scratch its way to the surface.

"But I don't believe any of that," Mary said. "I think this place simply *is*."

An insect crawled out of the crevice between the boulders. Its antennae and segmented exoskeleton were the precise same hue as the broken twig.

"It turned the stick into an insect!" exclaimed Taff.

"Yes," said Mary.

Kara reached her hand out for the twig insect, then thought better of it, remembering how Grace had used the grimoire to return Simon to life—or rather, something that had not really been life at all.

"This is wrong," Kara muttered.

Mary nodded.

"Can it bring anything to life?" Taff asked.

"Anything," Mary said. "Living or dead. That's why we have to be so cautious."

"Can I make a rock insect?" Taff asked, snatching a medium-size stone off the forest floor. "I really want to see what a rock insect looks like."

"It might not be an insect," Mary told him. "It might be something else altogether. Also"—she plucked the rock from his hand—"let's not play with dark magic." She squeezed Kara's shoulder. "Listen for the voice of the branch insect, *wexari*."

Kara listened. She did not need to close her eyes—not anymore—but instead let her natural instincts guide her past the eerily quiet morning and to the hidden sounds she had grown to know so well. She could hear the *TUNNEL* of the worms beneath her feet, the *BUILD* of the sickle-tailed bird nesting above her. But although she focused all her energy on the twig insect, there was nothing but a vacant silence where its voice should have been.

"I don't hear anything," Kara said. "Like it's not there at all."

"When you use your talent, you are hearing the very essence of a creature."

"You mean its soul?"

Mary winced. "If you will," she said.

"But how can a creature live without a soul?" Kara asked. "That shouldn't be."

"Precisely," said Mary Kettle, and squashed the scurrying insect beneath her boot.

EIGHT

As it turned out, Mary wasn't worried about the Draye'varg growing simulacra—as she called the creatures—from twigs or rocks; she was worried about it growing simulacra from *them*.

"We mustn't hurry," she said. "From one side of the Draye'varg to the other is but a few hours' journey, but we cannot risk someone falling. Even a single drop of blood can create a simulacrum."

Kara and Taff used strips of cloth and long tangles of vine to secure their meager supplies, though Kara wasn't sure they needed to fear a creature made from a spoon or coffee urn. While they did this Mary used a mortar and pestle to crush various cones into a thick paste. She spread this on their fingernails and it hardened in minutes.

"We'll be climbing a lot," she said, "and you'll have to use your hands to gain purchase on the stones. A piece of your nail could easily chip away."

"Would it be made of fingernails?" Taff asked. And then—Kara suspected simply because he liked saying the world aloud—he added, "The *simulacrum?*"

"No," Mary replied. "It would look just like you."

Taff stopped saying "simulacrum" after that.

It was Kara's hair that, more than anything else, worried Mary Kettle. "Why does it have to be so long? You probably lose a hundred strands a day and don't even notice." She suggested that Kara cut her hair off completely, and although Taff thought this would be highly amusing, Kara refused. In the end she bound her hair into a tight bun and secured it with a kerchief. Mary and Taff did the same.

Finally Mary spent an hour examining every inch of

her sack, making sure there were no holes or areas that needed to be patched.

"We don't want anything in here slipping out and becoming a simulacrum," Mary said.

"Why?" Taff asked. "What would happen?"

"I have no idea," Mary said. "But it would be *bad*."

The first hour of their journey across the Draye'varg was uneventful, and though Kara's calves grew sore from all the climbing, feeling the warmth of the sun on her body was more than adequate compensation. The boulders, gray and featureless, were indistinguishable from one another. On more than one occasion Kara nearly slipped on a surface worn smooth by hundreds—maybe thousands—of years of exposure to wind and storms.

To the north and south the trees of the Thickety, which ran parallel to the Draye'varg, had shrunk to the height of red willows before fading away altogether. Soon Kara was surrounded, in every direction, by a desert of boulders as far as the eye could see.

The sun, which she had at first welcomed, seared her shoulders.

The worst part, however, was the silence. Kara had grown accustomed to the constant noise in the Thickety: bleats, snarls, slithers, snapping in the night. She found, much to her surprise, that she missed the creatures of the Thickety. Their lives were so difficult here, and if she could only help them . . .

Stop it, Kara thought. *Sordyr's presence here is unfortunate, but the suffering he has wrought is not your responsibility. You're only going to get yourself killed, and who's going to take care of Taff then?*

Nonetheless, Kara reached out with her mind, just to hear the comforting voice of a single creature—and perhaps provide some comfort in return—but the nearest one was now only a distant whisper.

As they moved farther from the trees they began to see bones of every shape and size. Bones so small that the entire animal could have nestled in the palm of Taff's hand, and bones from a beast so gargantuan that a single femur stretched across five boulders.

"The urge to survive is strong," Mary said. "Dying creatures come here by instinct, not understanding what the Draye'varg is, thinking only that it can save them. This is especially true of creatures that have been touched by magic in one form or another." She took a short swig from her canteen and handed it to Kara. "Magic calls to magic," she said.

"Then why haven't we seen any simulacra?" Taff asked. "With all these creatures coming here something must have fallen between the rocks."

Mary dropped her sack and carefully loosened the vines knotted around its opening. The sun had vanished; clouds bulged and swirled across a storm-gray sky.

"No doubt the bones we've found thus far have created many simulacra," Mary said, "looking no different than the original flesh and blood. But once formed, a simulacrum is a damned thing, existing only to find its maker and destroy it. They are angry, you see, for they understand that their existence is nothing more than a shadow of real life. They have no purpose, and it makes them violent—so they seek out their creators and punish them. There are many stories of travelers who crossed the Draye'varg and left a piece of themselves behind, not realizing it—only to wake up a year later with a mirror image of themselves drawing a dagger across their throat."

Kara shuddered.

"But it would be different with the bones," Taff said. "Their creators are already dead. If they became simulacra, what would they do?"

"Mostly just wander the Draye'varg like ghosts until they perish from starvation or thirst. Without their maker to destroy, their false lives lack any meaning . . . so they simply stop living at all."

"But what about the bug you made from the branch?" Taff asked. "If you hadn't stepped on it, would it be wandering around attacking trees right now?"

Mary reached shoulder-deep into her sack, digging for something. "Simple simulacra die within a few hours," she said over the sound of shifting contents, metal clanging against metal, glass striking glass, the *whoosh* of something that sounded like sand cascading down a tube. "My guess is that these simulacra absorb something of the . . . Ah! I've found you."

From within her sack she withdrew a porcelain rabbit, the cracks in its face belying its wide smile. The rabbit was no larger than an apple and sat upon a bicycle crafted from several bands of wire. One of the wires, flaking rust, had uncoiled from its brothers and pointed off into space.

"What does that do?" Taff asked, reaching out for the rabbit. Mary twisted away before he could touch it, and the witch's petulant expression—like a child who did not want to share her toy—almost made Kara laugh.

Crouching down, Mary placed the rabbit on the boulder

and, withdrawing a piece of chalk from within the folds of her cloak, scratched a careful *X* to the left of the bicycle's front wheel.

She leaned over and whispered something in the rabbit's ear.

"Okay," Taff said, lying on top of the boulder so he was eye level with the toy rabbit. "I'm not going to ask any questions. I'm just going to watch and see what happens." He paused. "What did you whisper in its ear?"

"I asked it to show us the way to Imogen."

"You don't know?" asked Kara.

Mary gestured to the boulders that surrounded them in every direction. "I admit to being somewhat disoriented."

The three of them watched the rabbit. When nothing happened, Mary whispered her request again and then patted the toy rabbit gently on top of the head, as one would an obedient dog.

A minute passed. The toy rabbit sat there. Motionless.

The first drops of rain splattered against the boulder.

Mary looked like she was about to pound her hand into the boulder in frustration, but then thought better of it. "Blasted, useless bauble!" she exclaimed. "Sometimes this happens. Sometimes they don't do anything at all. More and more, lately."

"Let me try," Taff said. Before Mary could stop him, he bent next to the rabbit and whispered something in its ear.

The rabbit started to move instantly.

Its tiny feet, encased in red boots, pressed down against the pedals of the bicycle. Turning the handlebars slightly, the rabbit began to drift in small circles across the boulder. The little wheels of the bicycle creaked softly.

"It's moving!" said Taff. "It listened to me!"

Mary looked unamused.

Finally the rabbit began to cycle in a perfectly straight line. It picked up speed, and Kara stood near the end of the boulder in case it slipped off.

The last thing we need is a simulacrum of a toy rabbit, she thought. The image of a living, breathing rabbit on a bicycle should have been funny, but it wasn't—not even a little bit.

Just when Kara thought she was going to have to pick the rabbit up, however, it stopped at the base of her feet. Mary bent down and drew a chalk line from her original *X* to the bicycle's new position at the edge of the boulder, then measured the distance by using the span of her outstretched fingers.

"No more than three days' journey," she said, "though the Draye'varg will end long before then." Wiping a bead of rain away from her eyes, she pointed in the direction the bicycle had traveled. "The forest is that way, just out of sight. We're almost there."

Mary picked up the toy rabbit and gently returned it to her sack.

"How did you make it listen to you, Taff?" Mary asked.

He shrugged. "I just asked it to show us the way to

Imogen. I didn't do anything special."

"Hmm," said Mary Kettle.

"Does that mean I'm magic?" Taff asked. Kara could not tell if the trembling in his voice was from excitement or fear.

"Not at all," Mary said. "Using enchanted objects requires no craft, but it cannot be done by just anyone. It's a talent that might be——"

Taff screamed.

A millipede the size of a rat was gnawing on his ankle. Except the millipede wasn't made of flesh and blood.

It was made of water.

Mary hurled the writhing thing through the air. It struck the boulder next to them and exploded into a thousand droplets, most of which ran down the rock and vanished into the hidden ground below.

"I'm such a fool," Mary said. "The rain. Why didn't I think of it?"

From all around them, as far as Kara could see, water

creatures were pulling themselves out of the crevices between the boulders. Some looked like the millipede that had attacked Taff; others were spiderlike with spindly legs. And then there were those creatures cursed with no shape at all, slinking toward Kara like puddles with teeth.

Lightning flashed, revealing a sky awash with water bats and translucent ravens that swooped and darted above their prey.

No longer heeding Mary's warning to travel cautiously, Kara leaped from boulder to boulder. The storm had risen to a torrent and it was difficult to see more than a few feet in front of her, but even through the pounding storm she could hear the *tinkle-tinkle* of Mary's bag and used that to guide her instead.

The water creatures attacked them from every side—from below and above as well. With each bite Kara felt a mild shock shoot through her body; this rain, born from thunderclouds, had inherited some of its properties. She kept moving, doing her best to dodge the shapes that skittered across the rocky surfaces. There was no use fighting the creatures; for every one she stepped on or clapped between her hands, countless more took its place. The crevices between the boulders became jammed and swollen with new creations, anxious to escape and join the hunt.

And the rain kept falling.

Kara stumbled and landed on her knee, wincing in pain. Before her, less than an arm's length from her face, a translucent jellyfish splayed across the boulder on dozens of tentacles. The inside of the creature glowed faintly, and within its interior ocean creatures moved and swam and gnashed at one another with bestial violence. By instinct Kara reached out to the jellyfish's mind, hoping to build a mind-bridge, but this was a simulacrum and there was no connection to be made.

A single tentacle rose in the air and tensed like a python, but before it could strike, Taff sailed over Kara's head and landed on the jellyfish, smashing it into oblivion.

Pulling his sister to her feet he shouted, "We're almost there!"

Sure enough, through shards of rain Kara glimpsed the canopy and dark trees of the Thickety, the familiar shapes that had terrified her throughout her childhood now a welcome beacon of shelter and safety. Her knee throbbed with pain, but she knew she couldn't slow down.

Just a little farther. . . .

They neared the end of the Draye'varg, and the creatures began to attack with even greater fervor. A raven with rippling wings like waterfalls landed on Taff's back, pushing him to the ground. Kara punched it with an open hand. It was like passing her hand through a spout of icy cold water, leaving an angry red welt across her palm.

When Kara looked up, they were surrounded.

Banding together, the simulacra had tightened their forces around the children so that there was no escape in any direction. Boulders swelled with waves of false life, far too many to dodge, a glistening sheen of jaws and teeth and mandibles. Above the children looped water-birds, tiny bolts of lightning snapping between their open beaks.

Kara knelt next to her brother, her injured knee making a disheartening popping sound. Taff's blond hair hung down in dripping tendrils across his forehead.

"Stay close to me," Kara said.

She *listened*.

They were close enough to the trees that she could once again hear voices whispering *FEED* and *HIDE* and other common thoughts. Kara threaded her way through this storm of sounds, searching not for a particular animal but a particular *need*. When she found it she clenched her hands into tight fists and sent a message: *Come! I have what you seek! Hurry! Hurry!*

A tiny shock vibrated up her right calf. She plucked a water worm from her leg and squeezed tightly, sending droplets onto a dozen other shapes scurrying for position beneath her. "Leave us alone!" Taff screamed, slapping at his arms, his knees, his thighs. Some half-formed shape with four wings landed on the back of his neck, and Taff's mouth trembled as a particularly violent shock pierced his body. Kara—ignoring the pinpricks of pain exploding all over her own body—slid across the boulder and yanked the creature away, wringing it between two hands like a wet hand cloth. She enfolded Taff in her arms and covered him protectively as a dozen water-winged shapes plummeted toward them.

The simulacra never reached their target.

Something large and blue streaked across the sky and caught the water creatures in its gull-shaped beak. Kara saw at least a dozen of these new arrivals—with leathery skin stretched taut across long, sinuous wings—snatching the remaining simulacra from out of the air, or slurping the ones without wings from the surface of boulders with long, conical tongues.

Kara had not known what matter of beast would answer her call.

She had needed them only to be thirsty.

One of the creatures landed gracefully on the boulder next to her. It was somewhere between a reptile and a bird, with soft eyes and an absurdly long tail that sat coiled upon its haunches like a stored rope. A jagged scar split its flank, and its slightly protruding tongue was swollen with black mold. It wasn't completely Blighted—not yet—but it was well on its way.

The beast bent its head forward, and Kara, hesitating only briefly, stroked it.

"Thank you," she said.

Must keep you safe, Kara heard its voice in her head. *Witch Girl save us.*

"No," she said. "I can't help you. I want to, but I can't."

The creature looked up at her, its old eyes glowing with wisdom, and a hint of mischief too.

You will.

And then, with a squawk so loud that Taff covered his ears, the creature lifted off. The rest of its tribe followed, their bellies happily swollen with water. Kara watched them disappear into the leaves of the Thickety.

Taking Taff's hand, she skipped boulders until finally stepping onto black soil again, where Mary Kettle was waiting.

"Why didn't you help us?" Kara asked.

"You must learn to fight your own battles."

"We could have died!"

"Kara," Taff said.

"But you didn't. What exactly do you think Imogen is? A common sledgeworm? How do you hope to become strong enough to defeat her if I'm helping you every step of the way?"

"So this was, what? A test?"

"Kara," Taff said.

"No. This was training." Her voice softened. "If things had gotten truly dangerous, of course I would have helped you. But there was no need. You performed—"

"Kara!" shouted Taff.

Mary and Kara turned to face him. His face was ashen.

Blood dripped from a cut on his left palm.

"You're hurt!" Kara exclaimed.

"It's not that," Taff said. He raised his good hand and pointed toward the Draye'varg.

In the distance stood a small figure. It was too far away to make out all the details, but Kara thought she recognized an unruly patch of sandy hair.

"My blood—it must have dripped between the boulders," said Taff. "I'm sorry."

Kara shook her head. "It's not your fault."

"We can't let it live," said Mary. "It'll follow us. Hunt Taff."

Kara swallowed deeply and held out her hand.

"Give me your dagger," she said. "I'll take care of it."

Mary unsheathed the blade. She held it hilt-side out but as Kara reached for it Mary withdrew her hand.

"No," Mary said. She looked somewhat confused, as though surprised by her own decision. "This isn't right. I can't let you do it. You're his sister." With a look of resolution she stepped onto the first boulder. "Let me."

Kara looked past Mary. The figure had come closer. She could almost see the green eyes she knew so well.

"Thank you," Kara said.

She led Taff into the shelter of the trees, where she bound his wound. A few moments later they heard a familiar scream. Kara held her brother close, grateful that she had not been the one to wield the knife.

NINE

After dinner the following evening, Mary Kettle spread a scratchy old blanket across a patch of earth that had managed to dry beneath the feeble sun.

"It's time you know the whole story," she said, looking directly at Kara. "No more secrets."

Mary untied her sack and poured out the contents.

Toys in various degrees of disrepair cascaded to the ground: rose-colored marbles, a splintered wooden canoe, two tattered paper kites, a stuffed bear missing one eye, some kind of musical instrument with five airholes, a handheld rocking horse whose paint was chipping off, and numerous dolls of every description.

"Look at all this stuff!" Taff exclaimed, his face flushed with excitement. He picked up a wooden top with stars carefully stenciled along the ridge, but Mary snatched it away.

"Don't touch," she said. "Their magic might be weak, but many of these toys are still dangerous."

"What's this one do?" Taff asked, gesturing toward the top.

"It spins," Mary said, "until entire constellations of stars seem to pass before your eyes. You can't help but look. And as you look, you forget. Today. Yesterday. Where you've been. Who you are."

Silence descended over the group. The campfire crackled.

"I don't want to play with the top anymore," Taff said.

Mary was old that night, but as she shared the contents of the sack, her ancient eyes became as playful as a child's. Some toys still retained their magical properties—though Mary could not always count on them working properly—while others had lost their enchantment altogether. Eventually, Mary stopped discussing magic and focused instead on examples of craftsmanship in which she took particular pride: a ship with sails that unfurled by touching a tiny lever, a wooden puzzle completed only by shifting colored squares into a particular pattern.

"You must have been an extraordinary toymaker," Kara said.

"Aye," said Mary, her eyes distant. "Men and women would travel for days just to come to my shop. It was my life's work. Before I found the grimoire, that is."

"What are these things?" Taff asked. He held a small metal object between his fingers. "There's a bunch of them."

"It's a gear," Mary said. She leaned forward, her spine popping with age. "Do you know what a clock is?"

Taff stared at her blankly but Kara remembered

something Lucas had once told her. "It tells you what part of the day it is—if you can't read the sun and stars, I suppose. Some kind of meaningless entertainment for those with too many seeds to spend."

Mary said, "Someone very special gave me a clock once—another story for another night—and I used the grimoire to enchant it. This was one of my most clever spells, actually. When I turned back the hour hand before I went to bed, I would wake up years younger, and when I turned the hour hand forward, I returned to my natural age—even older, if I so desired, though I certainly did not. You must understand, I had only just discovered my abilities when I saw the first hint of gray in my hair, and the thought of growing old when I had only begun to live . . ."

"After you stopped using magic," Taff said, "the power of the toys began to fade. But the clock broke altogether, didn't it? You can't control it at all."

Mary nodded. "The grimoire's ultimate punishment."

"Where is your grimoire, anyway?" Kara asked.

"Far away from here," Mary said. "Where I will not be tempted to use it."

Mary turned her head, but Kara caught the look of longing that flashed through her eyes.

There's a part of her that misses it still.

"I found another one!" Taff exclaimed, pinching a second gear between his fingers. "Help me find the rest."

Noting Mary's confused expression, Kara said, "My brother has a talent for fixing things."

"Hmm," said Mary. "Perhaps that's why my little rabbit listened to you. It sensed your gift. Magic wants to be used—that's the one rule that never changes, no matter what type of magic we're talking about—so it makes sense that my toys would be drawn to a talented craftsperson. They think you can make them whole again."

Taff did not respond. He was lost in the work of separating the mound into smaller piles, categorizing its contents into groups that made sense only to him. Kara had seen him fall into these reveries many times before when working on a project back home.

"Taff," Mary said, touching his shoulder.

He looked up.

"I appreciate that you want to help me. But you must be trained from birth to build a clock—it is a most complex trade, passed down from father to son. This little gear is one of dozens hidden within the pile, and there are hundreds of other parts as well. It is a job for a master clockmaker."

"So you're telling me it's impossible."

"Yes."

Taff grinned. "Fantastic!" He continued searching for clocklike pieces with even greater enthusiasm. "That makes it even more fun. Besides, you've done so much for us—I want to do something for you for a change."

Mary Kettle watched Taff for a few moments, her startled expression gradually giving way to a bewildered smile. Absentmindedly she touched a hand to her eyes and seemed shocked to find a teardrop there. She flicked it away with two fingers, her smile suddenly shifting into a scowl.

"What's wrong?" Kara asked.

The old woman turned her back to the children and, hunched over, began sweeping the pieces back into the sack. "I shouldn't have showed you all this," she snapped, plucking the clock gears from Taff's hands. "And I certainly do *not* want you trying to put this back together. Stay away from my things. Do you even know how these objects *got* their power? Do you?"

Taff shook his head, unable to meet Mary's eyes. "You've been so nice to us. I'd forgotten."

"Well, that must be wonderful," said Mary. "That must be just fine. But as for me, I can never forget."

"Mary," Kara said, but the old woman ignored her, all her attention focused on Taff.

"Such magic requires *ingredients*. You understand

what I'm saying to you, boy?"

"You used children," muttered Taff. "I've heard the stories." He blinked away his tears and met her eyes. "But the grimoire was controlling you, like with Kara. It wasn't your fault."

Mary's gray eyes glinted in the firelight. She no longer looked like the woman Kara had begun to consider a friend. She looked like a woman who might linger in shadows or beneath the beds of unwary children.

"I lured them to my cottage with promises of sweet-cakes and silver coins and then I boiled them in my kettle until their souls had leeched into whatever object I felt like enchanting that day."

Kara wrapped her arm around Taff's shoulders.

"Please," Kara said. "No more."

But Mary was not finished. As she spoke, her upper lip lifted in a feral sneer.

"It was like boiling a chicken for broth. You know what happens then, right? The flavor gets sucked away and all you're left with is a bunch of useless meat. Except I didn't just throw the meat away or feed it to my livestock. I sent what was left of those children home to their mommies and daddies. Even though their souls were gone and they were nothing but lifeless husks, I sent them home anyway because it *amused me*."

She clasped Taff's face between her hands.

"Now tell me again, boy. Tell me that it was all the grimoire's fault."

"Stop it!" Kara exclaimed, pushing Mary away. "You're scaring him!"

Mary grunted deep in her throat and crossed to her side of the encampment, dragging her bag of broken magic behind her.

Taff, drawing in huge mouthfuls of air, trembled.

"Come on," said Kara, holding him tight. "You need to sleep."

But Taff broke free of her embrace and shouted, "You're not like that anymore! I know you! The real you!

You helped us! You're good! The witch who did all those terrible things is gone forever!"

There was a long silence. And then, from deep within the shadows, came a hoarse response: "Are you so sure?"

TEN

The next morning Kara woke to find Mary, middle-aged with crow's-feet, peeling fuzz-covered tubers for breakfast.

"What are those?" Kara asked.

"Jibs," Mary said. "They're like parsnips, except . . ."

She paused, as though pondering a way to explain the difference.

"Except what?" Kara asked.

"Except they're not. Your brother's a late riser today."

"He had trouble falling asleep last night."

"Because I frightened him?"

"Because you hurt his feelings. He likes you."

Mary scratched the greenish fuzz from her hands and clasped them together on her lap. "Doesn't he know who I am?"

"Of course he does," said Kara. "You're the woman who saved us from the branchwolves and taught his sister how to use her powers. You're the reason we're still alive."

"But—"

"Who you *were* is not who you *are*."

Mary scraped a jib clean with practiced swipes of her knife; the peel was still whole when it dropped to the earth. "I would give anything to undo my actions," she said. "But that doesn't stop me from missing it, you know. The grimoire. It gnawed a place so deep inside me that even now I feel empty without it." Using the knife, she traced the book's outline in the air. "It was red, the color of baked clay, with an elaborate pattern of gold filigree.

Red is my favorite color. I think the book knew that."

Mary stared into space, as though frozen in time, remembering.

After a few moments Kara slid the knife from her hand. "Let me help," she said, and began to peel the tubers. Kara had never enjoyed this kind of chore back in De'Noran, but now the monotonous action relaxed her.

"Imogen is but a few days away," Mary finally said. She withdrew a second knife and sliced a peeled jib into the boiling stew. "You must keep practicing. Some of these beasts may be reluctant to help you, but that matters not. You are their master. You must bend them to your will."

"No," said Kara. "I'll ask for their help, but I would never force another living thing to . . ."

"Serve you?"

Kara nodded. "It feels wrong. Like something the grimoire would make me do."

"They're just animals."

"You wouldn't say that if you could talk to them the way I do."

"You're right—and that allows me to maintain my perspective. You grew up on a farm, Kara. Did your father never slaughter a hog so your family could eat? So you could *survive*? This is no different. If you want to escape the Thickety you're going to have to make sacrifices."

Kara thought about building a mind-bridge to gain an animal's trust and then forcing it to do something against its will. The idea sickened her.

"What if I can't do it?" Kara asked.

"Then Imogen will kill you and your brother," Mary said. She dipped the ladle into the stew and took a sip. "It's as simple as that."

The following day they came to a village.

A wooden fence bound tightly with vine encircled a large clearing. Within its confines lay a row of black houses topped with peaked roofs and chimneys of yellow-hued brick. In the center of the houses—about thirty in all—sat a small play area with two seesaws and a scaffold from which dangled several rope swings.

There were no children to be found here, however—or adults.

"Where is everyone?" Kara asked.

"Gone," Mary said, the sack slung over her shoulder tinkling like mad as she hurried toward the houses. "It's best not to dwell on the specifics. There are dozens of ghost villages like this scattered throughout the Thickety. At one point, many years ago, this place was like your De'Noran. They cut Fringe weeds down every day before they could grow into full-fledged trees, hoping to keep the Thickety away. But no one can keep that up forever. Sordyr always wins."

"Why build a village here to begin with?" Taff asked.

Mary tried to open the door to the nearest house but it wouldn't budge. "Perhaps they were exiles and given little choice," she said. "Perhaps, like the Children of the Fold, they had lost their place in the World. We'll probably never know. But maybe we can all sleep in beds tonight."

"You've never been here before?" Kara asked.

"The Thickety is deceptively huge," Mary replied. "Sometimes I wonder if even *Sordyr* has seen all of it."

"Look at the windows," said Taff. "They're all boarded up."

"I've seen that before in other ghost villages," Mary said. "After the Thickety overtook this place, the villagers— the ones who were left, at least—did what they could to protect themselves. They had heard the stories. They knew that if they survived long enough, Sordyr would come and rescue them."

"*Rescue* them?" Taff asked.

"In his fashion," said Mary. "Sordyr would grant the survivors their lives, but in exchange they were forced to make a decision: either swear their undying fealty or be left to wander the Thickety on their own. You can imagine what most chose."

"What happened to them?"

"They were brought to Kala Malta. It's a settlement on the edge of the Thickety."

"Why does he need them?" Kara asked.

"I don't know," Mary said, refusing to meet her eyes.

Kara could hear the lie as clearly as the words themselves, but before she could ask the old witch about it, something caught her interest.

"What's this?" Kara asked, approaching the next house. She ran her finger along a narrow, bone-white object nailed into the door. It was the length of her forearm and sharpened at one end.

"Niersook fang," Mary said. "People who lived here thought they could carve an animal bone into a tooth and keep evil away." She shook her head in disgust. "Superstitious nonsense."

"Who's Niersook?" asked Kara.

"Not who. *What*." Mary paused. "You really don't know?"

Kara shook her head.

Mary whistled. "I'll give you the short version. There was a *wexari* named Rygoth who had power over all the animals of the world."

"Like Kara!" exclaimed Taff.

"In a way. But Rygoth—who was Sordyr's greatest enemy—could actually *make* animals. She created a beast named Niersook and gave it the power to take all of the Forest Demon's magic away. Only, Sordyr killed it first, and despite the fact that Niersook failed miserably people continue to honor it by carving bones into fangs, imagining they possess some sort of protective property."

Mary scoffed at the thought, but Kara did not find it so strange; in De'Noran, many of her neighbors had hung Fenroot branches on their doors for the exact same reason.

The details may change, but all people want to feel safe.

"What happened to Rygoth?" Kara asked.

"Sordyr killed her," Mary said, "but not before she cast

the spell that imprisoned him on the island. If it wasn't for Rygoth, Sordyr would be out in the World right now—assuming there even *was* a World anymore, once he got done with it."

"She's a hero," Taff said.

Mary shrugged.

"If you believe in that sort of thing," she said.

They crossed the narrow lane to the next house, identical to the others save a clay basket hanging from a wooden post. Kara thought the basket might have once held flowers—or at least what passed for flowers here—but now it was overgrown with sickly gray weeds that spilled over its edge like an Elder's hair. In the shadow of the basket was a patch of yellow grass. Crouching down she reached out her hand—

Don't touch it!

The voice came from the trees above her. The creature—Kara guessed some type of bird, judging from the songlike quality of the words—was too shy to show itself.

It just wanted to warn her.

Reaching out, Kara found the animal, felt its heart beating quickly in its chest. There was no need to build a mind-bridge. By approaching her first, the animal had already given its trust.

Why not? Kara asked.

Darkeaters. Go, Witch Girl, before notsuns rise. Make dark-eaters.

Kara did not know what a darkeater or a notsun was, but there was no mistaking the fear in the unseen creature's voice. She rose to her feet, intending to warn the others, and took in the entire patch of grass for the first time.

"Oh no," she said.

It was the perfect outline of a man.

"Taff!" she exclaimed. "Mary! You better come and see this!" She backed away and found herself stepping on another patch of grass, this one the approximate shape of a child. Kara scanned the village, ignoring the houses and other signs of life that had usurped her attention, focusing solely on the ground.

There were human-shaped patches everywhere.

"What is it?" Mary asked.

Notsuns rising! Go! Now!

"We need to leave," Kara said.

"And pass up the opportunity for a good night's rest? Why would we do that?"

Before Kara could reply, Taff shouted, "Look!"

A green vine was winding its way about the gargantuan tree that stood before them, slithering higher and higher before their eyes.

"There, too," Taff said, pointing to the other side of the village, where a similar vine coiled about a different tree. "And there."

No time, Witch Girl. Get inside.

"We have to get inside one of these houses," Kara said. "Now."

Kara ran to the nearest door, rattling the latch fiercely.

When that didn't work she threw herself shoulder-first against the wood. It didn't budge.

Kara glanced up at the nearest vine. At its tip a bulb swelled until it was as large as a sledgeworm, then unfolded. Bright-yellow petals stretched out from an orange stigma.

"The same thing's happening to all of them," Taff said, looking around. "They're pretty."

"That's what worries me," said Mary. "There's no place for beauty here."

"The seesaw!" Taff exclaimed. "I think we can use it as a battering ram and break into one of the—"

Too late. Kara heard the voice in her head.

The stigma of the giant flower above them began to glow, the orange sharpening to a fiery red and sending waves of searing heat in their direction. Kara, beads of perspiration already trickling down her neck, was certain the whole flower would burst into flame. It didn't. Instead a pool of crimson light flowed from the stigma—and the stigmas of the other flowers as well—bathing the entire village in its strange glow.

Notsun, Kara thought.

Taff turned his hand from side to side and watched the light reflect off his skin.

"It doesn't seem to be hurting us," he said. "Maybe it's just trying to keep us warm."

Kara gave him a look of disbelief.

"No," Taff said. "I don't really believe that either."

HUNGRY.

This new voice reverberated faintly, as though calling to her from the dark end of a tunnel. *HUNGRY*, it repeated. There was no emotion to the word, no need. It was just a cold statement of fact, and Kara knew that the owner of the voice—whatever it was—would kill them quickly and without remorse. *HUNGRY.* She clasped her hands to her ears, wanting the voice out of her head, but of course that didn't help—she wasn't using her ears to hear it.

"There's something here," Kara said. She pointed behind the flowers, where the dark forest remained untouched by the strange light. "We have to get out of this village fast. I think we'll be safe once we get past——"

Behind Mary, faint wisps of smoke rose into the air.

One of the grass patches had caught fire. The flames, small enough that Kara could have stamped them out with the heel of her boot, blazed out quickly.

Left behind was the charred shape of a man, which stretched its arms into the air and rose from the ground.

HUNGRY, Kara heard it say.

She felt herself moving, Taff grasping her hand and pulling her away as grass patches all around them burst into flames that quickly extinguished into flat, shadowy shapes rising from the ground.

HUNGRY. HUNGRY. HUNGRY.

"This way," Taff said.

He guided her to a house much larger than the others in the village. *Perhaps this is where their version of a fen'de lived*, Kara thought. Taff didn't even bother trying the front door, which was no doubt nailed shut. Instead, he unlatched the small wooden gate built into the side of the front steps and ducked beneath the floorboards of the porch.

"Come on!" he whispered, pulling Kara behind him. "Hurry!"

Kara was too tall to simply duck her head so she had to crawl into the space; her left knee, which had still not fully healed from their mad dash across the Draye'varg, throbbed with pain. Mary followed close behind, closing the gate behind them.

"There's nowhere to hide if they find us," Kara whispered to Taff. "Are you sure this is such a good idea?"

"Absolutely not," he replied, "but it's a lot better than wandering about in the open with those things. At least we're out of sight."

"Do you think they saw us go under here?" asked Kara.

Mary shook her head. "Look at the way they're moving.

Sluggish. Disoriented. Like they've just woken up from a long slumber. They're still regaining their senses."

"If that's the case," Taff said, "then maybe we should just put our heads down and run until we're out of—"

"No," replied Mary. "If there was an opportunity for that, we've missed it."

Through the gaps of the checkerboard skirting, Kara watched the black shapes roam the village. She tried to block out the rising voices (*HUNGRY, HUNGRY, HUNGRY*) in her head.

"I hear them," Kara said, "just like I would other creatures."

"Can you control them?" Mary asked.

Kara shook her head. "Their voices are like echoes of something that was once alive."

"Darkeaters," Mary said. "I thought—even here— that they were little more than a campfire tale."

"They're just monsters," Taff said, straining to sound brave. "We've defeated monsters before."

Mary sighed. "You haven't seen, have you?"

"Seen what?"

She placed a hand tenderly on Taff's forearm, and regarded him—for just a moment—with the protective expression of a mother.

"Look at their shadows," she whispered. "Both of you."

One of the darkeaters—tall and gangly, with arms nearly to its knees—had made its way to the front yard of the house. Kara leaned forward as far as she dared. At first she could not see its shadow—the angle was all wrong—but then the red light shifted and the darkeater turned to face it, as though to bask in its glow.

Taff whimpered softly next to her.

"No," he muttered, "no . . ."

The darkeater's shadow was not a shadow at all. It was a man in his late forties with a closely cropped beard and hazel eyes; he was perfectly flat, as though not a man at all but a slice of mirror bearing his reflection. As the darkeater moved, the man shadowed its movements, his face vacant and expressionless.

"That's what happened to the villagers," Mary said, "and that's what's going to happen to us if we can't think of a way out of here."

ELEVEN

They stayed beneath the house until nightfall, though there was really no night and day anymore, only the harsh red glow emanating from the flowers. Taff, who refused to look at the darkeaters again after seeing that first human shadow, had fallen asleep, his head resting on Mary's legs, his feet hooked across Kara.

"He looks so young when he sleeps," Kara said. "Sometimes I forget that he's only seven. No child should have to go through something like this."

Mary glanced in her direction, a small smile creeping over her lips.

"What?" Kara asked.

"Nothing."

Taff was still asleep and snoring soundly when an animal entered the village. It could have been mistaken for a fawn, were it not for twin sets of bulbous eyes that sat on opposite sides of its head.

The darkeaters hadn't noticed its arrival. Yet.

"What's it doing here?" Kara asked.

"I have no idea," Mary said. "Most animals know enough to stay away. There must be something wrong with it."

The animal, Mary told her, was called a paarn, and as it came closer Kara could see that it was indeed ill: it tottered when it walked, and its fur had fallen out on one side, leaving patches of flaky skin. Even from far away she could hear its wheezing breath.

Go! Kara tried to tell the paarn. *It's not safe here!*

But although Kara was able to find the animal's thoughts, they were too scattered and confused to allow her to build a mind-bridge between them. The paarn was ill in its brain as well as its body.

"They found it," Mary said, pointing to the first dark-eater rising behind the animal. Kara caught a glimpse of its "shadow"—an unsmiling girl with pigtails and a splotch of freckles around her nose.

In its last moments the paarn regained some of its lost senses and tried to run, but it was far too late. Kara waited for the darkeater to attack, for the inevitable rending of flesh as the shadowy shape fastened its jaws on the unfortunate creature. That never happened. Instead, the darkeater stood still while the pigtailed girl reached out her hands and snatched at the paarn's shadow, grabbing handfuls of blackness and shoving it into her flat mouth. The paarn bleated—a high-pitched, strident noise—bringing the attention of other darkeaters eager to join the feast.

"What?" Taff mumbled, half opening his eyes, but Mary rocked him back and forth and whispered, "It's okay, go back to sleep, go back to sleep . . ." and Taff drifted off again.

The pain focused the paarn's thoughts enough for Kara to build a bridge between them, and once the connection was made she sent the poor creature peaceful images—drinking from a puddle of rain at dusk, sleeping in a bed of leaves—in order to distract it from what was happening and provide some measure of peace. At the end, Kara felt the animal there with her, prancing through a meadow of freshly fallen snow before night fell forever.

She felt tears roll down her cheeks but refused to wipe them off. Not yet. Not until she saw what they had done.

The body of the paarn had evaporated, piece by piece, as its shadow was devoured. Motes of faintly glowing dust rose into the air, splitting off into equal sections and shooting across the village. Kara followed one cloud of motes as they were inhaled by the glowing stigma of the nearest flower. The petals trembled with satisfaction.

It was then, as she watched the sad remnants of an innocent life vanish forever, that Kara decided simply escaping this village with their lives would no longer be enough.

"I'm going to stop them," Kara said.

Leaning on one elbow, Mary regarded her with a curious expression.

"It was just a paarn, Kara. Animals die all the time. It's part of life in the Thickety."

"Yes," said Kara, struggling to keep her voice low in spite of her rising anger. "Animals get eaten by other animals. Predator, prey. I understand the natural workings of the world, and I would never presume to interfere." She pointed a trembling finger at the still-quivering flower in the distance. "But that is not natural. That reeks of Sordyr. And I intend to stop it."

Kara saw a flicker of something pass through Mary's face—something that might have been pride—before it returned to its typical stoic expression.

"Very well. But you don't need my help for that, *wexari*. You have an entire forest at your command."

Kara could hear them—*so easily now, as simple as reaching out my hand*—faint whispers in the trees but also along the outskirts of the village. The creatures were biding their time until the flowers sank beneath the earth once more and safety returned.

"They won't come," Kara said. "They're terrified of the darkeaters."

"They are nothing but beasts. You are their master. *Make* them come."

"I can't do that."

"Can't? Or won't?"

Kara wasn't sure. When she had used the grimoire she supposed it was possible—even likely—that the animals she conjured had come against their will. But she had never used her newfound powers as a *wexari* to try to force an animal to do her bidding. How would it even work? *If I had to*, she thought, *I could build the bridge strong enough to trap them.* Kara allowed her mind to drift to the canopy and felt the hundreds of flying creatures sailing through the night, the innumerable creepy-crawly things wending their way from tree to tree. Their minds were so simple, so weak. *Why hesitate when I have such weapons at my disposal?* she wondered. The voices of the animals rose in intensity, as though they wanted her to know how eager they were to be commanded. *I can use these beasts to destroy the darkeaters and the notsuns without even leaving the safety of this hiding place. What could be simpler?*

And yet Kara couldn't stop thinking about all the creatures that might die in the process of carrying out her plan. *Does it matter? Aren't human lives more important than the lives of animals? I must save Taff and Mary first if I have the power to do so!* The trees continued to whisper, beckoning her. *USE US. BE THE WITCH YOU WERE MEANT TO BE.* She remembered Mary's words: *If you want to escape the Thickety you're going to have to make sacrifices.* Yes. Sacrifices. And better those monsters than Mary or Taff—it was the right thing to do.

But then why did even considering such a plan turn her stomach?

"These creatures are tools," said Mary Kettle, "nothing more."

"I've heard grimoires described the same way," Kara said. "How did that work out for us?"

"This is different. A grimoire makes the user do terrible things. But here you would simply be . . . asking for help."

"Maybe the first time," said Kara, "maybe even the second. But eventually I think it would get too easy, and then it would be no different than using a grimoire at all. A living thing that allows me into its mind is granting me a gift, and to abuse that for my own benefit is . . . I think that might be the very nature of evil."

A darkeater passed their way then, so close that Kara could nearly touch its shadow——a rotund man whose beard was half-shaven, as though he had been transformed during his morning routine. Kara gently turned Taff on his side to diminish the sound of his snoring.

"If they were going to find us," whispered Mary after

the darkeater had wobbled away, "they would have done so by now. Besides, we should be safe here." She gestured to the wooden boards just above their head. "Blocks the light. Since we don't cast any shadows, they have nothing to feed on."

"So we're just going to stay here forever?" Kara asked.

"Let's see what the morning brings. I'm going to follow your brother's example and get some rest. Think on what I've said—you have the power to stop this."

"I told you, I—"

Mary placed a weathered finger to Kara's lips. "Just think on it," she said. Mary lay down next to Taff and pulled a blanket over her head. "Perhaps they'll simply leave on their own," she muttered. "Stranger things have happened."

Although her eyes were heavy, Kara couldn't sleep. She studied the darkeaters. *Are they searching for us?* If so, they were doing an exceedingly poor job; despite their sinuous form they were graceless creatures, lumbering about the village like moondrink-driven men on a festival night. Kara turned her attention to the nearest flower, the light from its stigma unwavering. *It was the notsuns that sensed we were here and woke up the darkeaters, and it's probably the notsuns that know we never left. The darkeaters are just servants used to gather food.*

So why haven't they found us yet?

Kara thought the answer to that question might be important, but her eyelids refused to remain open, and within a few moments she fell asleep.

Kara awoke to a blinding redness behind her eyelids, as though she had slept while looking directly at the sun. She slitted her eyes open and saw that their once dark hiding spot beneath the house was now flooded with red light.

Kara got up fast—too fast—and banged her head against the porch's floorboards.

"Taff!" she shouted, clasping a hand to her forehead. "Mary! You have to get up!"

Peeking through the lattice wall to her left, Kara saw that a notsun had changed position while she slept, looping around the chimney of a neighboring house and then lowering itself close to the earth so its red light could spill beneath the porch.

It wanted a different vantage point. So it could see new areas of the village that had been beyond the reach of the light.

So it could find us.

A small group of darkeaters began shuffling their way in the direction of the house, as though they smelled Kara's shadow stretching across the earth.

"Taff!" Kara screamed, no longer caring if the darkeaters heard them or not.

"What?" Taff grumbled. "Why is it so bright in here? Where's Mary?"

"What do you mean, where's Mary?" Kara twisted beneath the floorboards so she was facing the place where Mary had lain down to rest. She saw the bulging sack of magical items, but no Mary—only her lumpy old blanket.

"She must be in the village somewhere," said Kara. "Maybe she figured out a way for us to escape."

"Maybe," Taff said, but he did not sound very confident.

Kara peeked between the steps again. The darkeaters had drawn closer, and there were more of them now.

From underneath Mary's blanket, a baby began to cry.

TWELVE

Kara crawled across the dirt to find a baby, no older than six months, curling her tiny fists open and shut and kicking her chubby legs in the air. Sharp gray eyes left little doubt as to her identity.

"I didn't know Mary could become *that* young," said Taff.

"Yes," said Kara, "she might have thought to mention that."

The baby's frantic wails, breathless and piercing, sliced through the early-morning silence.

"Shh," Taff said, stroking Mary's cheek with the back of his hand. "Shh! You're going to bring all the monsters! Don't you understand me, Mary?"

The baby did not understand. The baby was hungry. Or wet. Or scared. Kara remembered all the long nights she had spent caring for Taff. Babies' needs were simple, but they had no concept of scale. At that particular moment, whatever Mary wanted was the most important thing in the world to her, and she needed it *right now*.

Kara pulled the baby onto her chest, hoping to calm her down, and then realized it didn't matter.

The darkeaters were here.

They sifted through the cross-checked lattice like fog, and their human shadows followed, stretching as far as the light permitted. Soon the earth beneath the porch resembled a red-tinged lake with a dozen people trapped beneath its surface, clawing for purchase. The angle of the notsun created a long shadow on Kara's right, so she spun, hoping to keep it away from the darkeaters, but that only created a different shadow behind her. One of the human figures—a woman wearing an odd hat covered with multicolored feathers—pinched a tiny piece of Kara's shadow hand between her fingers. She swallowed it eagerly, and Kara coughed out a tiny trail of floating motes.

Kara heard Taff scream next to her, saw a plume leave his mouth. She pushed him back against the house, where a narrow strip of darkness provided some protection against the red light. They were surrounded by the human reflections now, a sea of arms reaching not for Kara and Taff and Mary—but their shadows.

Kara winced as pain pierced her hand; she had been using it to support her body and gotten too close to the light. She drew it back into the shadows and spit out another mouthful of motes.

The baby continued to wail.

From Kara's right a second notsun appeared. New light began to flood the enclosed space. Once it reached their small section of darkness, there would be nowhere left to hide.

"I have an idea," said Taff.

Before Kara could stop him, Taff was crawling on his elbows across the human shadows. They were as surprised by his actions as Kara, and by the time they realized what was happening and began snatching at his shadow, Taff had already taken what he needed and slung it over his body.

Mary's blanket.

"They can't eat our shadows," he said, his voice muffled, "if we don't cast them."

Wearing the blanket like a turtle's shell, Taff crawled back to his sister. The darkeaters clawed frantically at him but their hands—both human and shadow—passed right through the blanket.

Taff lifted the blanket. Kara crawled next to him.

Darkness surrounded them.

Mary's wailing instantly stopped. She began to gurgle softly, suddenly content.

"Maybe she didn't like the red light," said Taff.

"I don't blame her," replied Kara. "What do we do now?"

"They can't hurt us as long as we stay under the blanket. I figure we can just crawl out of the village. Once we get past the flowers we'll be okay."

They moved slowly, Kara holding the baby in one arm while she maintained her balance with the other, Taff crawling beneath her chest. He unlatched the gate in the latticework and they moved out into the open.

As the red light descended upon them Kara expected to feel darkeater hands tear the blanket from their backs. *Since their human halves can touch only shadows*, she thought, *the dark halves must be able to attack more corporeal prey.* The blanket remained untouched, however, and the two children crawled undisturbed, their hands turning as black as the soil itself.

Once they had left their tight confines beneath the house, Kara rose to a stooped position. The blanket draped over them like a ghostly Shadow Festival costume as they advanced slowly through the village. Kara's thighs quickly started to burn, but it was much easier to hold the baby in this position than when they had been crawling.

Mary, whose energetic wails had no doubt taken a significant toll on her little body, fell fast asleep against Kara's shoulder.

"What if she wakes up and she's big again?" Taff asked. "There's not enough room for three of us underneath this blanket."

"I don't think that will happen," Kara said. "Remember all those nights you spent trying to stay awake so you could see her change?"

"I always fell asleep first."

"Or maybe the magic doesn't work if someone is watching."

Taff shook his head. "This magic of yours. There are so many rules."

Progress was slow. They had to stop every few minutes, not only to rest, but also so Taff could peek beneath the blanket and make sure they were heading away from the village and not farther into it. Kara might have felt better if she had heard some kind of sound from the dark-eaters: moaning, growling, anything. But the figures remained perfectly silent, and it was only the occasional glimpse of a dark shape through the fibers of the blanket that let Kara know they were still there.

It was nearly afternoon when they left the red light behind them.

"See?" said Taff. "That wasn't so bad."

Kara hesitantly rose to her feet—groaning at the pain in her stiff legs—and lifted the blanket. They were just outside the village. Darkeaters pressed against the edge of the red light, wanting to pursue them but unable to advance.

"They're trapped," Kara said, laying Mary on a soft blanket of moss. "They need the notsun's light to live. They can't follow us."

"What about the villagers?" Taff asked. "The ones that are part of the darkeaters. Are they trapped too?"

"I don't know," Kara said.

"Sordyr did this," Taff said. "I know it. He likes to change good things into bad ones, just like he did with Shadowdancer. Just like he did to this whole place. It's worse than killing them." Taff picked up a thick stick and hurled it toward the darkeaters. "I hate you! I hate you!"

Unexpected heat scalded Kara's back.

She turned to see a new notsun climbing up the tree behind her. Dozens more were blooming at great speed, cutting off their escape through the forest. Soon every step they took would be flooded with red light.

A familiar voice like rustling leaves scraped its way into her mind.

You didn't really think you could hide from me, did you? This is my Thickety. I know everything that happens here.

Everything.

Red light spread across the forest floor toward the waiting darkeaters, pressed against the barrier like beasts in a cage. Kara saw one of the human shadows, the same pigtailed little girl she had seen before, clap her flat hands with delight.

Taff reached for their blanket but a tree branch swept down like a bony finger and lifted it far out of reach.

You know what you have to do, wexari. *Command them. Use these creatures to destroy your enemies.*

"No!"

Then you will die. Your brother first.

The new red light met the light of the village and set the darkeaters free. Shadowy shapes stumbled toward Kara and Taff.

I have no choice, Kara thought. *But I'll do this on my terms—not yours.*

Her mind raced along ancient branches and drooping fronds, passing animals that would have willingly given their lives for her until she found just the right . . . *There!* The Blighted One sat high in the treetops, its jaws dripping with the fresh blood of its latest prey, its mind a bleak landscape of death and violence. Kara used the cruel ecstasy she had felt when sending the squits after Grace to build a bridge between them. The beast was a fighter by nature, and tried to push Kara away, so she focused her mind like a whip and struck it, again and again, until it whined with submission.

NO MORE!

You want blood. You want to hurt things. I promise both will come to pass if you serve me.

She felt the creature's bloodlust rising. In her chest, Kara's heart began to beat faster.

The bridge went both ways.

RAWTOOTH WILL SERVE. KILL FOR QUEEN.

The creature climbed down the trees, swinging from branch to branch on taloned arms. Kara heard the creak of its approach, the dash of animals as they avoided its descent.

This isn't right, Kara thought. *This is the grimoire all over again.*

"What is *that*?" Taff asked.

The rawtooth landed on the ground between the dark-eaters and the children, sending geysers of black earth into the air. Its legs were covered with tufts of sickly green moss, but its chest and back had no moss at all—or skin, for that matter. Within the labyrinthine pathways of its exposed chest, Kara saw two hearts pump in perfectly synchronized rhythm.

It turned to face her: four diagonal-slitted eyes that flickered open and shut with the speed of a humming-bird. The rawtooth rose to two feet and, tilting its head to one side, crossed its long arms in a disturbingly human fashion.

WHO? spoke a voice in her head. *WHO KILL FOR QUEEN?*

Kara pointed to the darkeaters.

"Them," she said.

Without hesitation the rawtooth pounced on the first shadowy shape, expecting to bite its head off, and grunted in confusion when its jaws passed right through it. The darkeater's human reflection—a wan woman with long hair—grabbed the rawtooth's shadow with two hands and bit down hard. The rawtooth shrieked in pain.

This is a foul beast, Kara thought. *If I did not command it to attack the darkeaters, it would have killed something else.*

Thinking that was one thing. Believing it was something else altogether.

The rawtooth shrieked again as another piece of its shadow was devoured.

It looked at Kara with something like betrayal in its eyes.

Kara, her mind elsewhere, focused on the task at hand. Her body was drenched in sweat. A fierce headache ground against her temples.

"Kara!" Taff exclaimed. "It's dying!"

The darkeaters had surrounded the rawtooth now. They chomped at its shadow with wild abandon, the children completely forgotten. Dust motes rose into the air and were devoured by the eager notsuns.

In Kara's head, she heard Sordyr's mocking voice.

Impressive to tame such a beast. But there is little it can do against my creations.

"I know," Kara said, gritting her teeth. "I just needed some time."

She sent the beetles.

It had taken her longer to build this mind-bridge—starting with one beetle and allowing her mind to spread among the others—all while commanding the rawtooth. She had known the beast stood no chance against the darkeaters. She had simply needed a distraction to keep Taff safe while she prepared her main attack.

It happened fast. Most of the beetles did their work underground, tearing through the notsuns' roots, but some scaled the trees and attacked the flowers directly. Kara looked up and saw a blur of black beetles cover the notsun above her. A brightly colored petal fell to the forest floor and wilted instantly.

The red light flickered out. The darkeaters vanished.

"I beat you!" Kara screamed. She tried to avoid looking at the rawtooth, bloodied and motionless. "I beat you, so *leave us alone!*"

Kara braced herself for a scream of rage blasting through the corridors of her mind, but there was only silence. And then, even worse than a scream, Kara heard a low, pleased laugh.

THIRTEEN

When Mary woke, an old woman once more, she was none too pleased to learn they had left her sack back in the village. Taff offered to retrieve it on his own, but after such a harrowing experience Kara was reluctant to let him out of her sight. There were things she wished to discuss with Mary out of his earshot, however, so she settled on following Taff at a distance.

"How much do you remember?" Kara asked Mary.

"I saw what was left of the notsuns," Mary said. "And the dead monster. So you decided to use your creatures. It was an easy—"

"I heard Sordyr," Kara said. "In my head. And I know I should be feeling victorious right now, but I can't stop thinking that I did exactly what he wanted me to do."

"And what is that?"

"Use my powers. Control the animals. But why would Sordyr want that? Wouldn't that just make me more of a threat to him?"

Mary withdrew a wad of yellow grass from her pocket and placed it behind her gums. She chewed it thoughtfully for a time before answering.

"I won't pretend to understand what the Forest Demon wants or doesn't want. I'm not sure I even *could*. All I know is that you saved our lives, Kara. How can that be wrong?"

Kara didn't answer. Instead she watched Taff crawl beneath the porch. He was humming something, though she didn't recognize the tune. Maybe it was just something he made up. Taff did that from time to time.

"The knees of his pants need to be mended," she said. "Do you have any thread?"

"Kara . . ."

"Is Sordyr close? I've heard him in my head once before, the first time I entered the Thickety. He was right behind me at the time."

"He might be."

"Does he know where we are?"

"I don't know. But we should hurry just in case. How do you feel, Kara? About everything."

A heavy wind blew through the canopy, but even over the trees' despondent whispering Kara could hear the creatures of the Thickety. They would do anything she asked. Fight for her. Die for her. All she had to do was use her magic.

"Kara?" Mary asked, a note of concern in her voice.

"I'm fine," Kara said softly.

Taff returned Mary's bag to her and she squeezed his shoulder. As they left the village they passed the ravaged body of the rawtooth. Kara averted her eyes.

They followed a narrow, winding stream pinched by gray trees. From low-hanging branches dangled succulent purple fruit that sweetened the air itself. No one touched the fruit. They all knew better. Instead they picked shrewberries and cadinuts—both bitter but safe—and chewed them as they walked. Near midday Mary pulled out the toy rabbit on its bicycle and Taff whispered Imogen's name in its ear.

"We're close," Mary said, watching the porcelain rabbit's brief journey. "Only a few hours now."

As they walked, tree trunks twisted together and formed walls to either side of them; soon the path grew so narrow that they had to proceed in single file. The ground sloped steadily downward, the air humid and slightly sweet. Taff kicked a stone, sending it skittering across the dirt, then kicked it again. And again.

Finally the path wound around a bend and opened into a narrow grove. The trees here were short, almost De'Noran-size, and barren of leaves.

Instead, they were teeming with other things.

Kara noticed the keys first, strung from the branches by thick cords of rope. Glittering keys of every shape and description: brass keys and gold keys, round keys and star-shaped keys, copper keys and glass keys encrusted with jewels. Those weren't the only objects in the trees, however. From thin, sickly branches dangled dolls and teddy bears, rings and bracelets, journals and scrolls. Taff pointed out a wooden sled perched precariously on some upper limbs.

"What is all this?" Kara asked.

"Lost things," said Mary.

Taff reached for a clay cup that hung from one of the lower branches.

"I wouldn't," said Mary. "There must be a reason Imogen keeps them. It's best not to find out."

"But how did they get here in the first place?" Taff asked.

Mary shook her head. "There's a clearing just over this

ridge. Let's set up camp and I'll tell you what I know." She pointed to a narrow path leading deeper into the grove. "Imogen lives right through there."

With one last look back at the trees, Kara followed Mary out of the grove. The soil felt strange beneath her boots, as though she were walking on pebbles. She bent down to have a look and instantly wished she had not.

The ground was covered with teeth.

They found a flat spot overlooking the grove and set out their supplies for the night. Taff piled kindling the way he had been taught—smaller pieces leaning against larger ones—and then Mary handed him two shiny marbles from her bag. Taff clapped them together. A soft blue light appeared in the center of the kindling and quickly spread into a blazing fire. Mary hung her kettle above the flame and began to brew something using a pungent mixture of brown and red herbs.

"You need to recover your energy," Mary said. "Your

fight against the darkeaters was a difficult one, but it was like hunting rabbits compared to a battle with Imogen." She dipped a ladle into the kettle and poured some of its contents into a wooden cup, which she handed to Kara.

"Thanks."

"Don't thank me yet," said Mary. "You haven't tasted it."

Indeed, the brew was only slightly less disgusting than the Clearer tea Lucas used to drink, but Kara forced it down anyway. In only a few minutes a revitalizing warmth swept through her body. She lay on the ground staring up at the canopy, many thoughts spinning through her mind.

"What is Imogen, exactly?" Kara asked. "We've been so busy just surviving that I haven't really thought about it much."

"She started out as a human being, though that was long ago. She was a sage of sorts. People would come to her when they had lost something truly important to them."

"And she would find it?"

Mary tipped her hand from side to side in an *almost* gesture. "She would give it to them."

"Isn't that the same thing?" Kara asked.

Mary shook her head. "No. What she gave them wasn't always what they lost—just an approximation, the best she could do. But her heart was in the right place, at least at the start, and more and more people came to her from all around the World, many of them rich nobles willing to pay anything for her assistance. Her parents profited greatly, and their greed blinded them to their daughter's growing unhappiness."

"That's terrible," Taff said. "They should have loved her."

Mary nodded. "Eventually Imogen fled to the Thickety to escape her parents' demands. Or perhaps she was called here. In either case, the Thickety changed her, as it changes all people, and instead of just finding lost things she developed an appetite for them."

"She *ate* them?" Taff asked.

"Not the physical objects, exactly. More like the feelings that went with them. But feelings are not meant to be devoured—not by people, at least—and in doing so Imogen sacrificed her humanity and became something different altogether."

Taff said, "That's impossible."

"Your sister talks to animals," said Mary. "Water falls from the sky. Food grows from the ground. The world is wondrously strange, if you really stop to think about it."

"How do I fight her?"

"Imogen is more monster than human now," Mary said, "which is not necessarily a bad thing, for you can use your magic to control her. But it won't be easy. She is full of deceit, that one. You might not even know—"

A fierce wind rustled the leaves around them. Branches creaked together in a keening, mournful wail.

"What?" Kara asked.

"It doesn't matter," Mary said. "There's nothing more I can teach you, Kara. You are as ready as you'll ever be."

Mary packed away their supplies so they would be ready to leave at first light. After this she knelt by Taff, who had quickly fallen asleep, and pulled the blanket closer to his chin. She kissed him on the forehead.

"Don't you dare tell him I did that," Mary said, refusing to look in Kara's direction. "I may not have a grimoire anymore, but I'm sure I still have something in this sack to turn even a *wexari* into a toad." She settled into her blanket. "Good night, Kara."

"What are you going to do?" Kara asked. "If . . ."

"If?"

"If I manage to defeat Imogen. If Taff and I make it to the ship and escape the Thickety. Sordyr will know you helped us. He'll come after you."

"I'm a crafty old witch. I know places even he can't find me."

"Why don't you come with us? Leave the Thickety. We'll go to the World together."

For a long time, Mary didn't answer—so long that

Kara thought she might have fallen asleep.

"Go to sleep," Mary said.

"There's no reason for you to stay here," Kara said.

"I can't return. Not after what I've done."

"But it's been so many years. No one would ever know. And you're *good* now. The grimoire has no hold on you anymore. You've redeemed yourself."

Mary wiggled out of her blanket and rose to her feet. She eased down next to Kara and placed a gnarled hand on her cheek, exhaling soft plumes of air as she spoke. Kara was shocked to see tears following the tracks of her wrinkled face.

"There can be no redemption for me . . . unless you can restore all the children whose lives I stole back to the way they were. Can you do that, *wexari*?" Her face brightened with a brief glimmer of hope. "Can you make everything go back to the way it was?"

"I can't," Kara said softly. "No one can."

"You would, though," Mary said, "if it were within

your power to do so. Perhaps that's enough. And perhaps I can still offer you a tiny bit of help in return." Mary leaned forward and whispered four words in her ear—words that made little sense.

"What—" Kara began, but Mary pressed a finger to her lips and shook her head. Without another word, the old witch crossed to her bedroll. Her back was hunched, as though the weight of all those extra years had finally caught up with her at last.

The canopy leaves were still dark when Kara felt a sharp pain in her knee. She opened her eyes, already reaching for the dagger hidden beneath her blanket, then gasped with relief when she recognized her visitor.

"Watcher," Kara said. "You scared me."

The bird's single eye rotated to the soft blue of early-morning sky, followed by an insistent, flashing mauve.

Quiet. Come.

"But Taff and Mary—should I wake them?"

Come.

Kara was reluctant to leave the warmth of her blanket on such a frigid night, but Watcher had already flown off. The bird perched on a tree at the edge of their campsite, waiting for her.

Just like in the hushfruit orchard, Kara thought, the memory of their first encounter bringing a slight smile to her lips. Her previous life of chores and classwork had begun to take on the faded quality of a barely remembered dream. *And then there are those memories I used to build mind-bridges,* Kara thought. *The ones I don't even realize I've lost.*

Hugging her body for warmth, Kara followed the bird deeper into the forest. *I hope Watcher's not taking me far. Otherwise I'm going to regret leaving my cloak behind.* Luckily it was a short distance indeed, a shallow gully still muddy from the previous rainfall.

Now that Watcher had stopped moving, Kara saw the deep gash beneath its eye and the odd way its left wing jutted out, as if some tiny bones had been broken.

"You're hurt!" she exclaimed.

Watcher's eye flipped from color to color. Kara had a bit of trouble understanding the last eyeball—cracked into a dozen shards like a mirror—but she was finally able to figure it out.

Sordyr knows. Watcher help. Witch Girl.

Kara gasped.

Watcher. Escape Sordyr.

"Good! You're safe now—you can stay with us! My friend knows the Thickety well—there are herbs that can help you heal. . . ."

No stay. Give warning.

A screech of pain cut through the night. This was immediately followed by a desperate flutter of wings, as though something was trying to escape but had been pinned to the ground. And then silence.

Watcher's eye spun, not as fast as usual, allowing Kara to see a steady streak of colors as they passed.

Oldwitch. Not friend.

Kara felt the trees above her start to spin.

"No."

Yes. Oldwitch. Not friend. Trick Witch Girl.

"No," said Kara, shaking her head. "That's not true. You're wrong. That can't be true."

Oldwitch. Sordyr friend.

"Mary saved my life. She's been helping us."

Helping you. Get stronger.

"Yes! She's been teaching me how to be a *wexari* so I can keep Taff safe and escape this place!"

No. For Sordyr. Needs Witch Girl. Strong magic.

"Sordyr tried to kill us! We've been running from him this entire time!"

No. Sordyr close. Always. Trick Watcher. Trick Witch Girl.

Kara found a black mushroom as large and solid as a tree trunk and took a seat. She wrapped her arms around her knees and squeezed them tightly together.

"If Sordyr knows where I am, then why doesn't he just come and get me?"

Witch Girl not ready. Sordyr needs wexari. *Strong* wexari.

"Why use Mary, then? Why not just teach me himself?"

But Kara didn't need to look at Watcher's eye to know the answer to that one. *I would never allow the Forest Demon to teach me. But a fellow witch, on the other hand . . .*

No. She didn't believe it. She had seen the way Mary kissed Taff, the love in her eyes. You couldn't fake that.

Have you forgotten who this is? Mary Kettle. She fooled hundreds of children into trusting her—you don't think she's capable of one convincing kiss?

"So you're saying that all of this has been a type of . . . test?"

Yes. Imogen. Last test. Then Witch Girl ready. Strong wexari. *Help Sordyr.*

Kara rose from the mushroom and pushed her hair back from her face.

"I will *never* help him," she said, her voice colder than the night.

Watcher's eye began to spin quickly again, though as it

did Kara heard a new, faint squeaking, like a wagon wheel ready to fall off its axis: *Yes! Witch Girl come! Witch Girl help Watcher friends. Save us!*

"That's right. You want my help too." A horrible thought formed in her mind. "How do I know *you're* not tricking me?"

Watcher opened its eye: the sandy color of a well-known shore.

Watcher friend.

"Mary has stood by my side and faced all the same dangers as me. What exactly have you done? Why should I trust you any more than her?"

Oldwitch enemy. Watcher friend.

Kara's thoughts spun.

Perhaps Watcher is right. How else could we have escaped the Forest Demon for this long unless Sordyr allowed it to happen? Unless it was all part of his plan. . . .

And Watcher is hurt. That shows he's no longer helping Sordyr, doesn't it? I can trust him. Unless Sordyr hurt Watcher just to make his story more convincing. Maybe that's the trick. *Sordyr is trying to get me to turn against Mary. She would never hurt us. She's my friend, my friend . . .*

Kara had no idea who to trust.

"Go," she said. "Leave me."

Watcher closed its eye. Opened it again.

Watcher friend.

"No! You're not! Mother left and Father left and Lucas left and I can't trust Mary and I don't have any friends!"

Watcher friend.

"Leave! Leave now!"

When the bird showed no sign of moving, Kara's frustration sparked into a red-hot anger. *I just want to be alone; I NEED to be alone.* She reached out with her mind, the bridge between them already there for her to cross, and *shoved* Watcher.

The bird catapulted off the boulder as though shot by an arrow and crashed into a tree with a muffled *thud*. A grave silence filled the forest.

"Watcher?" Kara asked.

There was no response.

She circled around the boulder, supporting herself with one trembling hand.

"Watcher?"

At first she didn't see the bird, its dark-blue plumage camouflaged by shadows and black soil. But then Kara caught a fluttering movement, ineffectual wings making tiny circles in the dirt.

"Watcher," she said. "I'm sorry! I didn't mean to—"

Kara bent down and reached out for the bird, meaning to lift it in her hands, but at her touch Watcher burst into the sky and flew shakily away. Its eye had been only the slightest bit open, but it was still enough to reveal the new color within: the gray flint of an arrowhead speckled with crimson.

SCARED! SCARED!

Kara watched the bird vanish, darkness into darkness, her heart thudding tremulously in her chest as she recognized the source of Watcher's terror and the bitter truth it implied: In this forest of monstrosities, she was the thing to fear.

By the time Kara returned to their campsite the canopy leaves had begun to glow dimly, sharing the collected sunlight from the previous day. Mary slept fitfully, tossing and turning. She looked like she was going to be young today, though a splash of gray remaining in her hair made Kara wonder if she was catching the tail end of Mary's transformation. Creeping silently to her brother's side, she whispered words in his ear until he was awake, then muffled his groggy questions with a touch of her finger.

"We have to go," Kara said.

Taff looked to Mary and Kara shook her head. For a moment Kara thought her brother might argue, but he simply got to his feet and began quietly gathering his things.

He trusts me so much, Kara thought. *I hope I'm doing the right thing.*

She took his hand. Together but alone, the two children made their way toward the grove of lost things and the monster waiting within its depths.

FOURTEEN

Kara awoke to the aroma of freshly fried bacon. After sliding into her school dress, she washed her face and dashed into the kitchen. Father, in the middle of pouring himself a fresh cup of coffee from the percolator, gave her a bemused look.

"I meant to save you some eggs," Taff said through a mouthful of food, "but they were just sitting there and I felt bad, so I ate them."

"Good morning, Father," said Kara. While reaching for a plate of biscuits she stuck her tongue out at her brother. "Good morning, egg thief."

"Does this still qualify as morning?" Father asked. His pants were dirty from the morning's chores, but he had taken his boots off at the door and scrubbed his hands clean.

"It's not *that* late," said Kara. "I'll still be on time for school."

"You say that like it's a good thing," mumbled Taff.

"It's important that you learn," said Father.

"But it's so *boring*. I bet you even grown-ups would have a hard time sitting in one room for hours and hours and hours."

"I spend my days toiling beneath the hot sun. Sit and relax while a wise man teaches me about the remarkable history of our people? I would trade places with you any day."

"Really?" asked Taff.

"Of course not! I suffered through school and now you have to as well. Such is the way of the world." He lifted his cup of coffee in Taff's direction. "You'll be having this same conversation with your own children someday."

"I'm not having children," said Taff, as though this was a topic to which he had previously given careful thought. "Too much trouble."

Kara giggled. "Let's see what your wife says about that."

"*Wife?* I'm *definitely* not having one of those!"

Kara and her father burst into laughter, Taff's confused protests of "What? What?" only making them laugh harder.

"Sounds like I'm missing all the fun," said Mother, stepping backward into the kitchen. She held a basket overflowing with freshly picked herbs in her arms; Father quickly rushed to her side and carried it into the house. As always, whenever Helena Westfall stepped into the room Kara felt a subtle brightening of the world around them. Part of this was Mother's beauty, but mostly it was just *her*.

"Taff has announced that he is never getting married," Kara said.

"How sad," said Mother. "Young girls all over De'Noran are headed for disappointment and they don't even know it yet." Father placed the basket on their counter. He had begun to grow a beard—trim and neat—and Helena ran her hand over it before kissing him on the lips. "Thank you, my love," she said.

"Gross," said Taff. He raised a finger in the air as though proving a point. "That is exactly the type of thing that happens to you when you get a wife."

Kara started to laugh along with her parents but winced as a high-pitched noise buzzed inside her right ear. For a moment Mother and Father wobbled up and down as though they were standing on a ship.

As quickly as it came, the noise vanished.

"What is it, Kara?" asked Mother, an unusually sharp note of concern entering her voice. "What happened?"

"It's nothing," Kara said. She tilted her head to one

side, as though trying to loosen an earful of water.

"Come here," said Mother. "Let me take a look at you."

But Kara, shrugging, had already slipped out of her chair.

"I'm fine," she said. "We'd better get to school. I don't want to be late."

Leah and Hope were waiting for her just outside the schoolhouse. The three friends usually chatted for a few precious minutes before class began, entering the building only at the last possible moment. But Kara was running late and barely had a chance to say good morning before the bell chimed, signifying the start of the school day. The girls had recently lost the privilege of sitting together—Master Blackwood, after chiding them one too many times for talking, decided this would be a simpler solution—so Kara reluctantly slumped into her new seat.

It was in the last row, next to Grace Stone. Kara

thought that might be part of Master Blackwood's punishment as well.

"Good morning, Kara!" the girl exclaimed, eager to see her as always. Her school dress, a size too small, was frayed at the edges and patched poorly in several places. Grace had tried to conceal her strange hair beneath a soiled bonnet, but a few white wisps, unwilling to be contained, dangled across her forehead.

"Morning," Kara muttered.

She took out her slate and began copying lines from the board. Though she steadfastly avoided looking in Grace's direction, she could feel the girl's piercing blue eyes watching her every move. It was Kara's own fault, she supposed. Last week some of the cattier girls had been teasing Grace, mostly about her father, and Kara had stepped in to defend her. From that point on, the former fen'de's daughter had trailed Kara's steps like a hungry puppy.

"I was thinking of picking washmallows today," Grace

whispered, tapping her fingers nervously against the desk. "You should come. I know a perfect spot."

"I can't," Kara said, not looking up from her slate. "I have chores."

"I could help you."

"I don't think that's a good idea."

"Because of your mother? That was such a long time ago, Kara. And it was my father, not me. I was just a child."

Seven years ago, Grace's father had falsely accused Kara's mother of witchcraft and tried to execute her in front of the entire village. Luckily Father and Aunt Constance had made the villagers see reason in time, leading to Fen'de Stone's excommunication from the Children of the Fold and Grace's subsequent adoption by duty-bound relatives.

The white-haired girl was a constant reminder of the night that could have destroyed Kara's life. For this reason, she could never be Grace's friend. It wasn't fair, but it wasn't wrong, either.

Kara felt a hand on her shoulder.

"What is *that*?" Master Blackwood asked, poking a trembling finger at her slate. "It is certainly not the Clen's fourth creed, I can tell you that much!"

"What do you mean, sir?" Kara asked. "I copied it directly from the board, just like I always—"

She looked down at her slate and gasped. Though the words were in her handwriting, Kara did not remember writing them.

She read the words—*truly* read them—for the very first time:

REMEMBER WHAT IT EATS.

That night Kara dreamed of a forest littered with lost things, keys and dolls and golden rings set with strange jewels. She followed a path deeper into the trees, winding her way toward a soft, beckoning light. Kara felt someone's hand in her own but when she tried to turn her head to see who it was, the dream did not let her. As Kara neared the light she heard an old woman whisper four achingly familiar words . . . and then she woke up, with no memory of having dreamed at all.

Years passed.

They were good years, stitched together not only from births and weddings and celebrations, but ordinary details like trimming nails and darning socks and waiting for various eggs to boil. Kara grew from a pretty child to a beautiful young woman, the spitting image of her mother. With her school days now behind her she began to take on more responsibilities at home, but though Kara loved spending time with her family, she did not believe she was destined to be a farmer. She had begun to earn a fair amount of seeds by tending to sick livestock, and she suspected there might be a place in De'Noran for a woman who specialized in doctoring animals. Kara was unusually good with them.

Occasionally, on what she came to think of as her

"strange days," Kara felt that she was not Kara Westfall at all but a thief who had stolen someone else's life. These days were few and far between, however, and in the end she did not pay them much mind.

Life was everything she had always wanted it to be.

On a morning just three weeks shy of her sixteenth birthday, Kara headed to the Fringe to gather herbs. Farmer Loder had a cow with the tremors, and he was willing to pay Kara two browns for a cure, a respectable day's work. Kara wished that Mother could have joined her, but since Master Blackwood's death the previous season, Mother had taken his place at the schoolhouse. She swore it was temporary, but Kara had her doubts; she heard the enthusiasm in her mother's voice when she spoke of her charges. Kara had asked Taff to come to the Fringe instead, but he was locked away in his work shed building some sort of machine he swore would cut their threshing time in half. She didn't doubt it.

Kara ate from a handful of berries and thought about the upcoming Shadow Festival. Two boys had already asked her to the dance. The first was a Clearer named Lucas, and though he seemed pleasant enough, Kara knew him on only a passing basis. She had refused him immediately.

The second boy presented a more complicated scenario. Aaron Baker came from a good family, demonstrated a fine singing voice at Worship, and was certainly not unpleasant in appearance. Despite this, Kara did not like him, sensing that beneath his smooth words lurked a dangerous combination of cruelty and cowardice. It wasn't the first time Kara had been granted a feeling of unwonted familiarity about another member of the village, as though she had a deeper pool of experience to draw from than just her day-to-day life. She had never told anyone about these inexplicable insights, not even her own family . . .

. . . *because you don't trust them they're not your real—*

Kara squeezed the thoughts away. *Nonsense. Just nonsense.* She hadn't been sleeping well lately, and as a result her thoughts were singular and scattered. That's all it was.

She walked along the border of the Fringe, searching for the herbs she needed. *A pinch of thistlerun, laberknacle, gill's ferry.* It would be easier if she could just enter the Fringe itself, of course, but that was forbidden. Instead, Kara snagged those plants beyond her reach with a long, hooked rod and dragged them back to her basket.

The wind rose to a feverish pitch and the trees of the Thickety creaked and groaned like stretching giants. Kara kept her eyes averted from them, as she'd been taught.

She heard footsteps.

"Hello?" Kara asked. She scanned the Fringe weeds, taller than they should have been; the Clearers, of late, had been lax in their work. "Is someone there?"

Parting two overgrown ferns, Grace Stone poked her head out.

"I found something interesting!" she exclaimed. "Come see!"

Grace's dress was torn in several spots and covered in dried mud, and her filthy white hair, littered with leaves, hung down her back in tangled waves. Kara could not remember the last time she had seen her wear shoes.

"I have to get back."

"This will take but a moment. I *need* to show you."

"Why?"

Grace shifted uncomfortably. "I don't know *why*. I only know *what*."

"You're talking nonsense," Kara said. "I have chores."

"Ah, yes," said Grace. "Chores. Sweep the porch. Till the field. Marry the boy." She tilted her head to one side and examined the ground in front of Kara's feet with keen interest. "What does *that* mean?"

Kara looked down. Using the sharpened end of her stick, she had scrawled something in the earth:

REMEMBER WHAT IT EATS.

As usual, she did not remember writing the sentence, but she recalled, with shocking clarity, its other appearances in her life. Whispered in her ear upon waking. Clapped out by ocean waves. Pattered by raindrops on the roof.

It's important. I don't know why, but these words might be the most important thing in my life.

"Remember what it eats," Grace said, considering. "The thing I found in the Fringe—I think it might have something to do with that. If you're interested, that is. I wouldn't want to distract you from your *chores*."

"Show me," said Kara.

Grace had to use her walking stick to maneuver across the unsteady ground of the Fringe, but despite her weak leg she kept a steady pace. Kara followed her along the outskirts of the border, refusing to enter the Fringe itself.

What am I doing? she thought. *I'm following the craziest girl in the village. Why?* The instincts that had served Kara so well the past few years were complicated when it came to Grace. For some unfathomable reason she trusted what the girl was saying, but she did not trust the girl herself. Not one bit.

"Here," Grace said.

Using her walking stick, she pointed to something on the ground. At first, Kara didn't even see it, camouflaged as it was against the other weeds. But gradually she was able to make out six green petals splayed across the ground, as though a flower had decided to spread out its arms and take a nap.

"Do you know what this does?" Grace asked.

Kara shook her head. It did seem vaguely familiar, though. Perhaps her mother had taught her about it at some point and she had forgotten? She tugged at a cloud of memory but it slipped away.

"Watch," Grace said.

She picked up a beetle from an overhanging tangle of purple vines and placed it next to the splayed leaves. The beetle hesitated a moment, its instincts telling it not to proceed, until Grace poked it with a stick and forced it onto the first petal.

The petals clamped together into a bell-shaped dome as large as Kara's head, then rose into the air on a single shoot and slowly began to spin.

"It's a trap," said Grace. "The beetle thinks it's still just going about its life and . . ."

Like a flash of lightning in Kara's brain: *lost things hanging from the branches.*

". . . doesn't realize the truth . . ."

More flashes. One after the other.

People.

Mouths agape.

Something wrong with their heads.

". . . until it's too late."

Slithering.

Screams.

Taff.

"My brother," Kara said. "He's in trouble. I have to go home."

"Do you?" asked Grace.

"Yes!" But another voice, a voice that was her own but different, stronger, said, "No. The boy at home isn't Taff at all."

Remember what it eats.

"Lost," Kara murmured. "It eats things that are lost."

The farm is not your home.

Remember what it eats.

"What's happening to me?" asked Kara. "I feel like my head is being torn apart."

Grace noticed something past Kara's shoulder. "You have visitors," she said. "I'll leave you to it." She paused and added, "See you soon!" before vanishing into the Fringe.

Kara turned. Her family stood behind her.

"Come home, Kara," said Father. "We need you."

"It's time to prepare dinner," said Mother.

"I got it to work!" Taff exclaimed, beaming. "My

threshing machine! Don't you want to see?"

Mother reached out her hands and Kara took a step forward, longing to fold herself in those lilac-scented arms and forget about this whole thing, but then . . .

The farm is not your home remember what it eats.

. . . she saw a younger version of her mother hanging from a tree, jerking as stone after stone struck her.

"You're not you," Kara said with grim certainty. "You're dead."

Mother straightened her back and sighed deeply.

"I don't have to be," she said. "Stay with us, and we can live like this forever."

Remember . . .

(Mary. That's Mary's voice!)

. . . *what it eats. The things you've lost.*

"Stay with us, Moonbeam," said Father.

Imogen. She has me right now.

"Don't go, sister!" exclaimed Taff.

She's in my mind.

"Stop it," Kara said. "None of this is real!"

Mother shrugged. "Real is what we make it. Come back to the farm, Kara. Forget all this foolishness."

"My brother needs me," Kara said. She looked at the boy wearing Taff's face. "My *real* brother."

The Taff-thing winced as though Kara had struck him, and a seam of nothingness zigzagged across his cheek, revealing the trees behind him.

"Mother," the Taff-thing said, jamming his fingers into the crack in his face. "Look what she did!"

"Is this what you want?" Mother asked Kara. "To hurt your brother?"

"I want to save him!"

Mother's arm vanished up to the elbow. A sizable piece of Father's torso disappeared as well.

"I'm very disappointed in you," said the Mother-thing. "You could have had me back again."

"You're wrong," Kara said. "My mother is gone forever."

Her family vanished.

Where a path leading back to the village should have been, a swirling nothingness expanded like a spreading stain across the horizon. Kara watched it approach, and in a few moments it took her.

FIFTEEN

Kara opened her eyes.

She felt the hunger first, gnawing and implacable. *How long have I been here? And where is here, exactly?* Kara opened her eyes wider but her surroundings remained hazy and unclear.

They've been closed too long. I have to give them time before they work again.

She heard vague sounds, dim and muffled. At first Kara thought her ears, like her eyes, needed time to recover, but this was not the case; there was something stuffed inside them. Kara raised a hand, even this small motion difficult in her weakened state, and took hold of a fleshy, tentacle-like form protruding from her left ear. She yanked it away, feeling suddenly nauseous as the tentacle, much longer than she thought it would be, slid out of her ear with a popping sound and released a stream of warm fluid. Before she lost her nerve Kara repeated this action with the right ear, and immediately fell to the ground. Pain shot though her left knee.

Kara didn't mind. Pain was good. Pain meant she was alive.

She lay there for a few minutes until her vision began to work again and the foggy shapes of her surroundings came into focus.

She was in a small pit. Luminescent moss, pulsing with red light, covered the walls. The opening of the pit, while not far up, was well out of jumping range, and the moss, warm to the touch, provided no handholds. Kara glimpsed her reflection in a puddle of water: She was dirty and bedraggled, but definitely no older than twelve.

Four years of my life. All a lie.

Her memory—her true memory—had begun to return to her in random images. A rabbit on a bicycle. An old woman with a sack. Keys and dolls in the treetops. These images were more confusing than helpful, but it didn't matter. She remembered the most important thing just fine: Taff was here, and he needed her help.

Kara heard movement behind her. The two tentacles she had torn from her ears were slowly rising through the air, returning to something—or someone—on the surface.

No time to think. Might not get this chance later.

Leaping into the air, Kara caught one of the tentacles with two hands. It sank beneath her weight, and for a moment she feared it would collapse altogether, but then it righted itself and began to lift Kara toward the opening above them. She waited until she was being pulled across the earth before relinquishing her grasp. The tentacles continued onward toward some unknown source.

Unsteadily, Kara rose to her feet.

In every direction her surroundings were obscured by swirling fog—not gray and cloudy, but dark red like the flesh of a dragonfruit. The air smelled of far too many things at once. Closing her eyes, Kara used her *wexari* training to pull the confusing medley of scents apart and pinpoint particulars: cinnamon-laced pumpkin pie, sandalwood soap, the mustiness of a seldom-opened trunk. Taken apart, the smells were common, even comforting—but their combined presence disturbed her.

A name rose from the murk of her memory.

Imogen. She's the one who has Taff.

Barely able to see beyond her outstretched hand, Kara took two steps forward and nearly fell into the second pit.

She teetered on the edge for a moment, and only by throwing her weight backward did she escape a nasty fall. The hole was the same size and shape as the one that had held Kara. Two tentacles crept into the darkness.

"Taff!" Kara called, leaning over the edge.

The tentacles suspended a small shape in the air like a marionette. It wasn't Taff. Kara couldn't even tell if it had once been male or female; the skin of its hairless head had long ago shrunk and tightened around a sunken skull. Despite this, the tentacles were still moving, still *pulsing*, like a greedy child using its finger to wipe the last bit of jam from the bottom of a jar.

That's what would have happened to me if I didn't escape. That's what will *happen to Taff if I don't find him.*

If she tried walking in this fog, however, Kara risked falling into another pit and breaking her leg. She would be no help to her brother then.

I need light.

She reached out with her thoughts and made a mind-bridge. An insect with three pairs of glowing blue wings landed on the edge of her index finger. It cast a round circle of illumination, the fog itself seeming to part at its arrival.

"A boy," Kara said. "Brought here the same time as me. Do you know where he is?"

Yes. Heard boy fight. Use wooden stick.

Kara smiled, her parched lips cracking. That was definitely Taff.

"Can you take me to him?"

Many-Arms have boy. Boy dreaming forever dream.

Kara reached deeper into the insect's mind and saw that by "Many-Arms," it meant the monster with all the tentacles.

Imogen.

You free boy? the glow-wings asked.

"Yes."

Bad. No free. Hurt boy.

"I'm his sister. I would never hurt him."

Disturb boy. During forever dream. Kill boy.

"Oh," Kara said, finally understanding. If she detached the tentacles from Taff while he was trapped in whatever world Imogen had created, it might kill him.

"There must be another way," Kara said.

Yes. Kill Many-Arms. End forever dreams. Save us.

Kara heard the eagerness in its thoughts. The glow-wings had no love for Imogen, and was eager for Kara to fight on its behalf.

"So if I kill this monster, Taff will be safe?"

Follow me.

The glowing insect led her safely past dozens of holes, a pair of tentacles exiting each one. Kara saw dim shapes at the bottom of each pit but tried not to look too closely. If it was Taff, she didn't want to get distracted. If it wasn't Taff, she didn't want to see.

As she walked, Kara tried to shake off the memory of the past four years, false events that had played only in her mind. It was hard. Even now she felt the urge to return home and finish her nighttime chores, after which she could talk to Mother about a design for her Shadow Festival gown. *None of it was real*, Kara kept repeating to herself. *It was just a prison in my head.* And yet she could not stop remembering the cadence of Mother's laugh, the warmth of her embrace. Wounds that had finally scabbed over were ripped open anew, as though her mother had died a second time. Kara had known darkness and violence and evil—but she had never known such cruelty.

I have to stop this creature so no one else suffers like that.

But how?

Before Kara could even begin to ponder this question, the fog cleared and Imogen was before her.

The *wexari* was more withered than a body had any right to be, as though the witch had skipped dying altogether but never stopped aging. A ridged black spine protruded from her back, and from this issued a single tentacle that branched into hundreds more, holding her aloft like some sort of malignant octopus. Kara turned and saw these tentacles disappear into the fog, feeding tubes between the monster and those trapped in the pits.

Imogen opened her eyes, revealing blind white cataracts.

"Kara Westfall," she said. "You escaped the world I created for you. Whatever for?"

"I'm here for my brother."

"Ah," Imogen said. "Little Taff. I had thought he might like to meet his mother, but this was not the lost thing in his heart of hearts, so I've given him his father back. His *real* father. They are currently fishing together—your brother's first ship ride."

"Let him go."

"Why? He's happy. He thinks he's having a lovely day with Daddy."

"But he's not."

"No," said Imogen, and her upper lip curled back in a feral smile. "He's not."

"Why are you doing this?"

"Because he misses his father so much—and that makes it *taste so good*."

Kara recoiled in horror.

"You're *eating* his *feelings*?" she asked.

Imogen crossed her arms in a disturbingly childlike pout.

"So quick to judge, are we? Do you not eat dead flesh? Do you not eat horrible green things that spring forth from the *dirt*? Clearly anything can be devoured, Kara Westfall. I myself have feasted on dreams and memories, and while these are certainly nourishing, nothing provides more sustenance than what might have been. Life *is* loss. The path not taken. The song unsung. The bittersweet nectar of true love left behind. Years ago a woman came to me whose only child had wandered off in the forest and never returned. She begged me to bring the child back to her." Imogen closed her eyes and inhaled deeply. "That was a banquet beyond compare."

Kara had learned to accept many things in the Thickety, and a creature that fed on emotions was no stranger than notsuns or Forest Demons. But there was something that didn't make sense. "Once you've fed," Kara asked, "why not just kill your victims? Why keep them trapped here in dream worlds?"

Imogen placed two hands over her stomach. Kara

thought she heard a low, liquid rumble.

"This would all be easier if I hungered for the simple emotions," she said. "Joy, jealousy, anger—such surface feelings can be consumed with a single kiss. But true loss anchors deep. You humans always seem so *surprised* by your little tragedies; you have such a difficult time accepting that what's gone is gone. That makes loss hard to get at, like a fleshy nut inside an impenetrable shell. Peeling away all the other emotions doesn't work; it just kills the host and the flavor. But if I use the dreams to convince people that their lives have been made whole again, they slowly let go of that delectable feeling of loss, which rises to the top, where I can get at it." Imogen moved a black-crusted tongue across her lips. "Like cream."

"You're a monster! You imprison people and drain them dry."

"I grant wishes. I give people what they want most."

"It's not real," Kara said.

"Isn't it? Did you know any differently, while you were

experiencing my gift to you? Don't you wish you could return there right now?"

"My mother is dead."

"But it's not your mother you want, Kara. She's part of it, to be sure, but there's so much more you lost. And I gave it to you! I restored your whole *childhood*! I allowed you to be a girl again, free from magic, free from responsibility. How is this cruelty?"

"Your *kindness* would have killed me."

"In time. But you will die in this world as well, no doubt sooner. Why not return to a kinder place? If you'd like, you can start from birth. Experience things fresh. I can even have your brother join you—your real brother, this time. Wouldn't that be nice?"

Kara remembered sitting around the fireplace with her family, the warmth of neighbors who did not believe she was a witch. She understood why some people might seek out such sweet oblivion. But she had not come this far to live a lie.

Kara stepped forward.

"You are going to return Taff to me and release all the people in these pits. Now."

A gurgling sound came from Imogen's throat. At first Kara thought it was laughter, but it wasn't—she was coughing something up, like a cat with a fur ball.

A shiny key fell from her lips and dropped to a small pile of objects beneath her feet: coins and rings and lockets, like some sort of bizarre dragon's hoard from a storybook.

"My apologies," Imogen said. "Occasionally some minor lost object, some bauble, gets passed along. Rather like a bone in one of those disgusting meals you people favor." She dabbed daintily at her lips. "This conversation was mildly diverting, and I do thank you for that, but I believe it's time for you to return to your pit. There is so much loss in you, Kara Westfall. My stomach growls just thinking about it."

A tentacle brushed against Kara's leg—not grabbing her, not yet. There was no reason to hurry; Imogen had all the time in the world. Kara reached out with her mind, searching for a nearby creature that could help her. . . .

A dark consciousness shoved her back.

Kara staggered backward in surprise, nearly losing her footing. *What was that?* It was so close that at first she thought it was Imogen, but if so, the *wexari* seemed completely oblivious to their encounter.

No. Something else is here.

Brushing away the second tentacle creeping up her leg, Kara built a mind-bridge from memories of loneliness and hunger. She offered it to the darkness and it shoved her again, harder this time. *It will never cross, not of its own accord,* Kara thought, so she used more memories (*I'm in my bed, waiting for Mother to read me a story, but then I remember that Mother will never read me a story again*) to seal the top of the mind-bridge and set it on its end. She reached out again, and when the dark consciousness tried to shove her this time it slipped into her mind instead, falling down the tunnel she had constructed like rain through a well.

Kara was only able to hold it for a few moments before

it squirmed away, but that was enough time to learn its secrets.

"It's not your fault," she told Imogen. "You were once a *wexari*, but your power has been corrupted. They used you, didn't they? Your parents? That's why you came to the Thickety. To escape. You were searching for solitude. You found something else."

Imogen's wizened mouth curled into a scowl.

"You are no longer amusing, Kara Westfall," she said. Something whipped around Kara's ankle and she was suddenly upside down, only a few feet from Imogen's face. "You think you know me? You think you know suffering? You know nothing!" Blind eyes like saucers of spoiled milk searched her out. "It doesn't have to be what you want, you know. I can create a world where you watch your mother die, over and over again. Or maybe a world where Taff becomes a witch hunter and slides a dagger across your throat." Imogen brought her closer, baring daggerlike teeth. "Then again . . . talking with you has reminded me that at one point I truly did enjoy the taste of meat. Perhaps it is time to revisit lost pleasures."

"'Remember what it eats,'" Kara said.

"What? What was that?"

"I thought Mary was talking about you, but she was really talking about that creature attached to your back." Kara could see it clearly now, black and spiny like polluted coral. Hundreds of tentacles narrowed to cilia as they needled its surface, delivering the sustenance of lost dreams.

The creature pulsated. *Swallowing.*

"You don't know anything," Imogen said. "This creature is my slave. It helps me gather what I need."

"It calls itself the Harthix. Did you know that?"

This gave Imogen pause. "You've spoken to it?"

Kara nodded. "It can bestow great power—or, at least, it can exaggerate power that already exists. But it cannot eat on its own. It needs a host. It transformed your magic into a way to gather food, like a farmer building a threshing machine. After all these years, you're still being used."

"That's not true! I am *wexari*. I am its master!"

"I'm so sorry."

The tentacle released Kara and she crashed to the ground, her fall broken by a pile of tattered old manu-scripts.

"What are you doing?" Imogen shouted. "Attack her! Attack her!"

"I'm sorry," Kara said, "because the Harthix lives for new tastes, new experiences, and I told it that while lost childhoods and lost loved ones must taste fine, imagine how grand it would be to feast on someone who has lost her *humanity*!"

The first tentacle slipped into Imogen's ear. Her blind eyes widened in horror, seeking Kara everywhere.

"Please," Imogen said. "You're like me. A true witch. I sense it. Please help your sister. Please."

"I can't do that," Kara said. "I made a bargain with the Harthix. It promised to let everyone else go. In exchange, I assured it that you would provide enough nourishment for *centuries*."

"No!" Imogen exclaimed as the tentacles began to drag her deeper into the fog. "No! Put me down! I am your master! I am your—"

The last thing Kara heard was Imogen's scream as she was pulled into the depths of an unknown abyss.

She checked six pits before she found Taff, standing with his back pressed against the wall so he remained hidden in the shadows. His eyes were wide and disoriented. She called his name and he slumped to the ground with relief.

"I thought I was all alone," Taff said, pressing his face to his hands.

"Never," Kara replied.

The Harthix's tentacles were nowhere to be seen, so Kara slid a long branch into the pit and Taff shimmied to the surface.

"Are you all right?" she asked, hugging him tight.

"Why are the inside of my ears wet?"

"You really don't want to know."

Kara gave him the brief version of her encounter with Imogen, skimming over the more horrific parts. Taff had been through enough.

"I'm glad that monster took her," Taff said. "She deserved it."

"Don't say that."

"Where's Father?" he asked, his voice still groggy. "Is he in one of the pits too?"

Holding him tight, Kara reminded Taff that their father was lost to them in this world. His body grew slack as he remembered. She felt his tears on the back of her neck but pretended not to.

There was more she wanted to tell him, but Taff's was not the only pit, and the calls of the others could no longer be ignored. Though Kara was almost too tired to stand, she and Taff spent several hours fashioning makeshift ropes from fancy cloaks and robes they found among the other lost things. Not everyone awoke; some had been too long under Imogen's spell to survive the detachment. Others were angry with Kara and refused to leave their pits, praying for Imogen to return them to their mind worlds. A few people, however, seemed happy to be freed again, and despite their dazed and bewildered states helped Kara and Taff free the others. When Kara asked them what village they had come from they simply bowed their heads and scrambled away, too frightened to speak to this strange girl powerful enough to destroy their captor.

Eventually she gave up asking.

"How many days do you think it's been?" Kara asked Taff. If her brother had been older, perhaps she could have judged time's passing by the length of his beard; his sandy hair seemed as unruly as usual but no longer than she remembered it.

"Just a few days," Taff said. "For us, that is. But some of the others—I think they've been here for years. Magic must have kept them alive."

"What was it like for you?"

"Perfect," Taff muttered.

"It wasn't real."

"It felt real at the time. But it's getting harder to remember."

Kara understood what he meant. The false years she had spent in Imogen's world had at first seemed as vivid as any recent experience but were now being supplanted by her real memories, like feeling returning to a limb that had fallen asleep. In time she supposed she might forget the dream world altogether.

"We're back in the real world now," Kara said. "It's best to forget what happened there."

"No," Taff said. "I *want* to remember. I want him back!"

Kara knelt next to her brother. She was still much taller than him, but the height difference was not quite as significant as when she first found the grimoire and their lives changed forever.

He's growing up. Faster than he should be.

"We'll get him back. Our real father. We'll all be together again."

"You promise?"

Kara hesitated. *Can I really promise such a thing? What happens if I can't do it? He'll be crushed.*

But in the end she decided that there was no other choice. She would promise this one thing to her brother and either do it or die trying.

"You have my word," she said.

Taff's upper lip trembled. Kara thought, at first, that he was going to cry, and moved to hug him, but instead he burst into a teasing giggle.

"In my dream," he said, "you married *Lucas*!"

Kara turned her face away before he could see her blush.

They traveled past the remaining pits and the fog dissipated, revealing fresh water and a field of edible mushrooms. These tasted horrible but restored a little of her energy, though what she really needed was sleep.

"Should we set up camp?" Kara asked. "Or go back and find Mary—"

"Feel this!" Taff shouted, holding his hand as high as he could. "Feel this!"

Kara joined her brother at the edge of the field. There was no need to raise her hand. Not only did she feel the ocean breeze on her face, she smelled it: briny and fresh and so different than the ever-lingering decay of the Thickety.

It smelled like freedom.

"Let's go!" shouted Taff.

They ran toward the scent of the ocean. At first Kara feared it might be some sort of cruel mirage, but the smell was undeniable now, the salty air tickling her nostrils. Kara heard fierce wind unshackled from trees, water clapping upon water.

And then she saw it.

Back in De'Noran, Kara and Lucas had spent many hours staring out across the ocean. Her friend, desperate for news of his lost family, loved discussing what life must be like in the World—and while Kara thought the ocean view was certainly pleasant, she had never understood her friend's obsession with it. After weeks trapped in the darkness of the Thickety, however, the staggering beauty of such unhindered blueness overwhelmed her.

She wished Lucas were here so she could tell him: *I finally understand now.*

"Mary didn't lie," Kara said. "This is the way out of the Thickety."

"Why would she have lied?" Taff asked.

It seemed pointless explaining Watcher's accusation; Kara felt guilty even thinking about it. *How could I have doubted her?* Mary had led them safely across the Thickety, taught Kara how to use her powers, and even given her the key to escaping Imogen. *She's a true friend.*

"I'll race you to the water," Kara said.

Taff took off, building a solid lead before Kara, her previous exhaustion forgotten, passed him. She leaped into the ocean first, nearly losing her balance when Taff crashed into her a moment later.

The water was icy cold. It felt wonderful.

"Cheater," Taff said, splashing her. "You're too big."

"That's not cheating," she said, splashing him in return. "That's just winning."

After playing in the water a bit longer they crawled onto the sand and lay out in the sun to dry.

"That was fun," said Kara, "but unfortunately we can't swim to the World. We need a boat."

Taff shook his head in disbelief.

"You may be really good at magic, but you're not so great at noticing things." He pointed at the trees just beyond the beach, where a small canoe lay half covered by weeds. It was battered and ill suited to travel such a long distance but looked as though it might still float.

"Please don't have a giant hole in your bottom," Taff said, rising to his feet.

Kara wanted nothing more than to take a nap in the sun, but she followed her brother toward the canoe.

"What about Mary?" Taff asked. "I'm worried that if

we leave, Sordyr will punish her."

"I believe there's enough room for three people in that canoe. You'll just have to convince her to come with us."

"Why me?"

Kara ruffled his hair. "You're too cute to refuse."

They stood before the canoe. It was stuck in a tangle of wrapweed but its bottom seemed whole and undamaged. Two thick branches leaned against a tree, their ends flattened into vaguely oar-like shapes.

As though waiting for us, Kara thought.

Taff began pulling at the wrapweed, attempting to free the canoe, but Kara stilled him with a touch.

"Taff?" she asked. "Didn't Mary say there was supposed to be a *ship* here? Some explorers who came to the Thickety and never returned?"

Taff shrugged. "Maybe they anchored farther out and took the canoe to shore."

"Then why is the canoe in the forest and not on the beach?"

"In case there's a high tide," he said. "So it doesn't float away."

The answers made sense—but something still didn't feel right.

"Help me push this thing into the water," Taff said, bracing himself behind the canoe. "Actually, toss those oars on top first! We don't want to forget them!"

Kara nodded, her eyes fixed on the motionless canopy. Not a single leaf moved, as if the wind itself had fled. She reached out to the creatures above her, hoping they might have some explanation, but they remained silent.

I don't like this, Kara thought, grabbing the branches against the tree. *The quicker we get out of here, the better.*

The branches grabbed her back.

Kara struggled to escape, but the supposed oars had formed twig-like fingers that wrapped around her wrists with unyielding strength. Setting her feet in the dirt, Kara yanked backward. Something jerked loose in the tree, and a figure cloaked in pumpkin-orange stepped into the failing sunlight with branch hands still firmly wrapped around her wrists.

Sordyr.

He slowly rose to his full height, and as she fell within his shadow all the joy Kara had felt at their impending freedom curdled to helplessness. Though Sordyr's face remained concealed within the darkness of his hood she felt his eyes considering her.

"You have done well, *wexari*," he said, the words crackling through the air like dead leaves. "Defeating Imogen was an impressive display of magic. You are finally ready to play your part."

"Let her go!" Taff exclaimed as the canoe before him disintegrated into black earth. Unsheathing his wooden sword, he charged the Forest Demon and swung at his back. Sordyr's cloak flicked out like the tongue of a snake and swatted him away.

"Did you really think I would let you escape?" Sordyr asked. "I could have captured you at any time. You must know that."

"Let Taff go. You don't need him."

"Who knows? The future is a fickle thing. I just might."

Kara reached out with her mind and sensed something with three wings and razor-sharp teeth swirling above them.

I need a distraction. Just enough time so we can get to the ocean . . .

As soon as Kara began to build her mind-bridge, however, the creature fled in terror.

"Your magic is powerful," Sordyr said, "but nowhere near as powerful as their fear of me. They will not help you."

Then there's no hope, Kara thought.

Sordyr ran a branched hand across her cheek.

"No," he said. "There really isn't."

BOOK THREE
THE SPIDER
BENEATH THE EARTH

"Magic is a plague.
It must be contained, or
the entire World will perish."

—The Path
Leaf 205, Vein 99

SIXTEEN

The Forest Demon led them past Imogen's now-empty pits to the orchard of lost things. Branchwolves nipped and clawed at one another in a violent display that might have been their version of playing. Kara did not try to reach out to them, nor any of the other animals she felt lingering nearby. She knew it was useless.

Near the remnants of their campfire lay Mary's sack.

"What did you do to her?" Taff asked. "What did you do to Mary?"

"I'm here, my child," said a soft voice.

Mary stepped out from the shadows of a tree. Though she was no older than forty today, the skin beneath her eyes sagged from lack of sleep. Heedless of the snapping branchwolves between them, Taff ran into her arms.

"I'm sorry," he said. "We brought you into this. It's all our fault."

The old witch hugged him tight and buried her face in his hair for just a moment.

Then shoved him away.

"You really are a foolish little boy, aren't you?" she asked. Taff winced as though slapped, tears already forming in his eyes. "Don't you get it? Your path through the Thickety was charted out a long, long time ago." She turned to Kara. "Every single footprint you've made is because he wanted you to make it. With my assistance, of course."

"We trusted you," Taff said, and Kara winced at the pain in his voice.

"You were meant to! That's why Sordyr, in his infinite

wisdom, allowed you to escape onto the bridge—so I could 'save' you from the branchwolves. After that it was all too easy. I *pretended* to guide you, but my true role was training your sister to be a *wexari*. The Forest Demon needs her to be strong if she's going to fulfill her purpose."

Watcher was right. . . .

"From the very beginning, it was all a test," Kara muttered. "The grettin. Crossing the Draye'varg. The darkeaters. Imogen."

"At last," said Mary, "you're beginning to understand."

"But why would you help Sordyr in the first place?" Taff asked.

"Have you forgotten? I am *Mary Kettle*. I'm *evil*."

"Not anymore. You feel bad about the things you've done. You want to be *good*."

Mary grabbed Taff by the chin and tilted his head to the side. She brought her lips to his ear, close enough to bite.

"Heed me and heed me well, child. *I will never be good*."

"Her grimoire," said Kara. "That's why she helped him. It's the only thing she's ever cared about in her long, sad life. Sordyr promised to return your grimoire to you, didn't he?"

"Even better," said Mary Kettle. "The Forest Demon is going to grant me a *new* grimoire. Think of all those blank pages waiting to be filled. I'm going to be a proper witch again. You understand, boy? You were nothing but a means to an end. I was never your friend!"

Mary picked up her sack and carried it toward a waiting horse with black flowers in its eyes.

"I don't believe you," Taff said.

Mary turned back, shock registering plainly on her face.

"At first it was like you said," Taff continued. "You were helping Sordyr. But as we traveled, you started to change. You began to like us. Maybe even love us."

"You don't know anything about me."

Taff crossed his arms and gave her a challenging stare.

"I guess we'll just have to see who's right, then."

Mary opened her mouth as though to reply, then shook her head in disgust. "Foolish child," she muttered. She mounted her horse and, with one last uneasy look at Taff, galloped down the path.

Sordyr led them farther into the forest, the branchwolves trailing behind them. They eventually came to a carriage constructed from black bark. Wheels of dried mud sat upon two parallel sets of roots, raised from the ground and extending along the path. Four horses with mossy flanks were harnessed to the carriage by red ivy.

Kara recognized one of them.

"Shadowdancer?" she asked.

Kara reached out a hand to stroke her old friend's mane, but the beast snapped at her with thorny teeth.

"It's me," she said. "Kara. Don't you remember?"

Maintaining a safe distance, she peered into Shadowdancer's eyes and saw nothing there but flowers and evil. The noble soul that had once blessed the horse's frame was gone forever.

During the walk from the beach Kara had felt cold and lifeless, but now coals of black rage flickered to life and warmed her body.

She turned to Sordyr.

"I want my friend back," she said.

"What makes you think my magic can be undone?"

Kara's reply died on her lips. The very idea of magic implied the impossible—that *everything* could be undone. The thought of such permanence unnerved her.

Shadowdancer might be beyond saving.

Father as well.

Sordyr waved his hand and the carriage door opened, revealing a floor of packed dirt from which grew a garden of lavender flowers. The interior of the carriage was redolent with the smell of spring.

"For you," Sordyr said.

"How considerate," replied Kara, making no effort

to conceal the sarcasm in her voice. She looked back at Shadowdancer. *There's nothing I can do for her. Not now, at least.* Taking Taff by the hand, Kara led him into the carriage. They huddled closely together on a bench that stretched along one wall.

"I have been waiting for someone like you a long time, Kara," Sordyr said. He curled a branch hand around the doorway of the carriage, and for one horrifying moment Kara thought he was going to come inside and sit next to her. "Things can go well for you here—if you do what I ask."

"And what is that, exactly?"

Just as Sordyr was about to reply, his hands shook with terrible force, rocking the carriage back and forth. A low, guttural moan clawed its way out of his throat.

Branches creaked and swayed.

Leaves rustled.

Branchwolves howled their dirt-choked howls.

"What's he doing?" Taff asked, pressing himself against

the back of the wagon. "Is he casting a spell?"

Kara shook her head; if the past few months had taught her anything, it was the sound of suffering.

"I think there's something wrong with him," she said.

"That's good, right? Wrong is good."

Before Kara could answer, Sordyr's hands stopped shaking. Within the darkness of his hood, his eyes burned a fierce shade of green, like kindle that had been relit.

"What just happened?" Kara asked.

"Nothing of consequence," Sordyr said. "Just her pathetic little attempt to control me."

"Who?" Kara asked.

The carriage door slammed shut.

The journey took two days, their passage remarkably smooth along the root tracks that threaded through the trees. There were no windows in the carriage, but it was quick and easy work to jab four eyeholes in the bark's exterior, allowing Taff and Kara a view of the outside world.

They passed through several more deserted villages—including one that seemed to be constructed entirely of glass—and a large swamp from which crocodilian eyes watched them with insatiable hunger. The carriage cut through a field of pink flowers that whispered their names and was home to a sad, shambling creature entirely overtaken by black fungus. They saw trees that grew upside down in an earthy sky, flocked by thrumming birds whose sole purpose was to catch and replace an ever-falling cascade of soil. They saw purple leaves enfold scurrying mice and then quickly open, releasing something new and terrible into the world.

On the third day they came to the outskirts of a village. Here the carriage abandoned the root tracks for a dirt road cleared of trees. Elderly men and women—some with beautiful ebony skin unlike anything Kara had ever seen—walked along the sides of the carriage, carrying baskets or pushing wheelbarrows. It could have been De'Noran, were it not for their brightly colored clothes and the canopy of glowing leaves impersonating sunlight.

"Who *are* these people?" asked Taff.

"I don't know," Kara said. "Maybe they came from the World like the Children of the Fold did, once upon a day."

"But all the other villages we saw were wiped out. Why not this one?"

"Because they've sworn their allegiance to Sordyr," Kara said. "Remember what Mary said? About the village where he gathered the survivors?"

"Kala Malta," said Taff.

Kara nodded. "This must be it."

They passed an old woman singing to a baby. Kara couldn't hear the words, but the woman's tone was sad, as though she did not want to make any false promises of happiness to her young charge. Kara noticed that many of the villagers bore scars across their arms and unsmiling faces.

"Something's wrong here," Kara said. Noting the questioning look on Taff's face, she added, "Even more wrong than usual."

They heard a loud squeaking noise, like a gate swinging open. Shortly after this the carriage ground to a halt.

The door opened.

Kara stepped out first, happy to stand on stable ground after so many days of travel. Without the walls of the wagon to impede her view she was able to see the village in its entirety. The buildings were smaller than those in De'Noran and constructed with red clay and straw roofs. Most looked like residences, but to Kara's left was a store of some sort; through the open doorway she saw shelves stocked with colorful glass beakers and an old man leaning against a counter. Just outside the store, a worn-looking woman with a leaf patch over one eye strung together black shells; farther down the road a little girl turned a skewered, boar-like creature over an open fire. The smell of roasting meat filled the air.

Taff took a step in the meat's direction but Kara held him back.

"Why aren't they coming to greet us?" she asked. "They're barely even looking in our direction." Deep within the Thickety as they were, Kara assumed that the residents of Kala Malta would be burning with curiosity about any new arrivals. Their attention, however, remained fixed on the entrance of the village.

They're waiting for something.

From the shadows on either side of the road came men and women with shaved heads and leafless wreaths of branches encircling their necks. They wore purple cloaks and their ears and lips were pierced with black thorns.

Kara felt Taff's hand slip into her own.

In the distance the main road branched off into two paths: one lined with more huts, the other scarred by sunken wheel lines and hoofprints. Along the latter path came Sordyr, his trot graceful and unhurried, cloak snapping even in the mild breeze. As he passed, each villager fell to his or her knees. Those wearing the purple cloaks raised their voices in long, ardent wails that sounded eerily like rustling leaves. It was not, Kara thought, a sound any human voice should be capable of making.

"No one's going to help us here," said Taff. "We're on our own."

Despite her growing terror, Kara managed to smile. "That's always been true," she said. "And we've gotten this far just fine."

Behind Sordyr stood a towering gate, part of a huge fence that encircled the village. The fence was constructed from numerous branches woven tightly together like a net. It looked, from this distance, as though it could be easily climbed, and yet something about the fence disturbed Kara even more than the men and women in purple cloaks.

She thought she might have seen it move.

Two old women led Kara and Taff to a nondescript hut in the center of the village. Here waited dishes of food and, even more important to Kara, two washcloths and a tureen filled with water. Kara tried to ask the old women a few questions, but they just shook their heads and departed as quickly as possible.

As soon as they were gone, Taff reached for the food. Kara pulled it away, handing him a washcloth instead.

"Fine," he said, rubbing the small towel unenthusiastically across his face. When he saw the amount of dirt he had removed, however, Taff grimaced with disgust and began scrubbing himself with sincerity. Two sets of clean clothes had been laid out for them, and after Kara was satisfied she was at least moderately clean, she hesitantly pulled on the dress, sleeveless and sewn from a thin, comfortable fabric. The lower half was sky blue and very pretty, but it was the upper half that caught the eye: a perfectly symmetrical collage of yellow and blue patterns. After a lifetime of plain dresses it felt odd to wear such vibrant colors. Kara was certain her brother would laugh at her, but he just shook his head and smiled.

"It looks good on you, but that's because you're a girl," he said, shifting uncomfortably. "All these colors look ridiculous on a boy!"

He wore tan pants, cut short at the knees, and a loose garment woven with red, green, and purple diamonds.

"I think you look very handsome," said Kara, biting back laughter. Noticing a spot of dirt he had missed on his neck, Kara bent down to clean it—when the door opened and a large, dark-skinned man with a bushy white beard stepped into the hut. Half hidden behind the man's imposing frame was a girl about Taff's age, with long, braided hair and delicate features.

"So you're them," the man said with a considerate expression—not unfriendly, but not exactly welcoming, either. He folded his arms across his chest. "Safi, go play outside. I need to talk to our guests."

If the girl heard him, she gave no sign. Instead she studied Kara with an openly inquisitive look, then nodded to herself as though something had been confirmed.

"Hello," Kara said, waving her hand.

The girl gasped with surprise and fled through the front door.

"She's a strange one," said Taff.

"My name is Breem," the man said. "That was my daughter, Safi. She is my light and joy. Gather? You are not to talk to her. You are not to go near her. Sordyr says you have to sleep in my home, and I am in no position to argue. I am just a simple worker. But I will protect my own."

"We mean your daughter no harm," said Kara.

"Hmm," said Breem. He worked his jaw from side to side, his deep-set eyes boring into Kara's. She tried not to stare at the patches of burned skin that had colonized his face and arms. "I must be honest. I was expecting someone different. You're just children."

"I'm almost eight," said Taff, with such an offended tone that Breem almost smiled.

"What do your people call you?" he asked.

Kara told him their names.

"And is it true," he asked, "that you come from beyond the Thickety?"

She nodded. "A village called De'Noran. Far south of here. We were forced to flee—"

"I do not need to know more than this," Breem said quickly. "My curiosity is limited—probably why Sordyr choose me to be your host in the first place."

Kara threw up her hands. "Our *host*? We're prisoners!"

"If that were the case, you'd be in the thorn cages. You are our lord and master's honored guests."

Kara took a step toward the front door.

"Then we can just leave any time, right? And you won't stop us?"

Breem stepped to one side.

"During the day, you may roam Kala Malta as you see fit," he said, gesturing toward the open door. "You must stay inside the Divide, of course, but that goes without saying. At night you may not leave the hut. If you break either of these rules . . . you've seen Sordyr's Devoted, right? Purple cloaks, thorns piercing their bodies."

"We saw them," Kara said.

Breem nodded. "They sing only their master's wishes, and their eyes will be on you at all times." Breem lowered his voice, as though realizing that one of the Devoted might be listening right then, and added, "They have strange ways. Don't give them an excuse to punish you. Understand?"

Kara nodded. And then, because Breem seemed in a sharing mood, she asked the most important question of all.

"Why are we here?"

"You need a place to sleep, don't you?"

"Not here in this hut. Here in this village."

Breem, who had been absentmindedly stroking his beard, suddenly stopped. He raised his eyebrows in astonishment.

"Has he not told you?"

"He has told us nothing," Kara said. "All we want to do is leave this cursed place and go—"

Kara was about to say "home" before realizing that they had no home, not anymore.

"Our father is sick," Taff said. And then he added, with great certainty, "Kara is going to save him."

"Hmm," Breem said. He took a seat at a circular table and poured himself a drink from a clay pitcher. "You're loyal to your father. I like that. But it matters not where you come from, where you're going. Sordyr has a plan for you and it is not my place to tell you. Only a fool angers the Forest Demon. Besides, you'll find out tomorrow."

"Why?" Taff asked. "What happens tomorrow?"

Breem gulped down the rest of his drink and stared at the empty cup, unwilling to meet their eyes.

"Your sister goes into the cave," he said.

SEVENTEEN

Kara awoke from a dreamless sleep to find Taff bending over her, his finger pressed to her lips.

"Shh," he whispered. "We're escaping."

She sat up, eyeing the silent hut. Safi was asleep in her bedroom and Breem, snoring heavily, lay on a mat close to the front door. He wasn't quite blocking the entrance, but his intent to dissuade any escape attempt was clear.

Taff held out his hand to help Kara to her feet.

"No," she said, and even in the darkness she could

see the confusion on her brother's face. "If we flee this place, Sordyr will just capture us again. We need to stay. At least this way I can find out why Sordyr needs me so badly. That might help us figure out what to do next."

"You can't go into the cave."

"You don't even know what's inside."

"It's a cave," said Taff. "Nothing good happens in a cave."

"I'll be fine," Kara said. "Just go back to sleep."

Taff shook his head.

"You spend so much time worrying about me," he said, "but it works the other way too. I don't know why Sordyr needs your help, but I *do* know that it's going to be really dangerous."

"I've been in dangerous situations before."

"Not like this. *Please*, Kara. We have to at least try."

"We'll go look at the fence," Kara whispered. "That's all."

Breem barely moved as they stepped over his sleeping

form. His scars were even more hideous in sleep, without words and gestures to distract from their grotesque appearance.

What is Sordyr doing to these people? Kara wondered. *And why don't they fight back?*

Kara peeked her head out the front door. A purple-cloaked Devoted with three black thorns studding each ear stood across the way, watching the hut. *I need a distraction*, Kara thought. She reached out and felt a needle-nose digging for insects in a neighbor's backyard. *Perfect.* There was no need to build a new mind-bridge, as Kara had communicated with needle-noses before, so she simply asked it to rustle some leaves and branches. The Devoted heard the sounds and, worried that Kara had somehow slipped past him, went to investigate. As soon as he left his post they dashed out of the hut and into the shelter of the dark.

Pairs of Devoted were patrolling the main road of the sleeping village, so Kara and Taff traveled behind the huts instead, stopping every so often to check for movement.

"They might be watching the main gate," Taff said.

"I agree," said Kara. "Maybe we should cross to the other side of the village. We've been traveling for such a long time—we might be close to the eastern shore of the island by now."

"We have to go back the way we came. Mary said the only way out of the Thickety was past Imogen."

"Mary said a lot of things."

"She didn't lie about that," Taff said.

"No. Just everything else."

Kara hadn't had time to consider the depths of Mary's betrayal, but she had at least accepted it. Judging from Taff's look of defiance, he had yet to reach that point.

"Where did she go, anyway?" Taff asked, his voice suddenly concerned. "Why haven't we seen her?"

"She's probably with Sordyr. Her best friend."

"Don't say that."

"If it wasn't for Mary, we wouldn't even be here," said Kara, her cheeks flushed with frustration.

"You're right," Taff said, "we'd be dead. She taught you how to use your powers."

"So I could help Sordyr," Kara said. She clasped her hand to her forehead and an unexpected chuckle bubbled from her mouth. "By the Clen, Taff—aren't you at least a little bit angry with her?"

"It's not her fault. It's the grimoire. It made her do this."

"Taff—"

He spun on his heels and snapped, "You should understand that better than anyone!"

They walked in silence until the fence surrounding Kala Malta loomed before them. It was absurdly tall, but Kara thought there were enough nooks and crannies to allow them to climb it. She gripped a lower limb, expecting to feel cold bark but feeling something else instead.

The fence moved; you saw it. . . .

"No," Kara said, snatching her hand back as though from a flame. "He couldn't have. That's too terrible, even for him."

Slowly, not wanting it to be true, Kara pressed an ear against the fence.

"What are you doing?" Taff asked.

"Shh," Kara said. At first she heard nothing, and then——there it was, what she had felt and not wanted to be true: the frantic beating of a heart.

The branch opened its eyes.

With a wild scream of surprise Taff leaped backward, falling to the ground. The fence shook as though awoken from its slumber. Kara looked closer, the sharp tang of vomit burning her throat as she recognized the once-human forms, their arms and legs transformed into branches and twisted into the pattern of the fence. Unblinking eyes stared back at her, and mouths opened in silent screams.

Sordyr hadn't used wood to make his fence at all. He had used people.

The branches began to shudder, and thorns as long as shoehorns made a dangerous whizzing noise.

"Sorydr did this," Kara said. "With his seeds. Just like with Shadowdancer. He turned these people into this . . . thing." The branches were just a blur of motion now; if they tried to climb the fence, the thorns would slice them into pieces. "That's why he didn't bother putting us in a cell. Kala Malta itself is a prison."

"It's warmer in the house," said a deep voice behind them. Kara and Taff turned around to see Breem standing behind them with two blankets hooked over his arm. Safi stood next to her father, holding a small doll—though she quickly hid it behind her back when Taff looked in her direction.

"Were these people from your village?" Kara asked.

"Of course," Breem said. "This is the Divide, the glory that awaits all residents of Kala Malta when they die. It is our eternal duty to join our ancestors and protect our children and our children's children from the dangers of the Thickety."

Two Devoted approached the group but Breem waved them away. "Sordyr wanted them to see the Divide," he said. "He knew they were going to try to escape tonight and we were told to permit it." When the Devoted refused to move, Breem added, "This is part of the plan he sings," and they finally left.

Kara turned back to the fence. The thorns had stopped buzzing but dozens of eyes were still watching her, as though waiting to see if she was going to touch the fence again.

"Are they suffering?" Kara asked.

"I don't know," said Breem. He checked to make sure the Devoted were out of earshot. "I'm not even sure they're still alive. Most were on their deathbeds when Sordyr fed them his seeds."

"Most?" asked Kara.

Breem pointed at the fence. "That one there, Thomas—I don't know if I would call him my friend, but he worked hard and did no one any harm. Except one day he made a mistake at the Bindery and burned half our stock. Sordyr decided that Thomas could better serve Kala Malta as part of the Divide. Such is the *wisdom* of the Forest Demon."

Breem's voice remained calm, but as he spoke, his body tensed with barely subdued fury.

I wouldn't want to be on the wrong side of this one when he loses his temper, thought Kara.

"You're prisoners here too," Taff said.

"Of course not," Breem said. "This is our home. Sordyr saved our ancestors from dying villages throughout the Thickety and brought them to Kala Malta, where we have lived in peace for many generations. Sordyr keeps us safe from the creatures of the Thickety. Without him, there would be no life."

"And what do you give him in return for such

generosity?" Kara asked, eyeing Breem's scars.

The man's bushy eyebrows narrowed in anger.

"My people do what we must to survive," he said. "Surely you know something about that."

Using the main road this time, they started back toward the hut. Nobody talked. There was nothing more to say.

After a few precious hours of sleep Breem took them to the cave.

They rode horses to a hollow cleared of trees. The Forest Demon was waiting for them, his head bent forward in repose, branch hands folded across his chest. He gave no indication that he had noticed their arrival. Next to him a cage woven from thick, pliable roots hovered above a hole. The rope holding the cage aloft wound through a series of pulleys attached to a thick wooden post, then spooled onto a large wheel. Several Devoted waited to lower the cage into the earth.

Kara noted, with a sinking feeling, that the cage was only large enough for one person. Visions of the hours she had spent trapped in the dark confines of the Well passed through her head. *I'm going down there alone*, she thought, trying to slow her suddenly rapid breathing.

Kara glanced down at Sordyr's feet and saw exposed, for just a moment, a three-clawed foot armored with black bark. Snakelike roots dug into the sole and sides of the foot, pulled taut against the earth.

He's connected to the ground, a part of it.

Kara was trying to think of a use for that knowledge when Sordyr raised his head and fixed her with merciless green eyes that seemed to hover in the darkness beneath his hood.

Kara looked away.

The Forest Demon flicked a hand into the air. Two vines, looped at the ends, descended toward them. Kara stood protectively in front of her brother, wondering what new horror was about to unfold, but the vines simply dropped in front of them like swings.

"Sit, *wexari,*" he said. "There is something you need to know before you enter the cave."

Kara and Taff sat. Sordyr turned away from them, as though unsure how to begin. After a few moments of silence Taff absentmindedly tucked and untucked his legs, breaking into a grin as the vine swung high into the air.

"Stop that," Kara whispered.

Taff dragged his feet along the ground, halting the motion.

"Sometimes you're no fun at all," he said.

When Sordyr spoke, his voice was softer than Kara had ever heard it before. She wouldn't have said he sounded *human*, but it was a passing facsimile.

"I felt your power all those years ago. The night your mother died. The night you first used your gift and forced the nightseeker to conceal your magical ability. Even if you didn't do it intentionally, it was an impressive display of self-preservation—and without the use of a grimoire. I knew then that you possessed the power of a *wexari*, a rare thing indeed. But I did not know how special you truly were until you killed Bailey Riddle."

Though she had only been five at the time, Kara remembered with uncommon vividness the man who had dragged her out of bed that night. Bailey Riddle had not only brought Kara to the execution, but he had also made light of Mother's death afterward, as though it were all some sort of game.

"I hated him," she acknowledged, "but I never harmed him."

"Are you so sure about that?" Sordyr asked. "Do you not remember the night after your mother's death? The dream you had? You hated Fen'de Stone the most, of course, but it had been beat into your impressionable little brain that he was to be revered, no matter what. You just couldn't imagine any harm coming to him. But Bailey Riddle was nothing more than a cruel, insignificant man. You needed to punish someone, and since you were too little to do it yourself, you imagined his death beneath the jaws of a terrible beast . . ."

"Stop it," said Kara.

". . . and something in the Thickety heard you, Kara. Heard you, and obeyed! I wonder. Did you feel it feasting? Did you taste that man's blood on your own lips?"

"You're lying."

"You know I'm not. I *felt* your hatred, Kara, and I knew then that there was a seed of true darkness within you—I only had to give it time to blossom. I waited until you were twelve and in full possession of your powers, and then I ordered one of my Watchers to guide you to the grimoire. I had hoped that its influence would help you accept the evil within your heart, at which point you would return to me for proper training in the ways of a *wexari*. For some inexplicable reason, however, you rejected the grimoire's powers and denied your true nature, *saving* those people in your village when you should have been *destroying* them. I knew then that you would never accept my tutelage, so

I sent the old witch to do my teaching for me. One way or another, I needed you to be powerful. The darkness, I knew, would come later. It always does."

Kara stared up at the canopy, starved for the few rays of sunlight brave enough to enter this cursed place. *Is it true?* she wondered. *Am I really responsible for the death of Bailey Riddle?* Sordyr's words had pecked away the shell of long-forgotten memories; she remembered lying in bed, her burning eyes beyond the point of tears, wishing with all her heart that some terrible violence would befall the horrid man who laughed at—

What if Sordyr is right? What if there is darkness within me? What if it's only a matter of time before it takes over?

And then, like a cool balm, she felt Taff's hand touch her arm. He shouted at Sordyr, "You may be powerful and scary and old, but you don't know *anything* about my sister! She saved my life! She's saved the lives of so many people that I don't even know enough numbers to count them all. She's brave and kind and . . ." He paused here and looked to Kara for guidance. "What's the opposite of evil?"

"I think just 'good,'" she said.

Taff turned back to Sordyr. "She's really, really good," he said. "Nothing you do or say is ever going to change that! I don't know why you've brought her here, but she will never help you! Ever!"

Sordyr lowered his face to Taff's and, squeezing the boy's chin between two twig fingers, twisted his head from side to side, like a farmer inspecting livestock at market.

"Interesting," said Sordyr. "I never considered you. The brother. What harm your influence might be doing to my fragile *wexari*."

"Don't touch him!" Kara shouted. Before she could intervene, however, brown tendrils sprouted from the swing and wrapped around her wrists, holding her in place. Sordyr flicked his fingers and a handful of dirt plastered itself across Kara's mouth, instantly changing to a black, viscous substance that stilled her lips.

"Shh," said Sordyr. "We're having a moment, the boy and I." The Forest Demon poked Taff's cheek with a branch finger as sharp as a stake. "I wonder," he said. "Perhaps the only thing separating Kara and her true nature is another family tragedy."

Kara struggled harder against the vines, but it was no use; they were as strong as chains.

Sordyr pressed his nail against the soft flesh of Taff's neck.

"It is in despair that true evil is born," said Sordyr. He dug inside his cloak. "But not to worry. I won't kill you. I have an even better idea."

Between two twig fingers he held a black seed.

Taff screamed, which was the worst thing to do, for it gave Sordyr a chance to pry his mouth open before he could clamp it shut. The Forest Demon tilted Taff's head back and lowered the seed to his mouth.

Mumbling through the dirt-gag, Kara screamed the

words Sordyr wanted to hear. For a horrifying moment she feared she was too late and Taff would be lost to her forever, but with the seed dangling between Taff's lips, the Forest Demon turned to her.

"What was that?" he asked.

The vines released Kara and the substance sealing her mouth was suddenly dirt again. Choking, Kara spoke the words: "I'll help . . . you. Whatever . . . you want. I'll do it."

"I know," Sordyr said. "I've known since you were five years old." He dropped both Taff and the seed. Taff fell to his knees, gasping for breath. The seed tunneled into the ground. In a few short moments a single flower emerged, slicing the air with knife-edged petals.

Kara knelt by Taff's side. He was shivering but otherwise unhurt.

"Do you know the story of how I became trapped on this island?" Sordyr asked.

Kara nodded. "Mary told me. You gave a grimoire to a

little girl. A lot of people died, so a *wexari* named Rygoth tracked you down and sacrificed her life so you couldn't hurt anyone anymore."

"That is the way they tell it here in Kala Malta," Sordyr said. "But does nothing about that story seem strange to you?"

Kara remembered a peaceful night outside a field of yellow grass, the song of the grettins. And the advice Mary had given: *You must learn to ask the right questions. . . .*

"How did Rygoth trap you here?" Kara asked. "She was just a *wexari*, like me. She could control animals, and even *make* animals, but she wouldn't be able to turn a forest into a prison. Unless . . . did she use a grimoire? Her Last Spell?"

"I wish she had," said Sordyr. "Rygoth would be suffering in Phadeen right now and I would be free." He paused. "At least, I don't think she used a grimoire. It was so long ago, *lifetimes* ago, and—" Sordyr clasped the sides of his head and screeched in torment. The Thickety creaked and howled with him.

"*Stop it!*" he shouted. "*Stop that this instance!*"

The chaos around them settled to a soft buzz.

"She likes to weaken me," he said, his voice unsteady. "What little she can. It's her only entertainment, I imagine."

"Are you talking about Rygoth?" Taff asked. "But— she's dead."

"Oh no," said Sordyr. "She's quite alive. And while her magic may keep me from leaving the island, *my* magic has kept her imprisoned deep within the earth for centuries. We have trapped one another, neither one of us strong enough to escape from a stalemate that has lasted far too long."

"How is that possible?" Kara asked.

"In our prime, we cast the right spells," Sordyr said, leading Kara to the cage hovering over the pit. "Grew the right flower. Created the right animal. At this point, you might even call us immortal. But magic has changed both of us over the years, and these days Rygoth is little more than a monster. That's why I need you, Kara. I've waited so long for a *wexari* with your particular talents. Bend her to your will! Go down there and *make* her release me."

Sordyr unhooked the gate of the cage. Ignoring her brother's protests, Kara stepped inside. Through the gaps in the floor she felt a rush of subterranean air.

"Free me and I will leave you in peace," Sordyr said, latching the gate. "You can have the island. I will even tell you how to break the spell on your father." Kara looked up at this, and she caught a glimmer of a smile beneath Sordyr's cloak. "That's right, Kara. There is a way."

"Even if I did believe you," Kara said, "you're asking me to sacrifice the rest of the world just so my family and I can be safe."

"Perhaps. But ask yourself, Kara: What has the rest of the world ever done for you?"

Working together, the two Devoted spun the large wheel holding the rope and the cage began to descend slowly into the earth. Taff pushed past Sordyr and threw himself against the gate, his fingers reaching for her between the wooden bars.

"Don't do this, Kara!" he exclaimed. "You don't know what's down there! It's too—"

Then all was dirt and darkness.

EIGHTEEN

The cage descended for what felt like an eternity. Kara gasped for air, the walls of the narrow shaft pressing against her. *If some ill is going to befall me*, she thought, *let it be in the open air. Not here in the dark.*

The cage squealed to a sudden stop.

Kara unlatched the door and stepped into a rocky tunnel. Globules of luminescent fungi dangled from the low ceiling like beaded necklaces, illuminating her path.

"Light," Kara said. "Light is good."

She moved forward, trying not to think about the

mountains of earth separating her from daylight. *If the ceiling were to collapse, there'd be nowhere to escape*, Kara thought. She found herself taking short, quick breaths, imagining how it might feel to gasp for air and swallow only dirt instead. . . .

Calm down. This cavern has obviously stood for a very long time. It's not going to collapse today. Probably.

The tunnel widened into a large chamber. The air smelled different here—dank, to be sure, but without the persistent rot that suffused everything aboveground, the taint of Sordyr's corruption.

I don't think he has any influence down here, Kara thought, and a calming sensation filled her. She proceeded to the end of the chamber, where three passageways led deeper into the cave.

Which one?

The last thing Kara wanted to do was get lost. Taff was alone with Sordyr, and she needed to get back as quickly as possible.

She reached out with her mind.

It shouldn't be hard to miss a creature as powerful as Rygoth, she thought, but despite her concentration all she could sense were the tiny inhabitants of the cave: quadra-pedes and ketchy-koos, tangle bats and blindteeth. Kara heard a scratching sound and caught sight of a six-handed creature scurrying for a nearby hole. She built a mind-bridge and the creature came to her almost immediately, maggot white with a toothless, sucking smile. Kara held one of its hands in hers and marveled at the dozens of joints, perfect for finding insects in even the narrowest of cracks.

"I seek Rygoth," Kara said.

The creature hesitated. It looked back at the crevice, perhaps wondering if it should have escaped while it had the chance.

"Maybe you don't know her by her name," Kara said. "She's a——"

Cavemole take. Honored to help Witch Girl.

"You know me?"

We all know you!

The cavemole, no taller than her waist, gazed at Kara with knowing eyes that shone in the darkness. Its smile widened.

You destroy hurt-hurt creatures. Eater of shadows. Eater of lost things. You will heal us all.

Kara looked away in shame.

These animals expect me to save them, she thought, *and instead I'm going to free their greatest enemy. I'm a traitor.*

Except that wasn't true at all, which was the worst part. By freeing Sordyr, Kara *would* be saving them. She would just be condemning the rest of the World.

Either way you look at it, someone is going to suffer, she thought. *There is no right answer.*

The cavemole led Kara into the center tunnel, which sloped downward across a natural bridge that had been eroded to glacial smoothness. A hole in the distant rock wall spat out water that plummeted through the darkness with an earth-shattering roar. Kara peered over the edge of the bridge but could not see where the water landed. They pressed onward. There were no forks in the passageway, no other way to go. The cavemole scampered onto Kara's shoulders and curled around her like a scarf, its skin cold against the nape of her neck. Kara's stomach grumbled. She wondered if she had made a mistake, assuming this trip would take hours instead of days.

Then they stepped through a fissure and into the largest underground chamber Kara had ever seen.

It was colder in this part of the cave—and windy too, as though all the frigid air had been funneled into this one area. The ceiling of the cave was a blurred, distant shape that reminded Kara of the canopy outside. From it hung stalactites as long as trees, their spires glowing with a powerful blue light that illuminated moss-covered walls—and something far less expected.

Draped from the stalactites and walls of the cave was a web.

It stretched across the gargantuan chamber, not flat like other webs Kara had seen but with *depth*: multiple levels and ramps and layers upon layers upon layers. Despite the web's intricate design there was an amazing symmetry to its construction; not a single strand seemed out of place or wasted.

"Hello?" Kara asked, her voice echoing off rocky walls.

There was no response.

Kara looked around some more. Though the web was truly impressive, it was not the chamber's only wonder. From a wide cleft in the rocky floor emerged a densely wound mass of black roots, thick as a tree trunk, which coiled to the lower layer of the web before splitting apart. Hundreds of individual roots then climbed the web to the ceiling of the cave, where they crept through crevices and into the black soil above them. From there Kara supposed they could reach almost anywhere on the island.

How do you like my trap?

Kara jumped in surprise, looking behind her for the source of the voice before realizing that it was coming from inside her head.

Of course it would be best to keep his roots from reaching the surface altogether—that would kill him, I think, as he is more tree than man at this point. But such a feat is, quite unfortunately, beyond my diminished powers.

"Are you talking about Sordyr?" Kara asked. She flashed to an image of the Forest Demon's foot, the roots that pierced his bark-like flesh. "Is that where all these roots go?"

Indeed.

"But there are so many of them!" Kara exclaimed.

How else do you expect him to move? At any given moment, there might only be a few roots connecting Sordyr to the sustenance he needs, but there are thousands more lingering just beneath the soil, anticipating his next step. Each time his foot touches the ground the old roots pull away and are instantly replaced by reinforcements. My web keeps him from getting too far, however. The voice added with amusement: *Like a dog on a leash.*

"But the roots are climbing the web. It's helping them reach the surface."

Is it? Look again.

Kara inspected the sections where web and root met and saw that there was indeed a full war raging between them. Some roots had managed to inch their way to the surface and escape through cracks in the ceiling, but others—most others—were cocooned to the web like unwary insects, their progress impeded. These cocoons shook slightly, the roots struggling to break free.

Kara nodded, finally understanding. The maker of the web had compared Sordyr to a dog on a leash, but Kara thought of him more like a kite attached to thousands of strings. Sordyr wanted nothing more than to fly free, but although a single string might unspool and provide him with a small amount of leeway, most were locked in place.

Kara walked along the rocky floor, continuing to search for the voice's owner. She had spoken to dozens of creatures in her mind by this point, but never any as intelligent as this one. The voice was female, with a comforting tone as lulling as a bedtime story.

"Where are you?" Kara asked.

Up, girl. Up.

In the shadowy recesses of the ceiling, a dark shape watched her. From this distance, the creature looked no bigger than a horse, but Kara knew that was only a matter of perspective. Up close it would be gigantic.

"Rygoth?" Kara asked.

I have been called this.

"My name is Kara Westfall. I am from——"

I know who you are. I might be trapped in this cave but my senses are still keen. You have traveled long and hard, my child. I see you've brought a friend.

It took Kara a moment to realize that Rygoth was talking about the cavemole still draped around her shoulders.

The poor thing had begun to shiver.

"It guided me to you."

A job well done. But perhaps you should return this one to its family. They await dinner, which our little hunter here has promised to provide.

Kara would have liked the cavemole to guide her back to the surface as well, but she supposed she could always call for it again if she got lost.

"Thank you," Kara said, stroking the creature's head.

Clearly relieved to be dismissed from its duty, the cavemole dashed back into the tunnel.

You care for these creatures. You do not use them ill, though it is certainly within your power to do so.

"They are my friends. Come closer. I want to see you."

I am a monster, child. It will be hard for you to trust me afterward. You are wexari, *but you are also human.*

"I've seen plenty of monsters."

Not like me. I used to be beautiful, you know, before Sordyr trapped me in this form. See the moss growing on the walls? That is his creation. *It keeps me from changing back into a human or any other animal small enough to escape this chamber. I am imprisoned not by locks or bars, but by my own size.*

Kara imagined being trapped in this place for thousands of years. *Does she even remember what sunlight feels like anymore?*

"That's terrible," Kara said. "Horrible."

Terrible. Horrible. So many ways of saying the same thing. But most terrible-horrible would be allowing the Forest Demon to leave the island. He is my prisoner as I am his, and I must keep him here. Otherwise all is lost.

A *snap* echoed throughout the cavern as one of the roots broke free of the web and slithered upward. In a blur of motion, Rygoth swung down from her topmost perch and grabbed the fugitive root, spinning a pocket of new silk that secured it to the web.

Rygoth was still a good distance away, but Kara could make out several yellow eyes and many, many legs.

When the creature spoke again its words were hesitant,

as though this unexpected chase had tired her.

Look below. Into the chasm. Understand.

Kara crossed the floor until she stood before the tangle of roots emerging from the depths. She laid a hand on one of them and recoiled at its touch; it was slick with moisture. She could feel something passing through it, a rush of liquid.

Kara peered into the chasm.

A labyrinth of roots extended as far as she could see, tangled together like some secret world of giant worms, shifting and squirming in a never-ceasing battle to reach the surface.

Kara looked away, suddenly dizzy. She had no idea how far down the pit went. For all she knew, it might have been bottomless.

In order to defeat me, Sordyr sacrificed what little humanity he had left and grew himself into something new. He was granted great power, but with a price—he had to remain forever anchored to the earth, just like a tree. Even with this limitation he could have still left the Thickety—his roots, allowed to extend their full length, would stretch to the ends of the World—so with the last of my strength I changed into a form strong enough to ensnare him from beneath the ground. Sordyr trapped me in return—and so it has remained for over two thousand years. Recently, though, I have found it more difficult to contain him. I try to inject him with my venom as often as I can in order to weaken his powers, but its effect has diminished through the years.

She remembered Sordyr's screams of pain outside their carriage and his words of explanation afterward: *Just her pathetic little attempt to control me.*

"It hurts him," Kara said.

I mean only to keep his power from growing too great. Nevertheless, it is only a matter of time before my web begins to snap and his roots are allowed the freedom to go wherever they'd like.

"Then he'll be free," Kara said. "And his Thickety will infect the World."

When are you going to stop lying to me?

"What?" Kara asked.

You act so concerned. So innocent. But I can sense your intentions as clearly as the walls of this cave! You aim to free him!

"No!" said Kara. "That's why he sent me here, yes. But I haven't decided whether or not—"

A strand of web yanked her high into the air. Kara screamed and kicked her legs as cold cavern air gushed past her, the walls blurring by at sickening speed. She closed her eyes for a few moments, afraid she was going to be ill, and when she opened them again the ceiling of the cave was dishearteningly close. The web against her back felt surprisingly frail. Its stickiness, like the flesh of some sweet fruit, clung to the bare skin of her wrists and hands.

"Listen to me," Kara said. "I am not your enemy."

Kara felt the web tense as Rygoth approached her from behind. She tried to turn her head, but her neck and hair were enmeshed in the web and would not allow any movement at all.

"You are Sordyr's servant," said Rygoth, her true voice this time, no longer in Kara's head but muffled, like a mouthful of fangs were getting in the way. "You wish to loose him on the world and undo everything I've done."

"I'm not his servant!" exclaimed Kara. "I hate him! He has my brother, and if I don't help—"

"One life? In exchange for multitudes?"

"What else can I do?" Kara asked.

The web tensed again, as though Rygoth were about to spring, and Kara reached out with her mind. The bridge was surprisingly simple to make. Kara knew that Rygoth must be lonely, trapped here in the darkness for so many centuries, and loneliness was something Kara knew all about. She built a bridge from years of being excluded from games and conversations, from long days spent walking the fields of De'Noran without a friend to take her hand.

The bridge held true.

Kara knew that Rygoth wouldn't come to her, so she

crossed the bridge into Rygoth's mind instead. Kara gaped, startled by the vastness of it. This was no simple animal, and Kara sensed that it would be dangerous to stay here for longer than a moment or two. She might not be able to find her way back again.

"I can't risk anything happening to Taff," Kara said, her voice weak and uncertain. "I'm sorry, but I need you to release Sordyr!" The web vibrated and a single root slipped away, madly unspooling from the crevice below them. *I'm helping Sordyr*, Kara thought. *Whatever he does with this newfound freedom will be my fault.* The thought sickened her. She lingered in Rygoth's mind, knowing she should release more roots but unable to issue the command. *I can't do this. There are other families in the World. Innocent people. Why should they suffer so Taff and I can live?*

And then Kara felt a gale dragging her back across the mind-bridge and into the recesses of her own consciousness.

A bridge goes two ways, wexari. *Let's see what your mind holds.*

Kara's body fell slack against the web. She tried to move but could not.

"Stop it," Kara muttered. "Stop it."

She felt Rygoth crawling along the lines of her mind as if it were a brand-new web.

You weren't lying. You really do hate him. With such passion too!

"Get out . . . of my head."

Don't fight me. I want to help you.

Taking a moment to calm her frantic thoughts, Kara tried breaking the bridge apart with her mind, but nothing happened. *That's not the way to do it,* she thought. *It's not a real bridge, made from stone and mortar. It's made from loneliness.* And so Kara recalled afternoons spent playing Hooks and Ladders with Taff, Mother teaching her the secrets of the Fringe, even—and this surprised Kara—evenings spent around the campfire with Mary Kettle.

She sent all these feelings of companionship toward the bridge, and it shattered into a million pieces.

The connection to Rygoth was instantly severed. Although Kara still couldn't move very much due to the web, her mind was her own again.

"Impressive," Rygoth said. "You escaped my hold. Only the most powerful *wexari* could do that. I needed to know."

"Know what?"

For a few moments Rygoth said nothing.

"I am old and weak," she finally said, "and I don't know how much longer I can hold Sordyr here. I need someone to help me stop him. Someone brave and powerful."

Kara's thoughts swirled. *She just attacked me—and now she wants my help? How can I trust her?*

Do I have a choice?

"I would do anything to destroy Sordyr," Kara said, "but you told me he's immortal." She brightened as an idea struck her. "Unless . . . what if we cut these roots?

That should hurt him, shouldn't it?"

"You are welcome to try, but they are immune to blade and fire," said Rygoth. "And magic too. A good thought, but I had something else in mind."

Kara felt the web vibrate as Rygoth crept close enough to whisper in her ear, her breath like the fetid air of a just-unsealed tomb.

"Niersook," she said.

NINETEEN

Kara sat silently through dinner that night.

"Eat," Breem said, nodding toward the roasted meat at the center of the table. "You are to go into the cave again tomorrow. You need your strength."

Kara, who had lost her appetite for meat many mind-bridges ago, took a dish of yellow mashed vegetables and spooned some onto her plate. She caught Safi, who had eaten nothing but a small bowl of red rice, eyeing the food hungrily.

"You want some?" Kara asked the girl.

Breem shook his head. "Sordyr's instructions were clear: This food is for our honored guests only. Not my daughter."

Kara spooned a heaping portion of the vegetables onto Safi's plate and added two slices of meat.

"Eat," Kara said. She met Breem's eyes. "Or your honored guest will be very displeased."

Sighing deeply, Breem nodded to his daughter. Safi glared at Kara with blatant mistrust, as though this act of kindness were surely some kind of trick. She tore into her food nonetheless.

"The Forest Demon seems pleased with you," Breem said. "This is good."

Kara would not have used the word *pleased*, but at least Sordyr had believed her story. "I can break Rygoth's hold on you," Kara had told the Forest Demon when the cage reached the surface, "but not all at once. She's far too powerful, and I'm still weak from my encounter with Imogen."

It was fortunate that Kara, during her time in Rygoth's mind, had managed to free Sordyr of the single root; he had felt its hold loosen, and taken this as a sign that Kara was telling the truth. After two millennia of being tethered to the ground, such a minor unshackling must have tasted like freedom. At the very least, she had bought herself some more time.

It was the first step of their plan.

"How long have you been in the Thickety?" Kara asked Breem.

"My whole life."

"What about Kala Malta? How long has this village been here?"

Kara saw, from the corner of her eye, Taff sneak Safi a piece of meat from his own plate. A conspiratorial smile passed between the two younger children. When Safi saw Kara looking in her direction, however, the smile faded from her lips.

Why does she hate me so much?

Breem folded his hands behind his neck. "My people have been here a long time indeed. As long as my grandfather's grandfather can remember."

"Have you ever left the island?"

"Why would I do such a thing? Here we are provided with everything we need. Food. Water. Shelter."

The man smiled, but Kara saw the strain behind it.

Sordyr won't let them leave. He needs them for some reason.

"The Thickety is a dangerous place to raise a child," Kara said.

"To others, perhaps. Not to us." He reached over and stroked Safi's hair. "The Divide keeps us safe."

Kara scanned the white scars stitched across the man's body.

"Not that safe."

"These?" Breem laughed. "These are nothing."

"I've seen others in Kala Malta with such marks."

"We are a hardworking people. Accidents happen."

"And what is this work that you do?"

Breem shrugged. "Farming and such."

"I grew up around farmers," Kara said. "And they bore all manner of cuts and bruises as a consequence of their labors. But those burn marks on your face? I've never seen the like."

Breem poured himself a cup of amber liquid. He drank it swiftly and rubbed the froth from his beard.

"These are nothing but common injuries," he said. "You might be *wexari*, but you are still only a child and surely cannot tell the difference between—"

"Don't treat me like a fool. Where I come from, there are people called Clearers who help burn the Thickety before it spreads. They have many marks like that on their hands, only flatter and wider. Yours, though—I don't understand. It looks like you've been whipped by fire."

The smile faded from Breem's face.

"Why are you pushing this matter?"

"Because maybe I can help you."

"Stop it!" Safi shouted, slamming her hands on the table. "Stop pretending that you care about us! It makes me sick."

"Safi," Breem said.

"But I do care," Kara said. "I see the scars. I see what he's done to people to make that terrible fence. You might be too scared to admit it, but I know that you're a victim of Sordyr's evil, just like us." Recalling a motion that Father made when trying to punctuate a point, Kara leaned back in her chair and crossed her arms. "We should be helping each other."

"I would never help you!" Safi exclaimed, springing to her feet. "You talk of evil, but I know what you did." She shook her head. "What you're *going* to do. I saw it!"

"That is enough!" exclaimed Breem. "I forbid you to talk about this."

"No," said Kara. "I want to hear."

"Safi," Breem said, his voice lowering to a harsh whisper. "*Please*. We can't let anyone know about your . . .

gift. He might . . . he might *make use* of you."

But Safi was not listening to her father. She leaned across the table, her green eyes centered on Kara.

"Villages will burn," Safi said. "People will die. The World will be covered in darkness. And it will all be because of you."

After dinner, Safi was ushered into her room, where she quickly fell asleep.

"Do not disturb her," said Breem. "She is frail and needs her rest."

"She didn't seem so frail at—" started Taff, but Kara nudged him into silence.

"I didn't mean to upset her," Kara said.

Breem studied her face for a long moment.

"I believe you," he said. "If I didn't, I wouldn't leave you alone with my daughter. Not for a heartbeat."

"You're leaving?" asked Kara.

Nodding, Breem picked up a small satchel that

looked almost silly in his huge hand; he had the type of body meant to hold sacks of grain and long axes. Breem slung the satchel over his shoulder, producing a clinking sound that was probably made by something as innocuous as tools but nonetheless reminded her of Mary.

"The original plan was for me to play host until your stay at Kala Malta ended, but that has changed. My presence is requested at—" Breem paused here, catching his words. "There is a problem that needs to be remedied."

"What sort of problem?" Taff asked.

Ignoring his question, Breem turned to Kara. "What Safi said about you—I wouldn't put much faith in it."

"Has she had these visions before?" Kara asked.

"Her whole life."

"And have any of them come true?"

Breem scratched his beard. "I'll be back by morning," he said, and slipped into the night.

Kara and Taff took a seat at the circular table. She traced a finger along its ridges.

"We need to talk," Kara said.

She had wanted to tell her brother what happened with Rygoth for hours now, but this was the first time they had been alone since her descent into the cave. Although Kara liked Breem, she did not feel as though they could speak freely in front of him. He was still their captor and would no doubt give Sordyr a full report of anything she said.

"I know why Sordyr can't leave the island," she said, and told Taff about the web and the roots, keeping her voice low in case one of the Devoted was stationed just outside the hut. Taff listened in silent amazement, gasping only when Kara told him how her attempt to make a bridge had backfired and Rygoth had ended up inside her head.

"This one sounds scarier than Sordyr," Taff said.

"She just wanted to make sure she could trust me,"

Kara said. "If she was going to hurt me, she could have done it anytime. I was trapped in her web."

"So she's a giant spider."

"I think so. I never saw her clearly."

"How do you not see a giant spider clearly?"

"Just listen to the rest," Kara said. "It's important. Sordyr can't be killed, not in the traditional ways. That's why Rygoth created a creature called Niersook that . . ."

". . . could take away his magic," Taff said. He shrugged. "Mary told us this story. Niersook's dead."

"But its bones are still here."

"In the Thickety?"

Kara nodded. "Rygoth's not exactly sure where, but she told me that in its body a few drops of the venom still remain. If we can find Niersook and get the venom . . ."

"We can take Sordyr's powers away!" Taff broke into a toothy grin. "I love this plan! When do we do it?"

"We don't."

Taff looked at her, confused.

"I wanted to tell you what happened," Kara said, "because you deserve to know. But nothing has changed. Just consider our two choices. One——I try to overpower Rygoth and get her to release Sordyr. Difficult and dangerous to be sure, but *possible*——I think she's a lot weaker than she seems. Our second choice is to somehow sneak to another part of the island without Sordyr noticing, find Niersook and this venom that may or may not still work, and then somehow——and this is my favorite part—— get said poison into Sordyr's body." She shook her head. "That's not even a choice at all. It's insanity."

"You can't free Sordyr," said Taff. "*That* isn't a choice at all."

He's right. But what if I fail? What if I can't get the venom?

This thought terrified her more than anything else, because she wouldn't be the one who got punished if they were caught. Sordyr needed Kara. He would hurt Taff instead to teach her a lesson.

"If we set Sordyr free he'll just——go somewhere else,"

Kara said weakly, wanting the words to be true. "The World is a big place. We'll never see him again. We can be safe. I'll return Father to the way he was and the three of us—"

"We can't let him leave the island," Taff said. "Remember what Safi said? 'The World will be covered in darkness.' It'll be our fault if we don't do anything to stop it."

"Why should we believe her?"

"Because I've never been wrong before," said a small voice behind them. They turned to see Safi, doll dangling from one hand. "If you free him, you *will* destroy the World. I've seen the people screaming. I've felt their terror."

"Tell us what you saw," Kara said.

Safi hesitated, as if wondering if she had said too much already.

"Maybe it was just a bad dream," suggested Taff.

"I don't have *bad* dreams," said Safi. "Only *real* ones."

Taff turned to his sister. "It was probably a bad dream."

"It was *not*!" exclaimed Safi, stomping one foot on the ground. "And I can prove it. Come with me now and I'll show you exactly how the World is going to end."

TWENTY

After creeping through the sleeping village and a thicket of tightly spaced trees, they entered a small clearing. Six buildings loomed in the darkness. Five were small, with huge metal rings affixed to their roofs, but the last building was larger than all the others combined. Its right end was completely open to the night. This allowed a row of freshly downed trees, stripped of leaves and branches, to stretch inside the building.

"Are those *Fenroots*?" Taff asked.

Kara nodded. Even in the darkness she recognized the

singular color of the tree, considered holy and untouchable by the Children of the Fold. The people of De'Noran had built their entire village around a Fenroot in order to respect it, yet here the tree was being treated like common lumber.

Several chimneys belched black smoke. A sickly sweet smell like burning sugar filled the air.

"What are they doing here?" Kara asked.

"Shh," Safi said, her voice quick and anxious. Kara wondered if this was the first time she had ever broken a rule. "No one but Binders are supposed to see this. I could get in a lot of trouble." She shook her head. "I should have never brought you here."

"What are Binders?" asked Taff.

"People who bind. Like my father."

"Bind *what*?" asked Kara.

"You'll see."

Past the buildings, shadowy branch arms wound together into the Divide. With their heads bent forward in false repose, the people trapped in the fence looked like grotesque scarecrows.

Taff took a step forward and Safi yanked him back.

"Stay out of sight!" she exclaimed. "If one of the Divide sees us, they'll sound the alarm."

As though registering Safi's voice, a head lifted slightly from the fence but quickly returned to its resting state.

"This way," Safi said.

They crawled through tall grass past the open end of the main structure, rising only when they reached the opposite side. The building was ravaged with holes and cracks through which dim light and snatches of movement could be seen. Some of the wooden boards were charred black, perhaps from a quickly extinguished fire. *The entire building looks like it's been through a battle*, Kara thought. *What are they doing in this place?*

The sweet smell emanating from the chimneys was almost unbearably strong here. Kara could feel it on her teeth, as though she had eaten too much rock candy.

"What is that?" she asked, pointing toward the plumes of smoke.

"The sap from the Fenroot trees," Safi said. "They burn it along with the leaves. It's not part of the process."

Though she would never again be a Child of the Fold, Kara winced at the thought of the holy tree being treated with such casual disregard.

"What are they doing with the Fenroots, then?" Kara asked.

"It's easier if you see for yourself," said Safi.

She gestured toward the nearest hole. Kara knelt before it and peered into the building.

The interior bustled with activity, lit by row upon row of candles. At one long worktable, several burly men shaved the bark from the Fenroot trunks that extended a third of the way into the open building, then sawed them into smaller sections. These were transported to the next table. Here, workers chopped the dark wood into tiny pieces that were gathered in wheelbarrows and rolled across the dirt floor to the water-filled trough running across the center of the building. Women with long paddles and blank expressions stirred the water.

"What are they doing?" asked Taff.

"They're making pulp," said Safi, "for paper."

"That's your big secret?" Taff asked. "Paper?"

Safi motioned for them to continue. Remaining in a crouch, Kara followed her along the side of the building. She stopped to glance through another hole and saw five villagers standing at a table, mixing white pulp with their gloved hands like bakers kneading dough. One man paused and tilted a half-filled beaker over the mixture. Three drops of a thick crimson fluid fell into the pulp.

"What's that stuff?" Kara asked.

Safi shook her head. Either she didn't know—or didn't want to say.

At the next table sat a dozen workers, each holding a wooden frame enclosing a rectangular screen of wire mesh. Kara watched one tired-looking woman take two handfuls of pulp from the wooden buckets stationed in the center of the table and spread it evenly over the screen. When she had pressed all the liquid out, the woman flipped the frame, and a thin rectangle of pulp fell onto waxed paper. A different worker took this to the adjoining room, where Kara assumed it would be left to dry. The woman shook out her frame and reached into the bucket, starting the process anew.

"There's plenty of other trees in the Thickety," Kara said. "If you want to make paper, why use Fenroots?"

"And why are they doing all this in the middle of the night?" asked Taff.

Safi shrugged. "That's the way it's always been done. Bind at dark. Use Fenroots for the pulp. It won't work otherwise."

"What won't work?"

"This way," said Safi.

They followed her to the far end of the building. Shifting from foot to foot, Safi pointed at a horizontal crack long enough for both Kara and Taff to look through at the same time.

"There," she said.

This section of the building felt completely different than the others. There was none of the soft conversation Kara had heard at the other tables, idle workplace chatter characteristic of any job, even one as strange as this. The villagers seated before her—at desks, not tables—worked in complete silence, focused on the task at hand.

One of them was Breem.

On his desk was a stack of paper. He fanned the pages and, with a well-practiced movement, hit the stack against the desk until the edges of the paper fell perfectly in line. Once Breem was satisfied, he placed the straightened stack in a wooden frame nailed to the side of his desk, then twisted a handle that squeezed the pages together like a vise.

Reaching beneath his desk, Breem withdrew a single spool of what looked like thread. He passed it through the eye of a needle and pulled it taut. Kara heard a thrumming noise. Slowly and steadily, Breem pulled the needle through a premade hole in the stack and began binding the pages together, pausing only once to wipe a glistening sheen of sweat from his forehead. Kara watched, mesmerized by his skill.

Why did Safi feel the need to show us this? This isn't dangerous! It's wonderful!

It was only as the binding drew to a close that everything changed.

Blue rays of light burst from the book's spine. Breem calmly leaned out of the light's path, squinting at the sudden brightness and twisting the vise tighter. He continued to sew with steady hands. The light sliced through a ceiling beam, raining ash onto his shoulders. Safi gasped. Breem looked up, just for a moment, and light nicked his forehead, puckering the skin there to a blackened welt. He shook his head at his own foolishness and continued sewing, faster now. The vise rattled as the pages of the book struggled against their captor. Even the thread offered resistance, vibrating fast enough to slicken Breem's fingers with blood. Safi's father never hesitated, however, stopping only after he had pulled the knot tight and cut the thread with a hooked knife.

As though a flame had been extinguished, the rays of light vanished.

"This one's ready!" Breem exclaimed.

An old woman with a hunched back slunk into the room. Breem handed her the neat stack of bound pages. Over the woman's left arm hung a rectangular cut of unusual black leather. Kara recognized the material immediately. It looked wet, but would be dry to the touch.

"But you can't just *make* one," she said. "That's not possible!"

But of course it's possible, Kara thought. *Everything comes from something else. Everything has an origin.*

Even grimoires.

Kara grabbed Safi by the shoulders. The girl's eyes widened in terror, but Kara didn't care about that right now. There was something she needed to know.

"How many?" she asked. "*How many has he made?*"

Safi's eyes shifted toward the smaller buildings behind them. In light of this new development, Kara recognized them for what they were immediately.

Storehouses.

She sprinted toward the nearest one and opened the door. It was unlocked. Kara supposed that made sense. The hundreds of books piled inside were useless to anyone except witches.

Grimoires.

Kara entered the storehouse, following a narrow path that wove between the carefully stacked piles. Most of the covers were black, but not all: one was the dark green of a long-extinct reptile, another the red of a dying sun. Another grimoire, leaning open on its side, had a splotch of fur still attached to its binding. *The tanner was careless with this one*, Kara thought, and as she touched the cover a sibilant voice squirmed into her head.

YES, WEXARI! USE ME! WE CAN CREATE SUCH TEMPTING SPELLS TOGETHER AND DRAW THE OTHER WITCHES LIKE MAGGOTS TO . . .

Kara withdrew her finger.

The voice sickened her, but even worse was the small part of her that *wanted* to hold a grimoire again.

The temptation is still there. It always will be.

"Be careful," Safi said, catching up. "These books have magic in them."

Taff gasped. "Wait? These are all *grimoires*!" He eyed the stacks of books. "That's not good."

Kara bit her lower lip as a disturbing thought occurred to her. "Are there any witches in Kala Malta?"

"No," Safi said, quickly shaking her head. "Definitely not. Sordyr tests us when we're very young. The girls, that is."

"How does he test you?" Kara asked.

Safi shrugged. "When we turn six he asks us if we see anything in the book. I guess if you're a witch you see a spell or something."

"No witches," Kara said, pondering the books before her. "Why does he need all these grimoires, then?"

"He's going to bring them to the World," said Safi, "and find witches to use them. That's what I saw in my vision." She closed her eyes, remembering. "A girl speaks words from a book and the village below her shakes into dust. Another woman speaks words that pluck the dead from their graves like weeds. More women, more books. Too fast to see. Raging wind. Black clouds that blot out the sun."

Safi opened her eyes.

"The scariest part of my vision," she said, "is when all the images stop. Like there's nothing to see anymore."

They stood in silence. Wind whistled through the gaps in the Divide, muffling the rhythmic sawing sounds coming from the large building.

"Please don't think ill of Father," Safi said. "It's not like he *wants* to help Sordyr. He doesn't have a choice." She trailed her fingers across the nearest grimoire, its cover as white as a blinding snowstorm. "My father says these books are the most dangerous things in the world."

Kara pulled Safi's hand away from the grimoire.

"Your father's right," she said.

TWENTY-ONE

Kara woke early the next morning, eager to make the journey deep beneath the Thickety. She needed to tell Rygoth about the grimoires. Sordyr's oldest enemy would surely know what he was planning. She might even know how to stop him.

During the ride to the shaft, however, a steady rain began to fall. Though it was a balmy morning the drops were frigid ice picks against Kara's neck and hands. Within minutes the drops began to fall harder, turning the ground into a sloshy quagmire. Kara's hair flattened against her skull.

"This isn't going to happen today," said Breem. "We're going back to the village." The burn mark on his forehead sheened red, and a fresh wound sheared through his thick beard. *The newborn grimoires had not been kind to him last night.*

"A little rain doesn't bother me," Kara said.

"That shaft is unstable to begin with!" Breem shouted. "Add water and it gets even worse. We send the cage down there and the mud might come loose, trap you in that cave forever. Does *that* bother you?"

Though Breem's tone was sharp, she thought she heard the slightest hint of concern in his voice. *He is not a bad man*, she thought. *He is simply trapped here. Like me.*

When they returned to the hut, Kara climbed beneath her blanket and fell instantly asleep. Though the past few months had taught her many things about magic, quite a few practical lessons had been imparted as well. Not the least of these was the value of sleeping when the opportunity presented itself.

It was late afternoon when she awoke. The rain had stopped. Kara laced her boots, expecting to head to Rygoth's cave directly, but Breem informed her that they would have to wait until the shaft dried out.

"How long?" Kara asked.

"At least two days," he said. "Could be more if we get another storm. The air has that feel about it."

"Sordyr won't be happy."

Breem shrugged. "There are some things beyond even the Forest Demon's control," he said. "You'd best get your rest. I'm sure he'll expect you to make up for lost time when the shaft is usable again."

"Where's Taff?"

"There's a place water gathers after a heavy rainfall, makes a pool of sorts. It drains quickly, though, and the children like to swim there while they have the chance. Safi took your brother."

"That was kind of her," Kara said.

"There are not many children Safi's age in Kala Malta," Breem said. "Really, there are not many children at all."

"It's good then. Taff and her being friends."

"I suppose."

After Breem left, Kara decided to take a walk. As she traveled along the main stretch of road, she was astonished by the variety of faces she passed: dark-skinned and light-skinned, blue eyes and brown.

This place is so different from De'Noran, she thought.

The road, rutted and muddy from the recent rain, ran parallel to the Divide, and every so often she passed a man or woman speaking to its shifting branches. Some spoke in hushed voices, others in a more conversational tone. *They're visiting their loved ones*, Kara thought, *like in a graveyard*. A little boy placed a wreath around a curved branch that resembled the sloping shoulders of a man, and Kara looked away, not wanting to trespass upon his grief.

Finally the road began to curve away from the Divide. Kara passed a few more villagers, most carrying baskets on their head, their eyes set dead ahead. Only one man addressed Kara directly, nearly making her scream when he fell to his knees before her.

"You will free our master," he whispered. He pushed back the hood of his purple cloak, revealing a twisted thorn driven through the bridge of his nose. "We sing of you! We sing your name!"

Kara backed away and the man followed her for a time, though he made no attempt to close the distance between them. Eventually he veered off the road and entered a ramshackle building coated with a thick, tarry substance. Rows of animal pelts covered the roof. From within, Kara could hear the chants and moans of an entire congregation.

She did not go inside.

The main road finally emptied into a grassy square. Here a group of children around Kara's age were playing a game that involved three clay balls that varied greatly in size. The children laughed as they ran up and down the field, passing the balls between them. Kara stepped closer, longing to be folded in that laughter, as warm and comforting as a blanket. *If I can just figure out how the game works*, she thought, *perhaps they'll let me play.* After watching the participants for some time, however, Kara could still make no sense of the rules, and no one offered to help her understand.

She moved on.

At the opposite end of the square lay a man whose pants leg had been cut away to reveal a long, bloody gash. A woman with strange feathers in her hair sat on a stool next to him. She crumbled dried herbs into a mortar half filled with milky liquid, then ground the two ingredients into a thick poultice. This she spread over the man's wound.

A healer, Kara thought.

After this she decided to return to the hut. Kara felt as though her walk had not been wasted; she understood the villagers better now. *They eat. They worship. They play.*

They heal. It turned out that Kala Malta was not so different than De'Noran after all.

That night Kara's body was restless, her thoughts even more so. When she finally grew bored of staring up at the ceiling she went outside. It was cold. She brought her hands to her mouth and blew warm air into them, then waved to the Devoted posted across the road. He watched her carefully but did nothing else.

What am I thinking? she wondered. *Stopping Grace was one thing. The grimoire made her dangerous, but she was still only a girl. Sordyr is something different altogether. He might already know I'm planning to hurt him. He might be playing with me.* She perused the night: the slumbering huts, the arching branches. *He could be reading my thoughts right now. . . .*

"What are you doing out here?" Safi asked.

Kara turned to find the girl standing in the doorway. Her thin arms hung by her sides, her doll nowhere to be seen.

"I can't sleep," said Kara. When Safi's eyes remained fixed on her, she added, "I'm not out here planning anything evil, if that's what you're worried about."

"I believe you," Safi said.

Kara dug at a piece of dried earth embedded in her knuckle. "So you've finally accepted that your vision about me might be wrong?"

"I believe that you want to do good."

"You didn't answer my question."

"My vision had two parts. First I saw you and Taff in the Thickety. Then I saw all the death and destruction that are going to happen in the World. The way the visions followed each other, I thought that you were the one who caused all the bad things. Does that make sense?"

"Yes," said Kara. "I probably would have thought the same thing."

"You coming here and what happens *are* connected," Safi said. "But maybe not in the way I thought. My visions, they sometimes play tricks on me."

Safi stopped, on the verge of saying something more. Kara waited. She heard stirring from inside the hut as Taff tossed in his sleep.

"I know you saw your mother die," Safi said. "Taff told me. I hope that's all right."

Kara nodded.

"How old were you?" Safi asked.

"Five."

"I was four when I saw my mother die," Safi said, "only it was in my mind, not in real life. Not yet. I saw her drown in a pond. I must have been terrified, but I don't remember that part. I only remember how relieved I was when I woke up and found my mother peeling vegetables—alive, still alive. It felt like the greatest present I would ever get. It felt like a miracle. I told my mother what I had seen, and instead of telling me it was just a bad dream *she listened to me*. I guess maybe I had seen things before and they had come true—I don't remember. Or maybe she just trusted me. Anyway, my mother stopped going in the pond, or the river, or anywhere else she might drown. A year went by. I thought she was safe."

Safi's lips began to tremble as she talked, but her eyes remained dry.

"My mother stayed out too long in the rain one day and grew ill. Spent her last few days in a fever, coughing blood. I heard my father and Mr. Tonkins, who knows some things about medicine and tried to help, talking afterward. Mr. Tonkins said there was nothing he could do because there was water in her lungs. 'She's drowning from the inside out'—those were his exact words. I remember that."

Kara didn't say anything. The girl's mother was dead. The right words didn't exist.

"These visions of mine," said Safi, "sometimes happen in a roundabout way, but they always happen."

"This is different," said Kara.

"Is it?" asked Safi. "It doesn't matter, I guess. We have to try to stop Sordyr. That's all we can do. But I'm not

sure it's going to change anything—not anything important, at least. My mother didn't drown in a pond, but in
the end she died just the same."

Despite Breem's prediction the weather remained dry,
and two days later Kara found herself deep within the
earth, summarizing her discovery of the grimoires to a
shadowy shape in the distance.

"Between all the storehouses there must be thousands
of them, and he's still making more," Kara said. "But *why*?
Can Sordyr even use a spellbook?"

Of course not, replied Rygoth. *Nor does he have need of*
one.

"But didn't he make the first grimoire? That's what
they believe in Kala Malta, at least. Last night a man
named Breem told me a story about a spoiled princess—"

Sordyr created the tree whose wood, once turned into paper,
enables the magic to be trapped. So yes, in a way he is the
grimoires' creator. But that doesn't mean he can use them. A

blacksmith doesn't wield the sword he fashions.

"Sordyr made *Fenroot trees?*" Kara shook her head. "This doesn't make any sense! I grew up as a Child of the Fold, who believe that all magic is evil. Why would they *revere* the Fenroot tree, then? Unless—maybe they don't know about the connection to the grimoires?"

Fenroots make magic. Your people hate magic. That can't be a coincidence.

"I don't know," Kara said. "It's hard for me to believe that the Fold would accept anything that involved magic. And Fenroots are such an important part of our religion! We can't even settle on a piece of land unless there's a Fenroot tree growing there."

Ah, said Rygoth. *I may understand now. Your people rose to prominence after I was trapped in this place, but the forest is full of spiders, and they bring me information overheard from those who have settled in the Thickety through the years. I have heard many things about your Fold. They were great witch hunters in their day, feared and merciless. No doubt they knew a Fenroot* tree was the source of a grimoire's pages.

"So why didn't they just destroy them all?"

Because Timoth Clen was much too clever for that. Instead of destroying the trees, he set his armies around the Fenroots as a trap for witches foolish enough to try to harness their power. When the witches vanished, the Fold lost its power; for many generations its members were scattered and disorganized. Almost all written records of that time were lost. My guess is the Fold remembered that Fenroot trees were important, but forgot the reason why. Time is a fickle sieve, catching the larger truths while the smaller ones spill through its slots.

"I think I understand," said Kara, "but that doesn't answer my first question. Why does Sordyr need all these grimoires?"

Why do you think?

Kara sighed. "My friend, the daughter of the one who told me the princess story . . . she sees things. The future, maybe. And she thinks these grimoires are going to cause great harm." Kara looked up at the dark shape in the web, an idea occurring to her. "When Sordyr gets to the World, is he planning to create an army of witches?"

The Forest Demon has no interest in armies or war.

"Sell the grimoires, then?"

Gold is like war, a province of man. Do not cloak him with human motives.

"Tell me," she said. "Please. What is he going to do?"

Nothing.

"Nothing?"

I believe he is going to spread these grimoires throughout the World and simply let nature run its course. Witches will find them. Witches will use them. Chaos will reign. Why destroy the World when you can watch the World destroy itself?

Kara instantly recognized the truth in Rygoth's words; that was *exactly* what Sordyr would do. There was nothing he loved more than corrupting the innocent. Kara. Shadowdancer. Imogen. The forest around them.

Why not everyone in the entire World?

"Wait," Kara said. "That plan won't work. I was raised

on the old stories. Even in the Dark Times, when magic was at its height, witches were few and far between. Not nearly enough for what Sordyr is planning."

And yet in your village alone, four possessed the gift. You. Your mother and her friend. Grace Stone. Why do you think that is?

Kara thought on it. Was De'Noran special for some reason? Her people despised magic in all its forms, so it hardly seemed a likely location for such fertile witch growing.

Unless . . .

"It's not the talent that's rare," Kara said, speaking her thoughts as they occurred to her. "It's the grimoires!"

Indeed, Rygoth said. *It is safe to say that every village has a witch—maybe two—but without the grimoire necessary to unleash her talent. Most of the original spellbooks have been lost forever, and the only one who knows the secret to their creation is—*

"Sordyr," Kara said. "And all this time he's been

making new ones, stockpiling them until the day a *wexari* could set him free."

She thought about how much damage Grace did with a single grimoire. What would happen if you multiplied that destructiveness by a hundred? A thousand?

The World would never survive.

"We can't let that happen," Kara said. "Niersook's venom. Are you sure it will still work?"

Oh yes. That sort of magic is eternal.

"Where do I find it?"

The resting place of Niersook is close—I can feel that much, but nothing more. I think Sordyr is somehow blocking its location from me, for though Niersook is nothing but bones, the Forest Demon fears what use I might yet make of it, as well he should. You will have to find it on your own.

"And then what?"

Trust your intuition. I do not think we should talk more of this. With every word grows the chance that Sordyr will sense our intentions. Which reminds me—we must make him feel as though you've done him good service today.

A section of web suddenly snapped, releasing the root that had been attached to it. Sordyr would feel this and hopefully keep believing that Kara was helping him escape.

"Did you really create Niersook?" Kara asked. "Like it says in the story?"

I did.

"Wow," said Kara. Her powers suddenly felt tiny and insignificant. "I could never do anything like that."

But you will someday! You have only just begun to realize your potential.

"You mean I'll be able to make my own animals too?"

Yes—but you'll be able to do more than just that. So much more!

Kara looked down at her hands. "Maybe you could teach me how to use my powers properly. When you're free."

Rygoth's reply was a long time coming.

I would like that, Kara Westfall, she said. *I would like that very much indeed.*

When Kara returned to the hut Taff and Safi were playing some sort of game with stones and cups.

"Another point for me," Taff said. "That's five."

"Four," said Safi. "If it were a point. Which it's not, because you can't use the same cup two turns in a row."

"Says who?"

"The rules."

"Really? How do I know you're not just making this up?"

"Because I can't!"

"Why not?"

"They're *rules*!"

Kara watched them for a few moments, just two children playing a game, their argument playful and good-humored. There was a lot to discuss, but Kara remained silent, not wanting to end this rare moment of normalcy a minute sooner than necessary.

Then Safi shook her cup, intending to roll a fresh set of stones across the table, and noticed Kara standing in the doorway.

"You're here!" she said.

Taff pulled Kara to an empty seat.

"Safi's father will be back any moment," he said, "so we don't have a lot of time. We'll have to talk fast."

"I still think we should tell Papa," Safi said. "He could help us!"

"No offense," Taff said, "but your father's a grown-up. That hasn't gone well for us in the past."

"I agree," said Kara. She met Safi's eyes. "But not because I don't trust him. He's your father. If he knew we were talking about making moves against Sordyr he would report us right away, before we got you involved in anything really dangerous. It wouldn't be a difficult decision for him to betray two near-strangers in order to keep his daughter safe."

"I guess," said Safi, but she didn't look convinced.

"Tell me what you've learned," said Kara.

Before meeting with Rygoth, Kara had told the two children to split up and stroll around the perimeter of the village, casually checking to see if there were any gaps in the Divide.

"I saw a small group of villagers leave," Taff said. "All the leader had to do was wave his hand and the gate just opened. Maybe this will be easier than we thought."

"Did they have a wagon?" asked Safi.

Taff nodded. "A long one, open and flat."

"They're Gatherers," Safi said, "chopping down trees in the Fenroot wood. They have permission to leave every day."

"Maybe we could hide in the wagon or something," said Taff. "Sneak out that way."

"It's been tried. The Divide always knows."

"Could we just climb over?" he asked.

"That's stupid."

"Why? Have *you* tried it?"

"Of course not! As soon as the Divide senses someone, the arms of those trapped inside the fence will grab you, and then these thorns come out of their fingers like claws on a kitten and—"

"Got it," Kara said. "No climbing."

Safi brightened. "I do have a different idea, one I think you'll both—"

"What about magic?" Taff asked. "Can you talk to some big birds and get them to fly us over the fence?"

"It's a thought," Kara said, "but don't forget, the Devoted will be on patrol, and any birds big enough to carry us over the Divide might be kind of noticeable. We need to keep this a secret. Even if we find Niersook and get the venom onto a knife or something, we still have to stab Sordyr with it, which means getting close to him. If he knows what we're up to, that will never happen."

"Then let's use my idea instead," Safi said. Her green eyes sparkled with excitement. "There's this huge tree on the eastern side of the village that extends over the Divide and almost meets a branch on the opposite side. I think we can climb up, make a short little jump, and climb down into the forest. No one will ever know we left Kala Malta."

"A short little jump?" asked Taff. "How high are we talking about?"

"If you're afraid of heights, just don't look down."

"Aren't *you* afraid?"

Safi stared straight into his eyes. "I used to be. But not anymore."

"I don't know," Kara said. "From below, what looks like a jump we can make might be really far."

"We can make it," said Safi.

Kara flinched at the word *we* but decided not to make an issue of it. Not yet, at least.

She can't come. It's far too dangerous.

"For now that sounds like our best idea," said Kara, "but it doesn't solve our other problem. We still don't know where Niersook is. Once we're outside, I'll ask some of the creatures if they—"

Taff leaned forward.

"We need Mary's toy," he said. "The rabbit riding the bicycle."

"Rabbit?" asked Safi. "Bicycle?"

Kara shook her head. "That's not an option," she said. "I'm sure once Mary got her grimoire she left Kala Malta. That's all she ever cared about."

"She helped you," Taff said.

"Because she was following Sordyr's orders!"

"Not always. Remember what happened at the Draye'varg?"

"Yes, Taff. I do. She left us behind to fight those water creatures and we only barely escaped with our lives!"

"Not that part. The part after. She didn't make you kill that . . . thing . . . that looked like me. Mary did it herself, even though Sordyr would have wanted you to do it."

"Why would Sordyr even care about that?"

"He wants you to turn evil, Kara. And something like that could have really changed you. Killing your own brother? I mean, I know it wasn't really me, but—Sordyr is always trying to get you to do bad things, and what could be worse than that? But Mary, she insisted on doing it herself. And then before you faced Imogen she gave you the clue that helped you escape. I'm sure she wasn't supposed to interfere like that."

Kara shook her head. "Even if you're right, it doesn't excuse what she did."

"Wait," said Safi. "Is this Mary person the old woman who's always carrying a sack over her shoulder?"

"That's her," said Kara.

"Is she still here?" Taff asked, and Kara winced at the hope in his voice.

After all she's done, why does he continue to believe in her?

"No," said Safi. "She stayed in an empty hut the first few days you were here, but no one has seen her since then. Her granddaughter says she has some sort of business in the Thickety, but she'll be back again soon."

"Her granddaughter?" Kara asked, shaking her head.

Taff burst into laughter.

"That's right, her granddaughter," Safi said, giving him a strange look. "If you need to find where your friend went, maybe she can help you."

TWENTY-TWO

T he hut sat off from the others in the village as though it were being ostracized for its decrepit appearance. Kara was considering whether or not she should knock when Taff walked past her and through the front door.

"Mary!" he called. "Mary!"

Nobody answered. Against the far wall a hammock swung gently. A half-burned candle waited on an uneven table. Pressed into the dirt floor were two sets of footprints: one big, one small.

"She's been here," said Kara.

They stepped outside, where a funnel of smoke swirled into the sky. As quick as lightning it flashed midnight blue before returning to its original color.

Magic, thought Kara.

Taff started in the direction of the smoke but Kara caught his arm, pulling him back.

"We have to be careful. She has a grimoire again."

"Mary won't hurt us."

"Taff, this is *Mary Kettle*. Think about what that name meant before we entered the Thickety. Forget the woman we thought was our friend. That was just a trick. Remember the stories instead."

"We just have to let her explain."

"I think you should go back to the hut."

Taff sat on the grass and stared up at her defiantly. "No."

The word, only one syllable long, struck Kara as sharply as a blow.

"Taff," Kara said, speaking slowly now, "go back to the hut. Now."

"I need to talk to her."

"Why? Why can't you just accept that she betrayed us?"

Taff took a deep breath and ran a hand through his sandy hair.

"I gave up on you," he muttered.

Kara sat on the grass next to him.

"What are you talking about?" she asked.

"When I was sick, after what happened with Simon. So many days went by. And . . . you had been acting so strange. You were scary, Kara."

She watched the next plume of smoke spiral into the sky. It flashed the color of overripe eggplant.

Finally, she said, "You know what happened. The grimoire was making me act—"

"I know. I know everything now. But lying there, I was so confused. I felt like you had abandoned me. And then you saved me, and there was part of me that didn't feel happy like I should have. I felt guilty. I had given up on you, Kara. I stopped believing. And I promised myself that I would never do that to anyone again."

Kara stretched her feet across the grass. Taff linked his legs over her knees.

"I'm not stupid, Kara. I know that Mary Kettle might just be . . . evil. But she *did* help us. Can't we give her the chance to explain? I think we owe her that at least."

Kara got to her feet and reached down for her brother. When he grabbed her hands she pulled him into the air and spun him around once, twice, three times. It was a game they had often played back in De'Noran, and his laughter now was a soft reminder of simpler times.

"You win," she said.

They found Mary standing in front of a bonfire in a field behind the hut. She was no longer a child; gray hair flowed unchecked down her back, and the skin of her deeply creviced face sagged with age. There was a slight tremor in her right hand, which held the wooden top that could make people forget things.

Mary tossed it into the fire.

The flame flashed yellow, and for just a moment its crackling noise changed to something different.

It sounded like a child's scream.

"Mary?" Taff asked.

The old woman nodded in his direction and smiled. Her gray eyes were distant, seeing them without seeing anything at all.

"Children," she said.

She reached into her sack and withdrew a tiny porcelain teacup spiderwebbed with cracks.

"I never told you about this one," Mary said, running her torn and bitten fingernail along one of the chinks. "One of my first creations. In its prime, you could fill it with water and wish any potion at all into existence. Invisibility. Death. Love. There are kings who would have given their entire kingdom for such a prize."

She tossed the teacup into the fire, producing a flash of red followed by a high-pitched scream.

"What are you doing?" Taff asked.

"Something that should have been done ages ago," Mary said. "The only thing I never tried. I was always too afraid."

"Afraid of what?" Taff asked.

As she replied, Mary dug in her sack. She was able to reach her arms to the very bottom now; the sack was much emptier than before.

"I was afraid that if I destroyed the toys it might also destroy the souls that fueled them. I didn't want that. Or at least, that's what I told myself. Probably I was just afraid of losing what little magic I had left."

She withdrew a stick with a small cup at its end. From this dangled a wooden ball attached by a frayed piece of string.

"I don't even remember what this one does," Mary

said. "Something with the weather, I think. But I remember the boy. Chubby little thing, headed for a lifetime of plainness but cute because he was a child. Only five years old. You figured he had what—fifty, sixty birthdays left? But no—I spoke the words, and this toy swallowed them all, every single uneaten birthday cake." She squeezed the wooden ball between two fingers. "And I *don't even remember what it does!*"

She dropped it into the fire.

"Did Sordyr give you your grimoire?" Kara asked, scanning the area near the bonfire. *I don't see it anywhere. She would keep it close. Maybe it's in the sack?*

"Oh yes," said Mary. "Say what you want about the Forest Demon, but he keeps his promises."

"Where is it?"

"You're nervous," Mary said. "You're afraid that I'm not thinking straight. That I might use my new grimoire to do terrible things. But you don't have to worry. The grimoire is useless."

"It doesn't work?" Kara asked.

"That's right. I needed it to do one thing—one thing!—and it refused."

From within the sack Mary withdrew the rabbit on the bicycle. She raised her hand, intending to throw it into the fire.

"No!" Taff exclaimed. "Please! Not that one!"

Mary turned to Taff. A long strand of gray hair dangled in front of her eyes.

"I'm sorry," she said, "I never meant to hurt you. Either of you. But I owed them. I had to at least try."

And suddenly, Kara understood.

"You wanted to bring them back," Kara said. "The children trapped inside the toys. That's why you needed the grimoire."

Mary slumped to the ground as though Kara's words had taken the last of her energy. The toy bicycle rolled down a sharp decline before clattering to its side.

"I'm just a foolish old witch," Mary said. "I don't know

what I was thinking. I betrayed the two of you on some ridiculous notion that . . . a grimoire can't bring the dead back to life without changing them in horrible ways. Nothing can undo the terrible things I've done!" She stared deep into the flames of the bonfire. "I was good once, you know. I really was."

Taff threw his arms around the old woman. At first she stiffened, but slowly she placed her wrinkled hand over Taff's.

"You'll be good again," Taff said.

"Can you find it in your heart to forgive me?" she asked.

"Of course," Taff said.

Mary's eyes found Kara's.

"And you?" she asked.

Kara shook her head. "You lied to us. You put my brother and me in grave danger. That's not something I can easily forgive. But I understand your reasons. I know that you meant to do a good thing. A noble thing, even."

"Sordyr told me you were a creature of darkness," said Mary. "I thought I would be training just another minion for the Forest Demon. I didn't know who you were, Kara—who you *really* were. And I didn't know about you at all, Taff. If I had——"

"It doesn't matter," Kara said. "We have more pressing concerns. Sordyr is planning to unleash thousands of grimoires upon the World. Do you know what will happen then?"

From Mary's horrified reaction, Kara saw that she did.

"We need your help," said Taff.

The old witch straightened.

"What can I do?" she asked.

Kara hesitated. *If I tell her our plan, she might go to Sordyr. For all I know, this entire scene could be a ruse to learn the truth. Another test.*

But then she looked at her brother, his head on Mary's shoulder. There was no doubt in his eyes. No doubt at all.

Kara still did not trust the old witch. But she trusted Taff more than anyone in the world.

"To start," Kara began, "we need to borrow one of your toys."

TWENTY-THREE

Back at the hut, Taff whispered "Niersook" into the rabbit's ear and its tiny feet pumped the bicycle forward. Safi gasped with delight and clapped her hands.

This is all new to her, thought Kara. *I keep forgetting that.*

Stretching his arm across the dirt floor, Taff measured the distance between the bike's starting and ending points.

"From the tips of my fingers to my elbow," he said. "A little less, actually."

"How far is that?"

"Mary said an arm's distance is about half a day by foot. So . . . a few hours?"

Kara grunted in frustration.

"Too long," she said. "And that's assuming we're able to find Niersook right away."

"And don't run into any trouble," Taff pointed out. "Sometimes that happens to us."

Kara slid a hand beneath her long hair and scratched the nape of her neck.

Why can't this ever be easy?

Breem had left for work just after dinner and would surely be gone until morning; Sordyr was pushing his workers to complete as many grimoires as possible before he left for the World. The children had exactly one night to sneak out of the village, find Niersook, get the venom, and sneak back. That plan had seemed unlikely to succeed from the very start, but now Kara knew it was completely impossible. The body of Niersook was simply too far away.

"It doesn't matter," Taff said when Kara expressed her

concern. "We have to try anyway."

"If Sordyr finds out what we're doing, we'll never get close enough to use the venom. This whole thing will be a waste of time."

"Why can't you just fight him?" Safi asked. The diminutive girl's eyes glowed with a fierceness that Kara had never seen before. "I mean, not *you*. That would be foolish. But the monsters of the Thickety. Make them fight for you."

Kara shook her head. "I won't do that. I've forced animals to do my bidding in the past, and they've gotten hurt, even killed. I won't put another living thing in jeopardy again. Not just to help me."

"But they're not just helping you. They're helping everyone. Sordyr is destroying their home. They *want* to stop him. All they're missing is someone to lead them."

Kara knew Safi was right; reaching out with her mind she heard the animals surrounding the village, hundreds of voices awaiting her command. Word of Kara's victories against the notsuns and Imogen had made its way through the Thickety, and creatures once too frightened to turn against Sordyr were now emboldened and eager to fight.

All I have to do is call them. . . .

"No," Kara said, closing her mind to their voices. "I don't want to be responsible for any more deaths."

"Then you need to do everything in your power to stop Sordyr," said Safi. "*Everything.* Otherwise all those people who die in the World *will* be your fault." Safi paused as a new thought occurred to her. "Maybe that's what my vision meant. You'd never really help Sordyr. I know that now. But if you have the power to stop him and refuse to use it? That might be even worse."

Kara picked up the toy bicycle. A thin new crack had emerged, running down the center of the rabbit's face along the left edge of the nose. Gently, so that she might not do any further harm, Kara placed the bicycle on the table.

"You're right," she said softly. "If my powers can save

these people, I have to use them. Even if animals die."

"What if we don't walk?" Taff suggested. He turned to Kara, a sly smile tweaking the edges of his lips. "I know you worry about these creatures risking their lives," he said, "but surely you wouldn't mind asking one for a ride?"

They set out at nightfall.

Kara had begged Safi to stay behind, but she stubbornly insisted on coming with them. There was nothing Kara could do. Safi was the only one who knew the location of the tree that extended over the Divide, and every minute spent arguing was a minute wasted. They packed small satchels with food and water and made their way through the quiet village. There were surprisingly few Devoted patrolling the roads; Kara wondered if they had been recruited into grimoire-making as well. In the distance axes struck trees in a rhythm as steady as a beating heart.

It wasn't long before Safi stopped. The section of the

Divide before them was taller than anywhere else. Deep within the mass of branches a pair of eyes opened, a hint of blue in the darkness.

"This will work," she said.

"Where's the tree?" Taff asked.

"What tree?"

"The one we can climb. You told us there was a tree that crossed over to the other side. . . ."

"*That* tree," said Safi. "Right. I made that all up."

Kara was too shocked to even reply. Taff, however, managed a soft, "There's no tree?"

"There's lots of trees," said Safi. "Just none that we can use to climb over the Divide."

"Then how are we going to get into the Thickety?"

Safi burst into a radiant smile. "That's the best part! That's the surprise! You ready?"

She withdrew a large object from her satchel.

"No!" Kara exclaimed, but Safi had already opened the grimoire. Strange words flowed from her mouth.

Kara felt herself jerked and tugged. Nausea clenched her stomach.

"What just happened?" Kara asked. Next to her Taff was bent over on his knees, his hands on his thighs. Kara gently rubbed his back.

"What did you do?" she asked Safi. "And where did you get—"

"Look!" Safi said, beaming.

She pointed toward the Divide. Kara examined it for a hole or other opening, but nothing was different.

"What?" asked Kara.

Safi rolled her eyes.

"*Look!*" she said.

Kara took in their surroundings, more carefully this time. The huts of Kala Malta were now in the distance, *behind* the fence.

The Divide hadn't changed at all. They were just on the other side of it.

"Safi," Kara began. She took a step forward, her arms

outstretched. "You need to give me the grimoire."

"Why? I can help you now!"

"You don't understand."

"Sure I do!" Safi exclaimed brightly. "I'm a witch too! Isn't that wonderful?"

Clutching the grimoire in two arms, Safi skipped along the path, deeper into the Thickety.

They found the gnostors playfully chasing one another just over the rise. Kara knew that the fast, ostrichlike creatures were a perfect choice to carry them to the resting place of Niersook, but it was dishearteningly difficult to make a connection with them. The fault was hers. Gnostors were an innocent species that responded best to simple amusement, and Kara struggled to find memories of fun strong enough to build a mind-bridge. Those moments felt so distant now, as though they had happened to a different person.

Finally she remembered a time she and Lucas had

raced downhill after a major storm, slipping through the mud until they slid to a stop at the bottom, laughing gleefully. Although Kara could picture the event perfectly in her head—could even recall the precise pattern of speckled mud across Lucas's forehead—she was still hesitant to use it. The memory was one of her favorites, and she did not want to give it up.

We need these creatures, Kara thought. *I have no choice.*

The mind-bridge snapped into place, and the memory vanished forever.

"These are the ugliest birds I've ever seen," said Taff.

There were three of them, with fat, unwieldy stomachs improbably balanced on two thin legs. They walked with a wobbling gait, giving the impression that they were just one misstep from falling over.

"I don't think they're birds," Kara said. "They can't fly."

The largest gnostor stepped forward. Kara ran a hand along its umber plumage—not soft like the feathers of other birds but rough like toasted bread. Its neck, long and graceful, split into two parts before coming together again, ending in a small head dominated by perpetually curious eyes.

None of the gnostors were the slightest bit Blighted. She wondered if their innocent nature acted as armor against the dark touch of the Thickety.

"Thank you for helping us," Kara said.

The gnostor whistled.

"Sounds like a bird to me," said Taff.

After checking the toy rabbit to make sure they were heading in the right direction, they mounted the creatures. Travel was difficult, the ground uneven and punched with holes. Their progress would have been agonizingly slow had they remained on foot, but the gnostors quickly navigated the unsteady surface by throwing the weight of their stomach from one side to the other.

It's not fat, Kara thought. *It's a balancing mechanism.*

Once they had settled into a steady pace, the trees

flashing by in a dark blur, Kara spurred her gnostor next to Safi's.

"How long have you known that you're a witch?" Kara asked.

"Since I was six. That's when I was tested. I opened a grimoire and saw the words to create a soonberry pie out of nothing." Safi shrugged. "I was hungry."

"What did Sordyr do when he found out?"

"He didn't," Safi said. "I pretended the page was blank. That was what Father told me to do. He said if I saw something in the grimoire and told anyone, the Forest Demon would take me away forever. I was terrified that I would never see Father again, so I lied. I told Sordyr that all I saw was a blank page, and he believed me."

Kara looked at the girl with newfound respect. "You fooled the Forest Demon. That is not easily done."

"I thought it would be harder, actually," said Safi. "Don't you find it strange? He's forcing us to make all these grimoires, yet he can't use them himself. I knew the

425

page in my grimoire wasn't blank, but there was no way for him to know that."

"He's not a witch," Kara said, but she saw Safi's point. *There are many different ways of destroying the World. Why choose to do it with a weapon you cannot control?* A realization lingered there, just out of reach. Something important. Before Kara could make sense of it, however, Safi started to talk again, and the half-formed thought slipped from her mind.

"Things were different after that," Safi said. She absentmindedly patted her gnostor, which whistled in appreciation. "I started to have dreams where I . . . did bad things. Things I would never think of doing in the real world. And sometimes I would wake up in the middle of the night and find myself at the storehouses." She looked over at Kara. "This must sound crazy."

Kara shook her head. "The grimoire was calling you. It wants to be used."

"After about a year, the dreams and the sleepwalking

stopped. It was like the grimoire just gave up. But then, the night after I showed you the storehouses, I woke up and heard something whispering my name. Not 'Safi,' mind you. My *true* name. I had never heard it before, but I recognized it. How could I not? It was like all the things that are me had been transformed into sounds and strung together." Safi touched her right ear, as though the word had left a pleasant imprint there. "I followed the voice to the clearing and opened the door to the first storehouse. My grimoire was waiting for me, right on top of the others. White as snow." She smiled, and her teeth gleamed in the darkness. "The spell to make soonberry pie is still there on the first page."

Kara glanced at Safi's satchel, noticed the way the girl's hand lingered near the opening.

"You can't use it again," Kara said.

"It's mine."

"It's evil."

"Are you sure? How else could we have gotten past

the Divide? That's the reason I took the grimoire in the first place. I would never use it to hurt anyone. Don't be ridiculous."

"I said the same thing."

"Well, clearly, I'm different!"

A moment of silence, fraught with tension, passed between the two girls. Finally, Safi looked away. When she spoke again her voice was soft and compliant. "If you think it's that important, I'll get rid of the grimoire as soon as we destroy Sordyr. Until then I think we need all the help we can get."

Kara wanted to tell Safi that it wasn't worth it, that she should bury the grimoire in some desolate spot she'd never be able to find again. But her practical nature, deeply ingrained by years in the Fold, intervened. *Who knows what dangers we're going to face? Having a witch by my side could be very useful. It might even save our lives.*

"Fine," said Kara, "but when this is done, you need to get rid of that thing. Promise?"

Safi nodded, her hand on the satchel again.

"Just this one time," she said. "I promise."

The trees opened up less than an hour later, revealing the broad expanse of a half-broken mountain with a gargantuan tail sticking out of it.

"Please don't tell me that's Niersook," Taff said.

"What else could it be?" asked Kara.

She dismounted her gnostor and looked more carefully.

Niersook must have crashed into the rock face at incredible speed; its body lay hidden beneath a mountain of stones. Only the tail was visible, as tall as a tree and covered by rich carmine scales that cast strange, shimmering reflections in the near darkness.

"How are we going to get the venom," Safi asked, "when we can't even see the mouth?"

"Should we climb over the rocks?" Taff asked.

"They're too unstable," Kara said. "One wrong step

and they could collapse beneath us."

"What about going around to the other side of the mountain?"

"We don't have time," Kara said. "Besides, even if we make it to the other side, who knows if the mouth is out in the open? It might be buried beneath rubble, or too high for us to reach."

"Or crushed completely," Taff said. "In which case, there's no way for us to get the venom at all."

"I don't think so," Kara said, pointing to the mountain. "Look carefully. You can see flashes of red here and there, like Niersook is just underneath the rocks. I think it crashed into the top of the mountain and slid down."

"Well," said Safi. "If we can't go over the rocks and we can't go around, how are we going to get there?"

Taff smiled and shook his head. "We're going *through* it, aren't we?"

Kara nodded.

"We're not *really*, are we?" Safi asked.

"Of course we are," Taff replied. "We just have to find a way in."

He approached the tail, which even at its shortest point was five times as tall as him. Taff tried to pry a few scales away from their moorings, and when that didn't work he withdrew his wooden sword and struck one. A deep metallic sound reverberated throughout the trees, like a gong calling long-dead armies to battle.

"Hmm," he said, tilting his head to one side. He struck the next scale, producing a similar sound. "Hmm," he repeated.

"Are you sure that's the best idea?" Safi asked.

Kara placed a hand on the girl's back. "You can wait here if you'd feel safer. No one would think less of you. You've more than proven your bravery by coming this far."

"But you might need my help," Safi said, and Kara saw her hand stray to the satchel.

She's looking for an excuse to use the grimoire.

"We won't," Taff said quickly, before Kara could reply.

He struck another scale, resting his hand on it in order to feel its vibration. "Besides, it's probably way too scary for you inside. Trust me. I have experience with these sorts of things."

"I'm sure it's not scary at all," snapped Safi, "if *you* can do it."

Taff shrugged. "Guess you'll never know." He moved to the next scale. When he struck this one the sound was no more melodious than an anvil striking stone.

"Here!" he shouted, waving them over.

Using all their strength, the three of them managed to peel the scale away from the tail. Behind it a narrow opening led deeper into the darkness. Mucus-like strings stretched between the scale and segments of pearl-white bone, shockingly pristine.

Before Taff could squeeze into the opening, Safi pushed past him.

"I'm not scared!" she exclaimed, vanishing into the darkness.

"I might have convinced her to stay behind," Kara told Taff. "I hope you're happy with yourself."

"Do you want to leave her alone with that book?" he asked, his voice suddenly serious. "She's better off with us." He winced at the smell coming from the opening. "You first," he said.

Kara turned her body so she could squeeze behind the scale. As she slowly inched her way through the darkness, Kara tried not to think about the soft, moist walls pressing against her, the stomach-churning smell that fouled every breath she took.

Finally she stepped into nothingness and fell, rolling down some sort of hill and onto a hard surface. Taff followed a few moments later, accidentally slamming his elbow into her neck.

"Sorry," he said.

"Safi?" Kara asked. "Are you all right?"

"Yes," Safi said. Kara heard the sound of flipping pages. "Ah, this should do the trick!"

Safi murmured a few foreign words and suddenly a glowing globe of light hovered above them, illuminating their surroundings.

Though not as big as Imogen's cavern, the chamber still dwarfed the children. Arches of bones held the scales in place, and a network of translucent veins, each large enough to walk through, weaved above them like a system of roads.

Thousands of bones littered the floor.

"What are these?" Safi asked. The ground cracked and snapped beneath her feet as she looked for a bone-free place to stand.

"Maybe this was its stomach," Kara said. "These bones must be what's left of its prey."

"But I thought its only prey was Sordyr," Safi said. "That's the whole reason it was made in the first place."

Kara shrugged. "Everyone has to eat."

"I don't think so," said Taff. He held up two skulls, each smaller than a human's but with exaggerated eye sockets. "Look at these. What do you notice?"

"They're the same," Safi said.

"*Exactly* the same."

"So?" Kara asked. "Niersook was bound to eat two of the same type of animal at some point."

"True," said Taff, picking up a third skull. It was completely identical to the first two. "But these skulls should still look a *little* bit different. Smaller, bigger—something!" He picked up a fourth skull, compared it to the others. "This is so strange," he said.

Kara scanned the floor and saw dozens of identical skulls staring up at her with those oversize eye sockets.

"What does it mean?" Safi asked.

"I don't know," said Kara, "but we have more important things to worry about. We have to find the venom and get back to Kala Malta before sunrise. Time is growing short."

They tried Mary's rabbit first, hoping it would lead them to the venom's precise location, but when Taff whispered his request, it refused to move at all.

"I guess it only works on big things," he said.

They headed in what they all agreed was the general direction of the mouth, thinking that it would be relatively simple to walk from one end of the body to the other, but after a few turns they became hopelessly lost.

"We need a different plan," Safi said. She withdrew her grimoire. "Maybe I could—"

"No," said Kara. "Emergencies only."

"How is this not an emergency?"

"Because nobody's screaming."

They journeyed through long passages and tall rooms, the surface littered always with the strangely identical bones, the large-eyed skulls. They found a tube that had collapsed onto the floor and followed it upward; it emptied into a room covered with a taut, fleshy material that began to tear the moment Safi stepped on it. Despondently, they retraced their steps to the previous chamber.

"What are we going to do?" Taff asked. "This is like finding a needle in a haystack, except you don't know how big the haystack is, and you don't know what the needle looks like."

"I think I can make the—" Safi started.

"No," Kara said. "I have a different idea. These bones—I don't think they're here because Niersook ate them. If that were the case, we'd only find them in its stomach, not everywhere."

"So what were they?" asked Safi.

"I think they were *part* of Niersook. Like workers. That's why they're all identical. Because Niersook"—she struggled with a way to explain the next part—"*grew* them, just like we grow nails and hair."

"Even if that's true," Taff said, "what good does it do us? If these creatures were alive, maybe you could ask them for help. But they're all dead."

"I know," Kara said.

She remembered Mary's warning: *You must never use*

your powers on the dead. The old woman had not gone into more detail than that, but the very idea was so obviously *wrong* that Kara didn't think it necessitated further explanation.

"Kara," Taff said. "Don't even think about it. There must be another way."

"There might be," Kara said, "but time is running out and this is the best thing I can think of." She picked up a skull. "If anything bad happens, make sure you . . ."

Kara hesitated. The skull dangled from the crook of her fingers.

"What?" Safi asked. "What should we do?"

"I have no idea," said Kara.

Holding the skull between two hands, she pressed it to her forehead.

TWENTY-FOUR

Kara listened closely for the skull's hidden language and heard nothing at all, no clues to help her build a mind-bridge. *Because it's dead*, a nagging voice in her head said, *and nothing you do is going to change that*. Pushing this doubt aside, Kara tried constructing a bridge from memories of those she had loved and lost. She remembered Constance holding Kara's locket in her hand, and Mother, always Mother, plucking weeds from their garden beneath a steady drizzle of rain.

Kara felt Taff's hand on her shoulder and realized she was crying.

"It's fine," she said. "Leave me be."

Taff withdrew.

The mind-bridge Kara had constructed was a strong one, but there was a major problem: It didn't lead anywhere. Since she was unable to locate the voice of the dead creature, Kara had no idea where the other side of her bridge should set down.

Because it's dead. . . .

Kara had never given much thought to ghosts, which had been a forbidden topic in De'Noran. Nonetheless, she had heard her share of spooky stories during Shadow Festival, but these had always seemed a little silly to her. Specters—the ones in the stories, at least—didn't seem to *do* much other than linger in the middle of cornfields or the rafters of old barns, wait for an unsuspecting child to make an appearance, and say some variety of "Boo!" Kara believed that half the reason ghosts appeared in the first place was because the foolish characters in the stories were convinced they were being haunted. They had welcomed the dead back to the world through their own curiosity.

Maybe that's it, she thought. *Maybe the dead need an invitation. I don't have to put the other side of the bridge anywhere. I just have to make it welcoming enough and wait.*

Kara set the mind-bridge down, anchoring one side in her mind, and lit it with memories of sunshine and warmth. She hoped the light of the bridge would be like a beacon in the fog, and waited for the owner of the skull to follow it.

She did not have to wait for long.

An old taste, like wagon wheels left moldering in the back corner of a barn, fuzzed her tongue. Kara felt a certain *shifting* inside her mind, and a weight like a painless headache throbbed behind her eyes. She exhaled a cold plume of air that was not her own.

"Hello?" she asked.

I will help you.

The words were high-pitched and delivered with brisk efficiency.

"You know why I'm here?"

Your thoughts circle in the darkness like glowflies. Pretty. Let me find the one I need.

She felt an odd sensation just behind her forehead. It didn't hurt, but it was hardly pleasant either, like walking on gravel in her bare feet. *It's sorting through my mind*, she thought, and while Kara didn't like the idea of some dead creature having access to all her secrets, she supposed it would make matters easier if she didn't have to explain anything.

You seek the elixir. I will help you. Hurry! Hurry!

The skull felt warm in her hands. She stared into its sockets, half expecting them to begin glowing with fire, but nothing happened.

"I don't know where to go," Kara said.

Just walk. You will know the way. There was a brief hesitation, and then the voice added, *I am part of you now.*

The words made Kara uneasy, but she sensed no malice from the creature. It really did want to help her.

"Follow me," Kara told the other two children. Holding the skull in front of her like a lantern, she put one foot in front of the other, slowly at first, then with increasing confidence.

The thing inside her head hadn't lied. She knew the way.

The creature called itself Konet and had been born inside Niersook, just like all its brothers and sisters. Konet and its brethren spent their entire lives with one purpose alone—to manufacture what they called the "elixir." Kara wasn't able to understand all the intricacies of the process, but apparently it was so complicated that it required the entirety of Niersook's massive body, which was really no more than an organic factory.

Niersook crashed into the mountain. Niersook died. We live. Continue to make elixir. No food. Soon Konet's people die too. Then Konet.

"That's very sad," Kara said.

Death not sad. Wasted elixir sad. Must use.

"I intend to," said Kara.

They followed a series of tunnels deeper into Niersook, Safi's floating light leading the way. The ground seemed solid enough but shifted from side to side like a rope bridge. Through the translucent floor Kara could see the surface far below her. They were going up.

They entered a tunnel that was larger than the others and filled with some sort of brackish, flowing liquid.

"What is this stuff?" Taff asked.

For transport, Konet said. *To move supplies from one end of Niersook to the other. Elixir requires many ingredients. Many steps. A lifetime to make a single drop.*

"Is this a vein?" Taff asked, poking at the dark liquid with his boot.

"It's a transport tunnel," said Kara.

"Right," said Taff. "A vein."

On Konet's suggestion, they cut away a piece of the wall and draped it over the surface of the liquid. It was as thin as a bedsheet but floated perfectly, even after Safi sat on top of it. Kara held it in place while Taff joined Safi. The membrane, like a lily pad, dipped only slightly beneath the liquid.

"I don't think it's going to support all three of us," Taff said.

Kara agreed. Reaching up, she slid her knife through the membrane and cut herself a new raft, a bit larger than the first one. She placed it on top of the liquid and hopped on before the current could carry it away.

They floated through the tunnel. Safi's sphere of light was a meager defense against the encroaching darkness.

"Do you think we're under the mountain?" Safi asked.

"I don't know," replied Taff. "I'm still getting used to the idea that we're traveling through something that used to be *alive*."

"It's pretty disgusting when you think about it like that."

"How else are you supposed to think about it?"

Kara allowed their conversation, amusing as it was, to drift away. She had a larger concern right now that she did not want to share with the other two children. Something was not right. Her mind felt *bloated*, as though someone had blown air into her head and inflated it like a balloon. Kara supposed she should be grateful that there was no pain, but in a way she would have preferred it. At least pain would have been something; this was just a vast emptiness stretching the perimeter of her mind far beyond its natural capacity.

The bridge. An open invitation.

No one new had attempted to cross over—not yet, at least—but it felt like her mind was readying itself to house a vast new number of occupants.

I have to get Konet out of me, as quickly as possible. I can't close the bridge until I do.

"Do you hear something?" asked Taff.

"Just you," replied Safi, "trying to scare me. It's not going to work."

"Shh," said Taff. "Listen."

Kara concentrated, trying to pinpoint what Taff was talking about. She heard the lapping sound of the raft as it cut gently through the liquid. A steady dripping just ahead of them. The ragged sprinting of her own breath.

There!

In the distance, back from where they had come, she heard the unmistakable sound of swimming. Drawing her knife, Kara held it before her with two slightly trembling hands. She opened her mind and listened, hoping to identify the creature. . . .

LET US IN! LET US IN! WE WANT TO LIVE TOO!

The chorus of voices assailed her like a physical blow. She dropped to her knees, nearly retching over the side of the raft, and the knife fell from her open hand and into the brackish liquid. She was aware of the bridge in her mind, still open, a welcoming beacon to those who hovered on the other side.

Mary warned me. She said it wasn't the creature I was

enchanting that would harm me. It would be the others: lonely
spirits who craved the same attention.

Kara thought about the countless bones they had carelessly stepped on, the hundreds, maybe thousands of spirits trapped in this never-decaying corpse forever. How angry they must be. And how jealous that Konet had stolen a tiny flash of mortality while they remained consigned to everlasting night.

They wanted a piece of Kara's life too.

"We have to hurry!" Kara called out.

Taff's voice slid through the darkness. "I'm trying to use my sword as an oar, but this stuff is all sticky!"

Kara reached out with her mind, searching for something—*anything*—that might still be alive, and found an ancient intelligence hidden in the cool depths below them. It was reluctant to move after so many years mired in the muck, but Kara pleaded with it, sacrificing the smell of her mother's meat stew in the process. She sensed one red-veined, reptilian eye creak open. The water parted, and the raft rose into the air on something far more solid than liquid.

They were on top of the creature.

The walls of the vein rushed by in a blur of speed. As Kara passed the other two children she made the creature slow down so she could grab their hands and pull them onto its back with her. They allowed the membranes to slide away and gripped bony ridges worn smooth by centuries in the deep. Their speed increased, the continual shouts of *LET US IN* fading to silence. The tunnel forked again and again, but Kara always knew the right path to follow. Through the translucent ceiling she saw the vast workings of Niersook: tall towers that spired into a branching network of veins, plump sacs the color of a ripening bruise that might have been some sort of organ, coral-like polyps brittle with age but still holding a vestige of their former beauty. Each of these structures was necessary, Konet informed her, to craft the elixir. As the paper-thin walls of the vein grew tighter, Kara marveled at what Rygoth had created, an entire world dedicated to one specific goal.

Finally the reptilian creature turned sharply, sending the three children tumbling off its back and onto solid ground. Kara reached out with her mind, meaning to thank their unlikely helper, but it had already begun the return journey to its resting spot, worn out from this unexpected exertion.

Kara examined this new area.

The spongy surface was the raging scarlet of an inflamed throat. The walls, equally red, oozed a thick yellow fluid. From the ceiling above them hung dangling shapes, hazy in the shadows. Safi's sphere of light seemed hesitant to get close enough to illuminate them.

In the center of the passage, a single, translucent sphere hung from the ceiling by a thin tube. Kara stepped over a huge pile of bones and bent before it.

Elixir stored here. Safe.

Kara heard unmistakable pride in Konet's voice. The

elixir had been its life's work.

"Why are there so many bones here?" Safi asked.

"I think they were guarding it," Taff said. "Everything about this place is centered around the venom. It makes sense that they would protect it."

Safi nudged a bone with her toe. "It doesn't make sense for living things to have other living things inside them," she said.

"Actually," Taff said, "I've often wondered if we have things living inside of *us*. I used to get sick before, so I spent a lot of time thinking about it. How does an illness spread from one person to the other if it's not alive? And how do we fight off an illness if we don't have living things inside us to do so?"

Safi gazed at him with complete disgust. "I'm never getting sick again," she said.

"Focus," Kara said. The word was intended for the children, but a little for herself as well. She had begun to hear the words like a drumbeat rising in the distance: *LET*

US IN, LET US IN. She feared the very bones beneath her feet were aware of her presence.

With the back of her hand, Kara wiped away a layer of pinkish fuzz from the sphere. At first it seemed empty, and a flood of panic threatened to overtake her. *This has all been for nothing!* But then Safi's floating light moved closer and revealed, at the bottom of the sphere, a few drops of red liquid.

"Look," said Taff, pointing to the tube that led from the sphere to the ceiling of the passage, then continued deeper into the tunnel. "This must be how the venom was delivered to the fang. We can follow this to the mouth and get out that way."

"Good idea," said Kara. "But we have to get this venom first." She carefully poked the pliant surface of the sphere, wondering how they'd be able to break it without losing the precious liquid, when it suddenly yielded and allowed her index finger to slide inside. The rest of the sphere remained undamaged, like an unpoppable bubble.

"Look at this!" she said, her finger hovering just above the liquid. "The sphere doesn't break! We can just slide something in here and . . ."

"Don't!" exclaimed Taff, yanking Kara's hand out of the sphere. "This stuff takes magical powers away! You can't go near it! Neither can Safi."

Kara glanced down at her hand as though it had betrayed her.

"You're right," she said.

"It has to be me," said Taff.

Kara had no desire to let Taff go anywhere near the sphere, but she knew he was right. *I have to let him help me. Safi too. There's no way to do this on my own.* Besides, the low hum of *LET US IN* was rising in her head and she was finding it difficult to concentrate. She thought about destroying the mind-bridge and setting Konet free, but what if they weren't able to exit through the mouth like Taff said? They might still need the dead creature's help.

"Just hurry up," Kara told him. She stepped away from

the sphere, intending to give Taff more space to work, and winced at a sudden onslaught of pain. It felt as though the space in her head—the room she was involuntarily making for the approaching dead—was stretching too far, straining the limits of her skull. Kara clasped two hands to her temples as though she could push her mind back into shape. It didn't work.

"Are you all right?" Safi asked.

"I'm fine," Kara said. She looked up and saw Taff watching her with concern. "The venom! Quick!"

Taff snapped back to work. "Give me your knife," he said.

"I lost it."

"Okay," he said, shaking his head. "That's okay. We just need something to get the venom into Sordyr's body. Something sharp. A dagger. An arrow tip." He eyed the bones scattered across the ground and smiled. "That will work. Help me find a sharp one." Taff and Safi rifled through the bones while Kara, the world around her spinning, slumped to the ground. "Hurry," she muttered, but she didn't think either child heard her. She closed her eyes, heard the snap of a bone as Safi cracked it in two and handed it to Taff.

LET US IN! LET US IN!

"Let's get at least three," Kara said. "In case something goes wrong."

Taff, his forehead furrowed with concern, was staring at her again. She waved him away.

"No time," she said. "Get it!"

The voices had risen to a wailing chorus of need. *There are so many of them. And they are so lonely.* They craved human companionship, living sensations.

They craved her.

Seeing no other option, Kara destroyed the mind-bridge.

Instantly the voices dissipated. She had one moment to touch Konet's spirit as a meager way of thanking the worker for its assistance, and then it was gone as well.

Kara's head still throbbed and she felt weak, as though she had not eaten in several days. But her mind was her own again.

And yet—her nerves still trembled.

"Got one!" Taff exclaimed. From the sphere he withdrew a venom-infused bone shard, now dyed a violent shade of crimson. Carefully he wrapped the shard in a rag and slipped it into his pocket.

On the ground, the bones began to quiver.

It was subtle at first, barely perceptible movements that could have been caused by an errant breeze or vibrations along the ground. But then a hip bone spun in front of Kara's eyes like an enchanted baton and she knew it was not her imagination.

"Bones," muttered Kara. Between her still-pounding head and the impossible sight before her, she was having difficulty forming the necessary words to warn the others. Taff and Safi had their backs to her, too absorbed in the task at hand to notice the movement on the ground behind them.

The hip bone locked joints with a curved, stubby little bone, and together they rolled like a broken axle, indiscriminately locking onto new bones as they passed. Joints jammed into sockets far too small for them, Nature's grand design rejected in favor of a more immediate need.

Reanimation.

When I built the bridge to Konet, I awoke all the spirits in this place. They wanted to touch life again, if just for a moment. Kara's cheeks burned with remorse; she had provided an irresistible temptation, a glimpse of warmth in a dark and frigid world. She sensed their fury at her inadvertent cruelty and felt the bitter weight of responsibility.

They hoped to cross the bridge and join Konet in my mind. I teased them and then closed the bridge. Now they have nowhere else to go, but their spirits are too angry to rest again——so they're breaking the rules and creating a new home instead.

"I lost it!" Taff exclaimed in frustration. He had dropped the second shard into the sphere and could not get his fingers deep enough to retrieve it. "Get me another one," he told Safi.

Safi turned, her eyes widening as she took in the mis-shapen creatures linking together before her eyes. Like malignant snowballs, bones rolled over one another and grew, until there were at least five or six of the unnatural creations . . . and then too many too count.

A six-legged horror with a skull perched on what appeared to be a tailbone looked up at Safi. Too many teeth packed its tiny mouth.

"Bones," Kara said.

Safi screamed.

Kara, amazed that such a fantastically loud sound could emanate from such a small frame, was shocked into action. She focused her mind on the raging voices of the bone monsters and began to build a mind-bridge from loneliness and hunger, intending to control them. She didn't get far. Before she could mold her first mem-ory into something usable she was assaulted by dozens of voices, desperate for entrance to her mind. With a scream of pain she shoved them away and abandoned the bridge.

Their furious wails echoed in her mind.

I can't control them, Kara thought. *There's too many. They'll push me out of my own head.*

One of the monsters, ill-placed rib bones extending from its skull like antlers, fastened its teeth on Taff's leg. Kara lifted it into the air and slammed it down as hard as she could. Bones exploded everywhere, but even as Kara was catching her breath she saw them rolling along the ground, looking for new creatures to join.

"Are you hurt?" she asked Taff.

"It's nothing," he said, but Kara saw the way he winced in pain, the blood matting his pants. He started to draw his sword, but Kara shook her head and slid it out of its sheath.

"We need the venom," she said. "Keep working. I'll protect you."

"*We'll* protect you," said Safi, the grimoire in her hands. Kara started to disagree, but Safi cut her off. "You told me if there was screaming that made it an emergency, and I *definitely* screamed!"

"Cast well," Kara said.

A bone monster like a hobbled dog charged her and Kara swung the sword as hard as she could, shattering the creature into two pieces and sending a cloud of white dust into the air. She stomped on a smaller monster, no bigger than a beetle, and swung the sword again at a shape spinning at her end over end like a windmill that had fallen off its base.

No matter how many monsters she cut down, however, there were always more to take their place. Her arms throbbed and the wooden sword grew heavier in her hands. She knew she couldn't keep this up forever.

The skull monsters exploded into flames.

The fire was strange and mesmerizing and seemed to be going in the wrong direction, as though the monsters were each surrounded by an invisible barrier that burned toward them, not away. In just a few moments all that remained were haphazard piles of blackened ash and a foul smell like burning sulfur.

"I did that," Safi said, pointing toward the destruction. She laughed gaily, a child chasing a butterfly. "I did that! Me!"

"Good job," Kara said, gently closing Safi's grimoire. "But let's put this away for now."

"Right," said Safi. "Of course."

But she made no motion to slide the book back into her satchel, instead staring at it with a kind of wonder.

"I did that," she whispered.

It was at that moment that the entire tunnel began to rumble, as if Niersook, after centuries of rest, had finally awoken from its slumber.

TWENTY-FIVE

Kara rocked back and forth, trying to keep her balance. Safi's grimoire flew out of her hands and she fell to her knees to retrieve it.

"What's happening?" Taff asked. "Is it Niersook?"

Kara listened with her mind; surely she would sense if Niersook had come back to life. There was nothing new, however, only a flurry of needy voices, too many to distinguish. . . .

Oh no.

"There's more of them coming!" Kara exclaimed. The

tunnel rocked again, as though a thunderstorm had been trapped inside the body of the ancient beast and was now headed their way. "Taff—are you done?"

"Two down," Taff said. He wrapped the shard carefully in a cloth and slipped it into his pocket with the other one. "One more left." The venom was almost completely gone, however, and he was having trouble immersing the last shard without dropping it into the sphere. "It would be a lot easier if this place would stop moving."

They heard the sound of footsteps. Dozens. Hundreds.

"The things that were following us before," Kara said. "They're here. We have to go."

Taff shook his head, steadying his hand against the sphere. "I almost have it . . . ," he said. "Just give me a little more time."

"Now!" Kara exclaimed, grabbing Taff's hand and yanking him away. He left the last shard behind, embedded uselessly in the sphere.

"Go," Safi said, flipping through the pages of the

grimoire. "I can stop them. All I need is the right spell—"

But Kara grabbed her hand as well, and Safi had to quickly get hold of the grimoire with her free hand or risk dropping it.

They ran.

Glancing behind her, Kara saw the horde of bone monsters slam into the tunnel, too many to count, an ever-changing army of ill-joined creations that was far faster than it had any right to be. Some were as large as cattle, but most were no larger than a skinless cat. Since there were no tongues with which to make sounds, their arrival was measured in clicks and cracks and snaps.

At first Safi's and Taff's hands tightened on her own, but they quickly let go, pumping their arms to better speed their flight. The tunnel split in two. Kara, following the tube along the ceiling, chose the passage to the right. It was narrower here, which seemed to slow their pursuers down somewhat as they struggled to fit into the smaller space. Kara did not waste any more time looking back. There was no need. She could judge the distance of the creatures from the sounds. *Click, crack, snap! Click, crack, snap!* More tunnels, more turns. Right, left. Left again. Then against her burning cheeks she felt cold air, the outside world. Kara reached out with her mind, difficult to do while running, and felt the creatures of the Thickety again, their comforting presence. She found the one she needed and built her mind-bridge, completing it just as two towerlike fangs came into view, hanging like stalactites. Behind them Kara saw the trees of the Thickety illuminated by faint morning light.

They were standing in Niersook's mouth.

"We made it!" Safi shouted, sprinting toward the open air. "We're safe!"

"Safi!" Kara exclaimed. "Wait!"

At the last moment Safi saw the fall that awaited her and came to a sudden stop, pinwheeling her arms. Kara pulled her back to safety. With cautious steps, the three children peered over the edge of the mouth. A gray, mossy tongue, as long as a tree, dangled lifelessly from the open jaws but came nowhere near to touching the earth, the hazy surface below more like a memory of the ground than the ground itself.

Click, crack, snap!

The bone monsters were coming.

"Did you bring rope?" Kara asked Taff.

"No," he said. "Who said I was in charge of bringing rope?"

"A rope will never reach the ground!" exclaimed Safi.

"I know," murmured Kara, frantically searching their surroundings. "I don't need it for that. . . . Here!"

Something red and stringy ran along the floor. It could have been ivy. It could have been the petrified muscle of some unfortunate beast devoured decades ago. In any case, it looked strong. Kara grabbed it with two hands and pulled with all her strength. It didn't break.

"They're here!" Taff exclaimed.

The bone monsters spilled out of the throat and fanned

across the floor of the mouth. They slowed down, under-standing that the children were trapped. A ball composed almost entirely of teeth clattered over the others, eager to take the first bite.

"No time to explain," Kara said. Standing on the very edge of the mouth, her feet balanced on a surprisingly dull molar, she looped the ivy around them and knotted it as tightly as she could.

"Hold hands," Kara said. "In case this breaks."

She wrapped her arms around the children and pulled them toward the edge.

"Wait!" Safi exclaimed, her eyes wide with panic. "We're not going to jump, are we?"

"No," said Kara. "We're going to fall."

She leaned forward and they plunged over the edge.

Free-falling was a lot louder than Kara had expected: the violent whoosh of wind, Taff screaming in her ear. At first she thought Safi was screaming as well, but the girl's eyes were pinched shut and what emanated from her mouth was little more than a series of small whimpers. The one screaming was Kara.

Please don't let me be wrong. Please don't let me be wrong.

Their speed multiplied second by second. Green and black flashed by. The hilt of Taff's sword dug into her stomach. Kara's eyes had gone blurry with the wind but she still managed to see Niersook's head poking out of the mountain, its tri-forked tongue unfurled like the banner of some lost civilization. From this angle she was unable to see the upper half of its face.

That's too bad, Kara thought. *I would have liked to have known what color its eyes were. . . .*

And then the sky disappeared and everything was dark. The air around them turned warm and moist.

Thank you, Kara thought, and sighed with relief.

"What just happened?" Safi asked. "Where are we?"

"My friend caught us," said Kara. "I reached out with my mind while we were in Niersook's mouth and asked for its help."

"Your friend?"

"A giant bird, more or less. We're inside its bill." She squeezed Taff's hand. "You all right?"

"That was *amazing*!" he exclaimed.

"He's all right," said Safi.

Though it was too cramped to stand, they managed to wiggle out of the red ivy and crawl their way along the bird's tongue. The beak was slightly open, affording them a view of the outside world. Leaning on their elbows, the children pressed their faces to the wind as the bird swept gracefully though the trees.

"We're flying!" shouted Taff. "We're really flying!"

"It's wonderful," agreed Safi, "but if it's all the same to you two, I'd rather not be inside anything's mouth for a while."

Kara laughed and stroked the girl's hair.

"I think I've had my fill of that as well," she said.

The bird landed just outside Kala Malta.

The children rolled out of its mouth, a little shaky on

their feet but otherwise unharmed. Kara turned to face their hero. Its beak was long in proportion to its body, like a gull's, and almost perfectly circular. Black plumage allowed it to camouflage itself in the trees. A thin line of moss wound its way between three copper-colored eyes.

"I'm going to fix this," Kara said, running her hand along the moss. The sharp tang of infection burned her nostrils, but Kara refused to embarrass the creature by holding her nose. "One way or another, the Thickety will be yours once again."

The bird flapped its white-tipped wings and slowly raised itself into the sky.

"What now?" Taff asked, retrieving his sword from Kara.

She had hoped to return before dawn, but the canopy leaves had already begun to burn with morning light. *Breem will have noticed we're gone by now, but he might not have reported us to Sordyr yet. When we get back to the hut I need to convince him that everything is all right. Then I can take the cage down to Rygoth, same as always, and inject the venom directly into Sordyr's roots. That would probably be the safest thing to do. And if that doesn't work, I still have the second shard.*

"We'll have to come up with some excuse," Kara said. "Safi, maybe you had a vision and couldn't sleep, so we all went for a walk."

"That'll work fine for Papa, but not for Sordyr. The Forest Demon can't know that I—"

"A nightmare, then," Kara said. "Or something. We'll figure it out later. Right now we need to get back over the Divide as quickly as possible. If we're found inside the village, that's one thing, but if we're found beyond the Divide, that will be *really* difficult to explain."

"They already know we're gone," Taff said. Though he had not spoken loudly, Kara snapped to attention, hearing a rare note of despair in his voice. "Look at the gate."

It was open. Around it stood a half-dozen Devoted, checking the ground for tracks. Even from this distance Kara could see the branch wreaths encircling their necks.

She pulled the children behind a large boulder.

"What do we do?" asked Safi.

"We can't let them see us," Kara said. "That's the most important thing right now."

"Maybe I can cast a spell to get us inside the village," Safi suggested. Then she added in a softer voice, "Or I could make something bad happen to the Devoted."

Before Kara could answer, a rising wail, like the whistle of a teakettle, shredded the quiet morning. *Stupid*, Kara thought, instantly realizing her mistake—she had been so worried about the Devoted that she had forgotten who else would be searching for them. The Divide. Hideous eyes framed by bark stared at Kara with malignant fury, while branch arms disentangled themselves and pointed in her direction. Dozens of twisted mouths wailed their alarm.

There was nowhere to hide.

"Give me the shards," Kara told Taff, holding out her hand.

"You can't touch them!"

"I don't have a choice."

"But—"

"Taff!"

He handed the crimson shards cautiously to Kara. She slid them into her pocket.

"We knew this might happen," Kara said. "That's why—"

A terrible squawk of pain shattered her next word. Kara followed the sound and saw, high in the sky, the bird that had saved them, caught within the clutches of several tree limbs. Kara heard its voice in her head—*SAVE ME, WITCH GIRL, SAVE ME, SAVE*—and then the limbs pulled it deeper into the black leaves and its voice stopped forever.

He knows, Kara thought, her grief for the bird overshadowed by more immediate concerns. *Was it the trees that told him? Does he know what we've done?*

When she turned her attention back to the village, Sordyr stood framed by the open fence, his orange cloak stretching back along the main road of Kala Malta. A dozen Devoted, most brandishing wooden spears, stood to either side of him. Other villagers, not directly involved but still curious, pressed up against the Divide. Breem was among them, holding an ax with two hands. His eyes fixed on Safi with a mixture of relief and concern.

"What have you been up to, Kara?" Sordyr asked.

"I went for a walk," she said, trying to control the trembling in her voice. "Is that forbidden?"

"A walk," Sordyr said in a mocking, childlike voice. "I don't think so, *wexari*. We both know where you were. Not that it matters. The venom is so old, I doubt its magic even works anymore. But I'll take it anyway. One can never be too careful."

"What venom?" Kara asked. "I have no idea what you're—"

From behind the Forest Demon's tall frame stepped Mary Kettle.

"Oh yes," said Sordyr. "The old witch told me everything. I'm disappointed, Kara. After she betrayed you once, you trust her again? I thought you were smarter than that."

Mary was a teenager today, but there was no mistaking those slate-gray eyes.

Kara swallowed hard.

"I'm disappointed too," she said.

"Let's not prolong this," Sordyr said. "You can still help me. Use the venom on Rygoth. Do this, and I will allow your brother to live."

"And my daughter!" Breem exclaimed. "Right?"

The Forest Demon clasped his branch fingers together.

"The girl is from Kala Malta and should have known better," Sordyr said. "An example must be made."

Turning his attention back to Kara, Sordyr did not see the way Breem clenched the ax tighter.

"You will not harm her," he said, walking toward the Forest Demon. A Devoted blocked his path and Breem slapped him across the face with the back of his hand. The man thudded to the earth like a sack of grain, blood gushing from his nose. Two other Devoted headed in Breem's direction. The other villagers—and Sordyr—turned to watch, drawn to the promise of violence.

The distraction was exactly what Kara needed.

She stretched her mind across the trees, as far and as high as she could reach, calling forth creatures of every wake and description. *I need your help*, she thought. *I can't do this on my own. But I will not lie to you. This fight will be dangerous, and many of you will die. But if we succeed, the Thickety will be yours!* It was the largest mind-bridge she had ever created, and it required a lot of building material. Kara dug through her mind. Since she wanted the animals to understand they shared a common enemy, she built the first part of the bridge from the hatred she felt for Sordyr, packing each wrong he had done her into an individual stone. She built the rest of the bridge from her love of animals. This was far more difficult, for she did not want to lose her memories of Shadowdancer or the grettin or the countless other friends that had colored her life. But she needed the Thickety creatures to know they could trust her, and sacrifices had to be made.

She waited.

Come on, come on. . . .

She could have forced them to come. But Kara refused to make the creatures do anything against their will, though she made it clear that once they crossed the bridge they would be hers to command.

Come on, Kara thought. She watched the skies, the treetops, the ground, looking for some sort of movement. *Come on.*

They came.

They came from everywhere, parting the trees with their trunks and claws, skittering through the undergrowth, slicing through the air on sharp-edged wings. A deafening storm descended upon Kala Malta: chitters and yaks, roars and squawks.

Sordyr took a single step backward.

A wolf with silver fur and a scorpion's tail settled by Kara's side. She stroked its head as she spoke.

"They're with me," Kara said. She pointed to her forehead. "In here. All of them. And they are so, so angry with you."

"An impressive display, *wexari*. But I know you. Your *goodness*. You would never sacrifice their lives to—"

She sent the birds first.

A cloud of winged creatures wound itself around Sordyr, a flurry of talons ripping at his cloak and bravely dashing into the shadows of his hood in an attempt to pluck out his eyes. Over the fluttering wings Kara heard the whiz of Sordyr's branch hands as they sliced through feathers and flesh with blinding speed. Kara felt the death of each bird as a clenching in her heart. Sordyr rubbed two branch fingers together, as though trying to light a fire, and from the canopy a storm of thorns was released. The ground was quickly covered with unmoving birds.

Before their numbers could be completely depleted, Kara sent the birds away. They left reluctantly. Despite Kara's protestations, they felt like they had failed her.

There is nothing more you can do, my brave friends, she told them. *Be proud. You have struck the first blow.*

Indeed, Sordyr's cloak was now torn and tattered, his hood pecked away in too many places to count.

In one motion, he pushed the hood from his face.

Sordyr's skin was the striated bark of an ancient tree, chipped and pitted with years. A tangled mass of wiry branches crowned his head. Swampy eyes swirled with their own secret history, impaled by the two thorns growing from Sordyr's eye sockets like ill-placed antlers.

These horrible eyes never left Kara as the Forest Demon slid a dead bird off his branch finger and tossed it onto the pile.

"Blood," he said.

At first Kara had no idea what he was talking about, but then she felt the warm liquid running down her face. She placed a finger to her left ear and it came back red and sticky. Frigid numbness spread through her head like a lake quickly turning to ice.

I used too much magic.

"You are still but a girl, *wexari*," Sordyr said. "There are too many of them for you to handle. You will only kill yourself."

Roots encircled Kara's legs. She bent down to pull them away but their grip was too strong. She lost her balance and fell to the ground. New roots wrapped around her arms and pinned her to the dirt.

"I can still forgive all this," Sordyr said. "It is not too late for us to help each other."

Kara called forth parasitic worms with double rows of stone-sharpened teeth. They made short work of the roots, allowing her to rise unsteadily to her feet. Kara sent the rest of her creatures forward—save the wolf with the scorpion's tail, who refused to leave her side. The animals charged like starving beasts suddenly uncaged. Several Devoted ran forward in an attempt to block the animals' path. Most were trampled underfoot, though one was tossed like a bale of hay by a beast with a fiery horn.

They were almost on top of Sordyr. For a moment, just a moment, Kara thought she might win.

But then Sordyr raised his hands and from the ground burst fully formed trees, catapulting dozens of unfortunate creatures high into the air. Those that remained were confused and disoriented, and their rising panic made them difficult to control. It didn't help that Sordyr was now hidden behind the row of entangled trees he had created. Natural enemies that had united against the Forest Demon were confused by his sudden disappearance and began to snap at one another instead.

I'm losing them, Kara thought as her spell began to fray.

She concentrated harder, trying to bring her army in line, and a fresh bead of blood leaked from her right ear.

They can't get to him anymore, she thought. *The trees are protecting him. . . .*

Lightning flashed across the sky. A tree wavered for just a moment and then fell, crashing into the Divide and bringing that section down.

Kara turned to see Safi, her nose in the grimoire. She mumbled a new spell. A second tree fell, this one taking down two others and producing a large gap in the trees that revealed Sordyr. Kara's creatures saw him, began to regain their focus.

"Look at that," Sordyr said. "Another witch."

"That's right," said Kara. She smiled back at Safi. "There's two of us now. You don't stand a chance."

Sordyr's thorn-pierced eyes glowed with amusement.

"There could be a hundred of you," said Sordyr. "It would not matter. You are in my home. I *am* the Thickety."

From the ground burst shambling monstrosities of moss and ivy, man-size rats with poisonous dandelions embedded in their fur, tangles of moving roots in the vague shape of something that had once been alive.

Kara's army faced this new challenge with raised hackles and low growls, but before they could charge, Safi read from the grimoire and a cyclone of wind slammed into Sordyr's monsters. Some flipped away into the trees, but most rooted themselves to the ground and withstood the blast. When the wind had died down the monsters continued to move forward. They did not shake the dirt from their flanks; the dirt was a part of them. Kara's creatures rushed into the fray and filled the air with snapping jaws and shrieks of pain. She tried to guide them, knowing that if they worked as one unit they would have a better chance, but death after death weakened her. Kara dropped to one knee and the wolf with the scorpion's tail slid beneath her, supporting her weight so she did not fall. Kara turned to look at Safi, who was in the process of casting another spell when a black toad the size of a large dog unfurled its tongue and snapped the grimoire from her hands. Taff attacked the toad with his wooden sword, trying to get the book back, but it hopped into the throng of battling creatures and was quickly lost to sight. Two branchwolves noticed Safi and crept closer, readying themselves to leap. Taff stepped in front of her and raised the sword above his head, but Kara could see his shaking hands.

"We yield!" Kara shouted.

With what little energy remained, she commanded her animals to leave and destroyed the mind-bridge between them. Most slunked into the Thickety, confused at this sudden turn of events. Only the wolf remained, staring up at Kara with a fierce expression, as though daring her to make it leave.

They don't understand why their queen gave up so easily.

"Kara!" Taff shouted. "What are you doing?"

"There's no point," she said wearily. "We can't win. Why should anyone else die?"

Framed by the gap between the trees, Sordyr watched her carefully for a moment and then, apparently satisfied, waved a single branch hand. The remaining trees thudded back into the ground, revealing the residents of Kala Malta pressed up against the Divide.

"Kara!" Taff exclaimed.

"Stay with Safi," Kara said. The young witch was crawling through the grass, looking for her lost grimoire. "Keep her safe."

Kara started toward the village, the wolf with the scorpion's tail following faithfully at her heels. The clearing was littered with the corpses of those who had fought for her. *All this death*, Kara thought. *Just as I feared.*

Sordyr's monsters crept closer but did not attack her.

It's not their fault. It's him. All him.

Kara removed a bone shard from her pocket and held it out to Sordyr.

"Take it," she said.

For the first time that afternoon, she saw genuine fear darken the Forest Demon's eyes. His creatures, sensing this change in their master, howled and scratched at the dirt.

"Come no closer!" he exclaimed. "Place the shard on the ground."

Kara did as she was told. The bone shard instantly sunk into the black soil and vanished from view.

"Now," Sordyr said, straightening the remains of his cloak, "let's discuss what's going to happen next. You are going to free me from Rygoth. Today. No more tricks. No more waiting."

"Yes," said Kara, moving closer. With achingly slow movements she inched her hand toward her pocket, where the second shard waited. "No more tricks."

Just a few more feet and I'll be within striking range.

He nodded toward Safi, who had come closer, Taff by her side. "This witch will come with me to the World. I can use someone like her to demonstrate the powers of the grimoire. As for you and your brother—"

"Stop!" Mary Kettle exclaimed.

She stepped in front of the Forest Demon.

"Master," she said. "Look at the way her hand is moving toward her pocket. I think she has another shard there."

Kara stopped short.

"Don't," she said, but Mary was already standing in front of her. Reaching into Kara's pocket she carefully withdrew the crimson shard.

"See!" she said, holding it up to show Sordyr. "You

can't trust this one. If you send her down to Rygoth, she'll just try to trick you again." She returned to Sordyr's side. "Master—why not let me go down to Rygoth instead? I deserve the honor of freeing you. We don't need this troublesome girl at all anymore."

Sordyr took a few strides forward and stood before Kara.

"The idea has merit," he said. He pinched Kara's neck between two branch fingers. "I must confess, I tire of this so-called *wexari*. She has been nothing but a disappointment since—"

The Forest Demon wailed in sudden, uncontrollable pain. His body went slack. He released Kara, who landed awkwardly on the ground.

"*WHAT HAVE YOU DONE?*" he screamed.

From this angle, Kara could see the bone shard poking out of Sordyr's neck. The Forest Demon tried to remove it, pulling on the shard with all his strength, but it was a part of him now.

"We knew you'd never let me get close enough," Kara said, "once you suspected I had the venom. And I knew I wouldn't be able to defeat you with magic."

"That's why we decided that I should do it," Mary said. "You trusted me, even more so when I told you that Kara had snuck out of the village. It never occurred to you that I might do something good for once."

"*TAKE IT OUT!*" Sordyr exclaimed. "*I COMMAND YOU TO TAKE IT OUT!*"

From the shard's entry point a crimson glow was spreading across Sordyr's body, changing the bark into something new.

Skin. Human skin.

Sordyr wailed in agony.

"You did this," he said, pointing toward Kara. "You!"

Sordyr thrust his branch hands forward, too quick for Kara to react, and she braced herself for the sharp rush of pain as the branches sliced through her body. Before that could happen, however, Mary slipped between them, shielding Kara's body with her own. Kara heard Mary's soft gasp and saw the sharp ends of Sordyr's fingers protruding from her back, red with blood.

Mary and the Forest Demon fell to the ground.

"No!" Taff screamed, running to Mary's side. He took the witch's hand. "Kara," he said. "Fix her!"

"I can't," Kara said. "I don't know how—"

"Then, Safi," Taff snapped. "You must be able to make that book of yours do a healing spell!"

"I might," Safi said, "but I don't know where it is."

"Look for it, then!"

"But I don't—I don't—"

"Stop talking and just look for it!" Taff exclaimed, and Safi rushed away, her eyes brimming with tears.

Kara pressed her hand against Mary's wound but the blood was flowing too fast and kept escaping between her fingers. *Why can't Mother be here right now? She would know what to do.*

Why does it always have to be me?

"Let me," said a man's voice, gently removing Kara's hand from Mary's wound. There was nothing remarkable about his appearance: brown hair, green eyes, hooked nose. He looked to be around her father's age, maybe a little older.

And then Kara saw the orange cloak—far too large now—wrapped around his body.

"No!" she shouted. "You're him! Sordyr!"

"Not anymore," he said. "Let me see if I can just fix this one last thing before my powers vanish completely." He opened his fingers and a few grains of black soil vanished into Mary's wounds.

"What did you do to her?" Taff asked.

"Look," said the man.

The bleeding had already stopped.

"She'll need rest," he said, "and certain medicines from the Thickety. But she will live." He stroked her hair. "She was very brave to stop me the way she did."

"You *helped* her. Why did you help her?"

He placed his hands on Kara's shoulders and stared into her eyes.

"We don't have time for questions. She'll be coming soon."

"Who?"

Beneath the earth came a rumbling sound and the ground in front of them collapsed inward, as though the dirt supporting it had simply vanished. Black soil spun as rapidly as a whirlpool. A few of Sordyr's remaining creatures were caught in the current and vanished beneath the earth.

A woman, her eyes closed, rose from the ground.

She should have been filthy but her white dress was pristine, her face clean and unblemished. She looked to be in her twenties, her features as cool and beautiful as a statue.

The woman opened her eyes. Instead of pupils, spider-webs stretched across her sockets.

"Hello, Kara," Rygoth said. "Thank you for freeing me."

She stepped onto solid ground and held her hand in front of her as though testing the air.

"It's colder than I remember," she said. "Not that I'm going to complain. Two thousand years in that cave. In that form." She glared at Sordyr. "All *your* fault."

"You were the one who wanted to destroy the world," Sordyr said. "I'd say you brought it upon yourself."

"Hmm," Rygoth said. Elbow-length white gloves appeared in her hands; she pulled them onto her arms as she spoke. "I didn't want to *destroy* the world. I wanted to *remake* it. Big difference."

"Not to all the people you were planning to kill."

"I have to admit, it was fun forcing you to do my bidding. Good, virtuous Sordyr. I made you into a monster. You have to live with all the things you've done, all the lives you've taken. You may have trapped me beneath the earth, but——"

"I kept you trapped," Sordyr said with pride. "There was enough of me left inside that monster to do that, at least."

"Whatever helps you sleep better, dear," said Rygoth. She faced Kara and smiled coldly. "That hideous spider form did give me one advantage—a venom I could inject into our friend here to keep him doing exactly what I wanted him to do. I couldn't leave, sure—but neither could he. He couldn't even warn you, Kara. I wouldn't let him."

"This wasn't about freeing Sordyr from you," Kara said. "It never was. It was about freeing you from him. You fooled me into helping you."

"And I feel just terrible about it," Rygoth said.

"What now?" asked Sordyr.

"I continue where I left off. The World. I'm going to make it mine. Thank you so much for assembling all those grimoires, by the way. They are going to be *ever* so useful. Speaking of which . . ." Rygoth scanned the crowd until she found Safi. She held out a white-gloved hand. "Little girl. You show promise. Do you want to come with me? Learn some real magic?"

Safi shook her head.

"As you wish," Rygoth said. She turned to Kara, and the wolf by her side bared its teeth. "And how about you, Kara Westfall? Would you like to learn all the secrets of a *wexari*?"

"You know my answer," said Kara.

Rygoth sighed. "I do. I don't even know why I asked, really. I've been in your head. I've experienced its . . . purity."

Rygoth spit on the ground.

"Oh well. I guess I'll be going to the World by myself, then."

"You're not going to the World at all," said Kara. "You've been in that cave for a long, long time, and my guess is you're still weak. I'm not letting you leave this island."

Rygoth shrugged. "Let's get this over with."

Kara ordered the wolf to attack Rygoth, trying to buy time while she reached out with her mind and called forth as many creatures as she could in her weakened state.

The wolf bit Kara's hand instead.

She screamed in pain and horror as her former ally leaped onto her chest, pushing her to the ground. It stared hungrily at her throat while its scorpion tail rose high into the air, ready to strike.

"That's enough now," Rygoth said. She stroked the wolf's ears and the beast shook with pleasure. "Feel free to call more creatures, but I think we know what's going to happen. I've been *wexari* for a long, long time. Compared to me, you haven't even learned to walk yet."

Kara turned her head from side to side. *Why isn't anyone helping me?* And then she saw. Hundreds of webs, attached to nothing but the air itself, held them all in place. Taff. Mary. Sordyr. The villagers. Even their mouths were sealed shut.

"So while I don't consider you a threat," said Rygoth, "I do believe in being cautious. You're clever. And persistent. I don't like that. I don't want you following me to the World and causing trouble. I could kill you, of course, but you did free me, and I think I owe you your life at least. I'm that kind of person."

Kara turned her head to see the crimson shard of bone rise from the earth.

"However," Rygoth said, "I can't allow you to keep your powers. I know you understand. In fact, I think you understand so well that you're going to prick yourself with that bone shard all on your own."

Kara watched her hand reach over and pick up the shard between two trembling fingers. She tried to stop it but her body was no longer under her control. She sat up like a marionette and pressed the shard against the flesh of her hand, not quite puncturing the skin.

Rygoth leaned forward and whispered in her ear, "We have the same power, Kara. But what you never understood in that pure little heart of yours is that *people are animals too*. They are ours to command. You don't deserve your gift."

Unable to stop herself, Kara pushed the shard against her palm. She winced in pain as a single drop of blood welled to the surface and ran down the inside of her wrist.

The piece of bone shed its hue and crumbled in her hand.

She felt tired, so tired. Each time she blinked entire minutes seemed to pass, images jumbling together in a too-fast stream. Rygoth vanishing before her eyes. Taff and Safi bending over her, looking concerned. Voices, screams, running people. Someone moving her. Dust on her face, a rain of woodchips. Tree limbs falling to the ground, sending geysers of dirt into the air. A beast crashing through the canopy with a thunderous roar, the tiny figure of a woman sitting astride its back.

Kara recognized the storehouses grasped in its talons.

"That's why the roofs had metal rings," she mumbled. "So Niersook could . . . carry them. Bring . . . grimoires to the World."

"Shh," a familiar voice said. Kara felt a warm hand brush her cheek. "It's over now, dear. You don't have to worry about magic anymore. It's all over."

"Mother?" Kara asked.

Before she could turn to see the owner of the voice, darkness took her.

EPILOGUE

After Kara had regained her strength she began to take long walks outside Kala Malta. Taff always offered to come, but Kara preferred her solitude. She told him that she needed time to think, to plan their next move.

This was a lie.

Instead, Kara spent entire days searching for a sign that she had done any good at all. The Thickety, as far as she could tell, remained unchanged. The flora was as dank and unforgiving as ever. Blighted animals still lumbered through the undergrowth.

Mary told her that she needed to give it time. "The Thickety has been diseased for hundreds of years," she said. "You cannot reasonably expect it to recover in a single day. Maybe not even a single year."

Kara wasn't certain she believed her.

She passed beneath two gray elms, their putrid-smelling leaves leaking some sort of yellow pus, and saw sitting on the branch above her a familiar shape.

"Hello, Watcher," Kara said.

The one-eyed bird stared down at her impassively. Kara flushed with shame as she remembered their last meeting. She had accused Watcher of trying to trick her and then hurt the bird with a spell.

"I'm so sorry," Kara said.

Watcher's eye turned a light mauve, holding there for just a moment before spinning to the color of a freshly ripened peach. And then, before Kara could say anything in reply, the bird flew away.

Those were such beautiful colors, she thought. *I think*

Watcher forgives me. I really do.

Kara, however, couldn't know for sure. She didn't understand what the bird was saying anymore.

The next morning, she found herself knocking on Sordyr's door. The word *DEMON* had been scratched into the wood. The villagers had left him alone at first out of fear, but their courage was growing. It was only a matter of time now before they attacked him directly. Though they had followed him willingly enough when he had provided protection against the dangers of the Thickety, the people of Kala Malta now blamed Sordyr for leading them astray. Mary had tried to explain that he was under a curse and therefore not responsible for his actions, but it was useless. Once people believed you were evil, there was really no changing their mind.

Kara knew that better than anyone.

"Good morning," Sordyr said, opening the door. He was wearing all black: breeches and a borrowed shirt that was far too large for him. Not a hint of orange.

"Mary said you wanted to see me," Kara said.

"Yes. Come inside."

Kara took a step backward, shaking her head. She would talk to Sordyr if she had to, but not in such close quarters. He might look like a man, but in her mind he would always be the Forest Demon. She supposed she was being as unfair as the villagers, but there was nothing she could do about it.

"Outside," she said.

They walked along the main road. The Divide had been dismantled, the wood burned. Kara didn't know what this meant for the unfortunate people who had been absorbed by the fence. She didn't plan to ask.

"Is Sordyr even your real name?" Kara asked.

He shrugged. His hair, completely brown only a few days ago, was now streaked with gray. New wrinkles lined his face.

"I don't remember," he said. "I suspect it might be, but

the details of my life before she changed me into that monster are clouded. I was a *wexari*, as was Rygoth. I believe we were even friends at one point. But Rygoth used her magic with wild abandon and sacrificed too many of her memories for power. Eventually she began to forget she was even human."

Kara bit her lip nervously. Though her magic was gone she had not regained her lost memories, and their absence gnawed at her.

"Is that when you trapped her?" she asked.

"It's not quite as simple as that," Sordyr said. "The villagers tell a story here. Perhaps you've heard it? A spoiled princess in a castle . . ."

"I've heard it," Kara said. "But my guess is the roles are reversed. Rygoth was the one who brought the grimoire to the princess. You're the one who tried to stop her."

"You're partially right," said Sordyr. "When I began telling the story to the villagers—or rather, when Rygoth planted the story in my mind and forced me to tell it—she did indeed switch our roles. I think it amused her to cast me as the villain, and it fit my new persona as the Forest Demon. But it *was* me who brought the princess her grimoire." He paused, looking down with regret. "Her name was Evangeline, and occasionally she *could* be kind—especially to me, the king's adviser. The story always leaves that part out."

Two former Devoted—one man and one woman—were approaching from the opposite direction. They had shed their purple cloaks and thorned piercings. As Sordyr passed they watched him with vacant, lost expressions.

"It was supposed to be a gift, nothing more," Sordyr said. "I thought the princess could use it to make her toys fly or for other such frivolous entertainment. I never imagined the grimoire would be as powerful as it was. Even as I handed it to Evangeline, I wasn't even completely sure it *worked*."

He shook his head.

"I was such a fool," he said.

"So that part about the princess destroying the king-dom . . ."

"True, all true. And when Rygoth saw the magic that a simple child like Evangeline could wield with a grimoire, she wanted the power for her own. She demanded that I make more grimoires, promising me that together we could remake the world into something new. Of course I refused, so she created Niersook and threatened to take away my powers if I did not comply. I still could have said no. I should have. But the thought of losing my pow-ers . . . I was weak. And then, when I finally resisted, Rygoth changed me into the Forest Demon. Before she gained control of me completely I was able to trap her as well, but it took all my focus to keep her there. There was none of me left to fight back as she injected her venom into my roots and controlled me."

There was a long, awkward silence. Kara searched for forgiveness in her heart, sensing that now was the time to offer words of compassion. *He was under a spell. It wasn't his fault.* But when she looked down at Sordyr's shadow her mind twisted his hands into branch fingers. She couldn't see him as anything else.

The moment passed.

"Might I ask you a personal question?" he asked.

"I suppose," said Kara. "But I make no promise to answer it."

"What world did Imogen craft for you?"

The question surprised Kara, and it was a few moments before she responded. "I was back in De'Noran," she said. "Except my mother was alive, of course. And the people in my village liked me. It was a normal life."

"Were you happy?" Sordyr asked.

"I was."

"You can have that now," Sordyr said. "You are no longer a witch. Nothing is stopping you from finding a nice farm and restarting your life."

Kara supposed he was right. She and Taff could find a safe place to live, a place far from Thicketies and Forest Demons and magic. *It's what Father and Mother would have wanted*. But could she ever be happy planting turnips knowing what wonders—both fantastic and terrible—existed in the world? Wouldn't she miss it, just a little?

"Imogen's world was a lie," Kara said. "At one point I might have desired such a life. But not anymore."

Sordyr looked at her for a few moments with his sad green eyes, then reached into his cloak and withdrew several leaves of rolled parchment bound together with a strand of dried ivy. He handed it to Kara. "Read this. After you've left the island. It's all I remember of the truth."

"Why does it matter?"

"The more you know about Rygoth, the better. That is, if you're planning on stopping her."

"I don't have any magic," Kara said.

Sordyr nodded. He popped a sunflower seed into his mouth and spit out the shell.

"These little human pleasures," he said. "How I've missed them."

Kara tucked the parchment away.

"Was that why you wanted to see me?" she asked, anxious to leave.

"Half the reason. Mary told me what happened to your father. I thought I could help."

Kara felt a rush of excitement. "You know how to save him?" she asked.

"It's dangerous," said Sordyr. "Beyond dangerous. And you are no longer a witch."

"I made a promise to my brother. Whether I can still do magic doesn't change that."

Sordyr folded his hands in front of him. The nails had been well scrubbed and carefully trimmed.

He told her what she needed to do.

"No!" Kara said, a burning sensation in the pit of her stomach. "That's impossible! Surely there must be something—"

Sordyr shook his head. "I'm sorry," he said. "If you truly want to save your father, there is no other way."

Kara sat in the center of the road and folded her knees

to her chest, too stunned to speak. *Not that*, she thought. *Anything but that. It's too much to ask.* When she looked up some time later, Sordyr was a small figure in the distance just vanishing around a bend in the road. Kara knew she should have thanked him for giving her the key to restoring Father, but she was too full of cold dread to be grateful right now. All she could think was, *Why did you have to tell me?*

By the time the ship was completed, winter had grabbed the Thickety with an icy hold. Mary suggested that they wait until summer to make their journey to the World, but Kara refused. Safi's visions had become more frequent and vivid.

Burning cities. Darkening skies. Screams of horror.

Kara didn't know how she was going to stop the spider witch, especially without magic, but she had to at least try. She was the one who had set her free, and each death Rygoth caused was her responsibility.

"I can't believe Safi didn't come to see us off," Taff said, staring out at the crowd of people gathered around the ship. A small number of the villagers had decided to make the trek with them, but most had stayed behind. "I looked for her all morning, but I couldn't find her."

"You two have become close friends," Kara said. "It was probably too hard for her to say good-bye."

"I guess," said Taff.

At some point Kara would tell him the truth, but not today. Safi had assured them that after the battle with Rygoth she had been unable to find her grimoire, but Kara had recognized the haunted look in her eyes, the shaking hands. She had followed Safi one night into the Thickety and saw where she had hid it, and then watched, in horror, as Safi cast spell after spell, unable to stop.

The night before, while everyone was sleeping, Kara had crept into the Thickety and stolen Safi's grimoire. No doubt the girl was searching for the book right now—the real reason she hadn't seen them off.

Even if she hates me forever, it's for the best, Kara thought. *I'm saving her.*

Mary walked them to the gangplank. She was an old woman today, the same age she had been when they first met. Kara was glad. This was the way she wanted to remember her.

"It's not too late to come with us," Taff said.

She stroked his hair. "My place is here. These people need my help—they *deserve* it. They have Breem, of course—he'll do a fine job leading them. But they aim to stretch their numbers across the Thickety, and no one knows this place better than I do."

"Especially now that Sordyr's gone," said Kara.

He had vanished several nights ago, and the villagers had quickly burned his hut to the ground and scattered the ashes to the wind. Although Kara could never find it in her heart to forgive him, she was surprised to find some pity there.

"I have a gift for each of you," Mary said.

"We don't need any gifts," Kara said, while at the same time Taff shouted, "What is it?"

Mary handed him her sack. Inside, the magic toys that had escaped the fire tinkled together.

"You have the heart of a true craftsman, Taff, and these work better for you. Plus you may find some use of them in the World."

"Mary," Taff said. "You can't give these to me. They're yours."

"I don't need them anymore."

Dropping the sack, he threw his arms around her.

"I won't forget you," he said. "We'll be back."

"I know you will," Mary said, fighting back tears. "I'll be waiting." She turned to Kara. "Your gift is on the ship already. She came into the village last night. I was going to bring her to you right then, but I thought it'd be a nice surprise."

Mary gestured to one of the lower portholes of the ship, where Kara saw two brown eyes staring back at her. Though the eyes were familiar, she did not recognize them right away; many of the memories her mind wanted to pull from had been exchanged for magic.

And then she remembered.

"Shadowdancer!" Kara exclaimed.

Not caring that she was flooding her boots, Kara splashed through the water and stroked the mare's head. She looked thinner, and maybe a little older, but otherwise no different than the first time Kara had met her in the Lambs' stable.

"I thought I'd lost you," Kara whispered.

"She's not the only one, Kara," Mary said. "The animals are coming back. And that's not all. Come with me."

"But the ship is leaving. . . ."

"These people have waited their entire lives to leave this island," she shouted in the direction of the captain. "They can wait a few minutes longer. Unless they want to anger an old witch!"

Mary brought them to a small glade bordered by gray willows sweeping the ground. A strong breeze shook the branches. Kara braced herself for the resultant sounds of despair but heard only a gentle rustling.

The trees whispered no more.

"Look!" Taff exclaimed, a smile brightening his face.

In the center of the glade was a rose.

It stood out against its drab surroundings like a child's laughter on a cloudy day, the red of freshly painted wagons and bright summer dresses. Kara knelt next to the rose and stroked its petals lightly. Taff did the same. When their eyes met, Kara laughed, a soft, girlish giggle. She couldn't help it. If the Thickety, of all places, could be saved, then there really was hope.

There was always hope.

Read on for a sneak peek of

THE THICKETY
Well of Witches

PROLOGUE

The afternoon had been sunny and full of promise when Bethany set out, but since then night had claimed the land and draped the dusty road in darkness. Just beyond the Windmill Graveyard the ocean crashed against high cliff walls, spitting geysers of dark water into the air. Bethany pulled her cloak tight around her shoulders.

I should have waited till morning before leaving. Mrs. Redding would have felt obligated to set a bed for me, had I asked. No doubt that would have been the more intelligent choice— what her mother would have called the *grown-up choice.*

But after Bethany had handed over that week's delivery of glorbs and collected payment, Mrs. Redding had begged pardon to attend to an unfinished chore and never returned. Bethany knew that Mrs. Redding was not being intentionally rude; she had simply forgotten that Bethany remained on her property. Things like this happened to Bethany all the time. Her mother claimed it was because Bethany was shy, but that wasn't it at all. She *loved* to talk to people; the trouble was keeping their interest. Bethany was serious by nature, and the jokes and effortless banter that came so easily to her peers eluded her. She wasn't particularly pretty, or athletic, or quick-witted; nor was she ugly, clumsy, or doltish. In fact, the only thing notable about Bethany was how spectacularly average she was in every sense of the word, fading into the background of most gatherings like a ghost.

There's nothing special about me, she thought.

The road curved away from shore between two rows of low-growing trees. Bethany thought about swirling a lantern but decided against it. The stars were illumination enough.

Someone was coming.

Though its source was yet obscured by darkness, from farther down the road Bethany heard the sound of squeaking wheels. A few moments later a covered wagon came into view, drawn by a single horse. From the wagon's roof swayed a single lantern that did little to reveal the identity of the driver.

Bethany tensed, slipping her hand downward until her fingertips grazed the dagger concealed beneath her cloak. Though more common farther inland, brigands were not unheard of this close to shore. She quickly unhooked the pouch filled with Mrs. Redding's copper and slid the majority of its contents inside her boot.

If they intend to rob me, I'll claim I have only a few coins.

As the wagon drew closer, however, Bethany decided she was just being skittish. Though the driver's downturned face remained hidden beneath a hood, Bethany recognized a woman's soft form. Hands covered by pristine white gloves held the horses' reins.

Probably just a traveling merchant, Bethany thought, *come from peddling her wares in Tear's Landing or Hendon. Harmless.*

Bethany slid her hand away from the dagger and waved.

"Evening," she said.

"And not soon enough," the woman replied. "You would think I'd have had my share of darkness by now, but I still prefer it to the sun. I always have."

The driver's words were strange, but Bethany hardly heard them. Her attention was absorbed by the old-fashioned wagon that had squeaked to a halt in front of her, details hidden until this point now illuminated in the soft glow of lantern light. The wagon's mud-splattered wheels were bone white, and a row of bows arched from one side of its bed to the other like the ribs of some deep ocean beast. Instead of white canvas a strange translucent material stretched between these bows, providing Bethany with a glimpse of the wagon's shadowy cargo. She leaned forward to get a better look, cupping a hand over her eyes to shade them from the glare of the lantern. . . .

"Would you like to know what's inside?" a voice whispered in her ear.

Bethany turned in surprise. Without making a sound the hooded driver of the wagon had somehow slipped next to her. The woman's face remained hidden, but Bethany thought she glimpsed the hint of a smile.

"I'm sorry," Bethany said. Her voice was faint and hoarse. "I shouldn't have looked without your permission."

"One should never apologize for curiosity," the woman said, and pushed back her hood.

Bethany had never seen such a beautiful woman. She looked to be in her midtwenties, with porcelain skin and delicate features. Straight blond hair grazed her shoulders, framing large eyes that were not just one shade of green but a collage of slight variations. Barely perceptible lines separated each hue, like a stained-glass window that had been cracked into pieces and then reassembled.

"Now tell me," the woman said, "why is a child wandering alone on such a cold, dark night?"

Bethany's mind had suddenly grown dull and sluggish.

"I don't know," she said.

Not broken glass, Bethany thought, unable to look away from those crystalline eyes. *Webs. It looks like spiderwebs have been stretched across her eyeballs.*

"Were you looking for me?" the woman asked.

Bethany shook her head.

"Are you sure about that? *I* was looking for *you.* Maybe not you, specifically, but someone with your special gifts." The woman ran the back of her hand along Bethany's cheek. "You are the first, Bethany. I saw you all the way from the night sky. You *shine.*"

Despite the strangeness of the woman's words, Bethany felt a slight thrill at being thought so worthy of attention.

"How do you know my name?" she asked.

"How do you *not* know mine? No matter. It's Rygoth." The woman straightened her gloves. "Soon all will know it."

A splinter of fear needled Bethany's spine. This was not the workaday fear of rats and dark passageways and stormy, sleepless nights with her father still out at sea, but rather the gasp-inducing terror conjured by her grandmother as she told little Bethany the old stories, the ones her parents claimed were nonsense, of a time when witches and monsters roamed the World.

Bethany pressed her back against the wagon, trying to get as far from Rygoth's eyes as possible, and the strange material shifted inward.

It's warm, Bethany thought, feeling its sticky heat against her back. *Why is it warm?*

"I'm late," she said, finally managing to peel away from those variegated eyes. "My parents will be worried."

"Will they?" Rygoth asked, and in her tone Bethany heard a second question: *Have they even noticed you're gone?* "I wouldn't dream of stopping you, love. Mommy and Daddy shall have their daughter back, safe and sound. *More* than safe and sound."

The beautiful woman spoke with soft, measured tones

that held within them far more threat than any brigand. Keeping her eyes on Rygoth's feet and her hand near her dagger, Bethany slowly backed away toward the front of the wagon. *Once I pass the horses I'll make a run for it along the open road. . . .*

"Have you ever noticed how infrequently your name is spoken?" the woman asked.

Bethany wanted to stop listening. She wanted to run. But her feet remained rooted to the ground, unwilling to follow directions.

"Think about it. How often do your neighbors, those who have known you from birth, even, identify you only by your relationship to others? Ansen's sister? Martha's daughter?" Rygoth leaned forward, as though imparting a secret. "It's because they can never quite remember your name. It's always on the tip of their tongue—it really is—but . . . sad. To be so tragically forgettable."

Warm tears flowed down Bethany's cheeks. She wanted nothing more than to get away from this woman and her truth-poisoned words, but though she screamed for her body to move, it was like a wall had been built in her mind, blocking the message.

"I can't move," Bethany said. Her heart beat madly. "What have you done to me?"

"I didn't want it to be like this," Rygoth said, "but you need to hear the truth. You're *special*, Bethany. You don't have to be Caleb Jenkins's dough-faced daughter anymore, the unseen girl behind the counter. Let me help you, and everyone will learn how extraordinary you really are."

"I just want to go home!"

"Shh, Bethany. Listen."

From inside the wagon came a chorus of hushed whispers. At first the words were indistinguishable from one another, but as Bethany listened she was able to make out distinct names. *Annabeth. Lenowy. Karin.* Bethany felt her body turn and face the wagon. She wondered if it was Rygoth forcing her to move or if she was doing it on her own. She wasn't sure anymore.

Rachel. Cordelia. Emily.

Rygoth watched her with a considerate expression, her eyes as beautiful and unforgiving as an unbroken landscape of snow.

"Do you hear that?" Bethany asked.

"I hear everything," Rygoth replied, and waved her hand. The strange material covering the wagon folded back, revealing hundreds of leather-bound books. Given the bumpy dirt road, such cargo should have been scattered all over the wagon bed, but though they had not been secured in any visible fashion the books remained in precise, even stacks.

That's where the names are coming from, Bethany thought. *The books. They're calling to their owners.* It shouldn't have made any sense—books couldn't *talk*—but she knew she was right.

One of the books whispered her name.

It wasn't the name her parents had given her but Bethany's *true* name, a combination of sounds that depicted her inner self as accurately as a mirror's image reflected her outward appearance. *The dull drone of insects filling lonely summer afternoons that stretched into forever. The scrubbing of a brush as she tried to straighten her hair into the same style as the other girls. The teasing giggle of conversations she would never be a part of.*

These sounds and others coalesced into a single word: her true name.

The names of the other girls faded away; there was only this new sound, *her* sound, drawing her forth. Bethany searched madly for its source, knocking entire piles of books down until she found it: a light gray tome with a black star, easy to miss, stitched into its lower spine. Bethany held the book to her chest, the leather smooth and oddly damp. Her heart pounded with a strange combination of exhilaration and fear, as though she were about to leap off some great precipice.

"This one's mine," Bethany whispered.

She turned to Rygoth, ready to offer all her copper, all her *anything*, in exchange for the book, but the beautiful peddler, apparently uninterested in payment, had already returned to her seat.

"I must go," she said. "There are so many others out there. I can feel their potential, waiting to be unleashed. Yours is not the only spellbook I aim to bestow tonight."

"Spellbook?" Bethany asked, turning the book in her hands. "But I'm not a witch. Witches aren't even *real*!"

The wagon pulled away and bolted down the road, rumbling hard enough to shake the trees. Bethany expected its wheels to crack into bits or slip off their axles but instead the wagon lowered itself, like a beast ready to pounce, and then sprang high into the air, where it swelled outward and sprouted long wings. The shape, now a wagon no longer but a monster large enough to blot out the stars, sailed through the night with a small figure perched upon its back.

As the shape vanished, a dark cloud lifted from Bethany's mind and she noticed the grimoire in her hands. She tossed it away as though it had sprouted nails and razor-sharp teeth.

I have to go home and tell the Mistrals what I have seen, she thought. *The old stories were right. Witches are real! But I'm not a creature of darkness like her, no matter what she said. I won't touch the book again. I'll just leave it here and come back with . . .*

Only when Bethany looked down the grimoire was somehow open in her two hands, the pages not paper as she had expected but impossibly thin mirrors stitched into the binding. *What kind of book is this?* Bethany wondered. She stared at her reflection, the short hair that never grew out the right way, her drab brown eyes. It was the type of face you would forget the moment after seeing it.

I wish people would notice me, she thought.

As though in answer, strange words that Bethany had never seen before etched themselves across the mirror-page, fragmenting her reflection into a monstrous distortion.

ONE

The village of De'Noran was no more.

Where wooden buildings had once stood were now only charred debris. Even the grass was blackened and dead. Kara walked farther down the main road, remembering how loud it had been at midday with the bustle of commerce in full force. The rattle of wagon wheels. The soft buzzing of barter and gossip. The delighted screams of children playing in the square.

All was silent.

They should have been on their way to the World right

now, but Kara, upon seeing the changed village from the deck of their ship, had insisted on docking. Several men had followed the children ashore, quickly spreading through the abandoned farms to forage for supplies.

"Are you sure it was a good idea to stop here?" Taff asked. "If anyone sees us . . ."

He didn't have to finish this thought; the dark events of that day were deeply branded in her mind. It had started out so well. Grace Stone had been defeated, and the villagers had gathered together to formally announce their new leader: William Westfall, Kara and Taff's father. It should have been the happiest day of their lives—but Grace wasn't done with them yet. She had used her Last Spell to possess Father with the spirit of Timoth Clen, the most merciless witch hunter of all, and he had ordered the villagers to kill them. The two Westfalls had escaped only by fleeing into the Thickety.

"What if they're still here, hiding?" Taff asked, looking around the remnants of the village. "Watching us? We barely escaped the first time, and now—"

"Don't worry," Kara said. "No one's here."

"What about Father?"

"He's gone too."

Taff swallowed deeply.

"Are they dead?" he asked.

Kara shook her head. "Just gone."

Taff did not look convinced. He stared across the flattened village, his brow furrowed with concern.

"I hope nothing bad happened to them," he said.

Kara couldn't help smiling, amazed as always by her brother's ability to forgive others no matter how badly they had wronged him. He had been equally quick to absolve Mary Kettle after she had betrayed them, and in the end it had been his compassion that won her to their side.

"They might have moved to a different part of the island," suggested Taff. "They could have been fleeing something. Thickety monsters, maybe. I know they don't usually cross the Fringe, but when Sordyr lost his power maybe things changed."

Kara stopped at the place where the general store had once stood, now nothing but charred earth and barely identifiable lumps that used to be shelves and jars. She picked up a half-melted spoon and absently gazed at her upside-down reflection, remembering the day when Grace had tricked her into giving up her seeds. At the time, such childish cruelty had been the biggest problem in her life. She wished that were still the case.

"No animal could have done this," Kara said. "It's too organized. If it had been a beast from the Thickety there would be debris everywhere. Wood, glass . . ."

"People pieces."

"Taff!"

"What?" he asked. "You were thinking it too." He lowered his voice to a whisper. "Could it have been Rygoth?"

"No. Rygoth only does things for a reason, and this gains her nothing. I'm sure she's in the World right now, distributing her grimoires and gathering new witches to her side. After two thousand years stuck on this island this is the last place she'd be, now that she's finally free."

All thanks to me, her foolish little pawn.

Kara kicked a blackened piece of rubble that might have once been a clay pitcher and watched it skip across the ashes of the store.

"Ms. Westfall," said a man behind her. "There's something you should see."

The voice belonged to Anders Clement, a tall, wiry man with dark skin and a dusting of white in his hair. Before leaving Kala Malta, the villagers had appointed him captain of the ship that would transport a third of their number to the World. As a leader he had proven competent enough, but though he was friendly and gregarious to other members of the crew he remained strangely aloof toward Kara.

"What is it, Clement?" Kara asked.

"*Captain* Clement," he snapped.

Clearly he was still upset with her. Clement hadn't wanted to dock at the island in the first place, and it was only when Kara had demanded they do so that he reluctantly agreed. She wasn't sure what had hurt his ego more—taking orders from a child or from a girl—but Kara was certain she had caused him to lose face in front of his entire crew. Luckily she had listened to Mary's advice and concealed the fact that she no longer had any magical powers. If Clement knew the truth she doubted he would have listened to her at all.

"My apologies," Kara said. "What is it, *Captain* Clement?"

"There's something you should see." He nodded toward Taff. "Might be best if the boy stays here. Too scary for little ones."

Taff stared at him in disbelief.

"Seriously?" he asked. "Do you have any idea what kinds of things I've seen? I could give nightmares nightmares!"

"Suit yourself," said Captain Clement.

They followed the tall man deeper into the village, passing sooty rectangles that used to be buildings but were now little more than scorched wood and memories. *That's where the tannery used to be*, Kara thought. *And that long stretch is the barracks where the graycloaks lived. Over there was Baker Corbett's place—you can still see the stones from the oven.* A surprising feeling of nostalgia swept over her. She had never been happy here, but it *had* been home—and now it was gone.

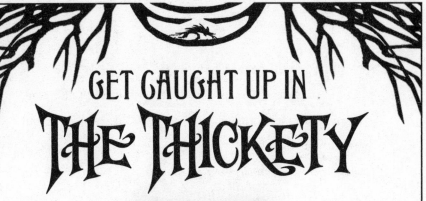